GRAND OAK BOOKS

The Complete Short Stories of Émile Zola

Published by:
Grand Oak Books Publishing, Ltd

ISBN-10 0983473811
ISBN-13 978-0983473817

Library of Congress Cataloging-in-Publication Data:

Zola, Émile (1840-1902)/The Complete Short Stories of Émile Zola, Volume. iii
                    p.   cm.

First Edition

The Complete Short Stories of Émile Zola

VOLUME III

Edited by Stephen R. Pastore

Introduction by Mark Prendergast

Grand Oak Books

2011

The Complete Short Stories
of Émile Zola
VOLUME III

INTRODUCTION to
The Complete Short Stories of Émile Zola in Four Volumes

Mark Prendergast

ÉMILE ZOLA was born on April 2, 1840, in Paris. His father was an engineer of Italian-Greek descent. The family went back to Aix-en-Provence, where the boy was brought up. After his father's death in 1846, poverty and the possessive love of the mother for her only child molded his character and left their marks on him forever. Emile attended the Lycée St. Louis at Aix—one of his school friends was the future painter Cézanne—and, later, universities in Paris and Marseilles.

In 1860, Zola settled in Paris and worked for six years as a clerk at Hachette's bookshop. Hachette rejected his first volume of stories, which was published by Lacroix in 1864 under the title *Contes à Ninon (Tales for Ninon)*. Shortly after, Zola acquired French citizenship and began to meet such leading literary figures as Saint-Beuve and Michelet. In 1865 his novel *La confession de Claude (Claude's Confession)* was published—and denounced to the Public Prosecutor as a dangerous book. At about that time he married, but his marriage turned out a failure and, in 1888, Zola took as his mistress a laundry maid from Médan, Jeanne Rogerat, who bore him two children.

Zola's first "realistic" novel was Thérèse Raquin (1868), which made a great stir. He then started to map out his twenty-volume ROUGON-MAC-QUART series, the complex chronicle of two interlinked families living in the late sixties, during the decline of the French Second Empire. As a safely entrenched but always controversial author, he intervened publicly in the infamous Dreyfus Affair, at a critical stage when the innocence of the Jewish officer of the General Staff, wrongly convicted of spying and sent to Devil's Island for life, had become the subject of bitter political controversy. Zola published an open letter, the celebrated "J'Accuse" (I Accuse), in which he indicated the War Office for hushing up the truth about the case. He was prosecuted and sentenced to a year's imprisonment but escaped to England and returned to France a popular hero, after Dreyfus's final vindication in 1899.

Zola's last work was the planning of a series he called *The Four Gospels*. Only three were completed and published: *Fruitfulness, Work, and Truth. Jus-*

tice would have followed, but Zola died suddenly on September 28, 1902, from carbon-monoxide poisoning caused by a blocked chimney in his bedroom.

In 1908, his body was transferred to the Pantheon.

When Zola wrote of Balzac, "What a man! He crushes the whole country with his weight," his words could have applied equally to himself. His hypersensitivity, his constant preoccupation with smells and sounds and color, made him a poet, while his analytical powers and a deep conviction of the evil that lay at the roots of society supplied by both his force and his realism. These combined gifts, and a monumental capacity for ceaseless work, enabled him to achieve his incomparable picture of France and the French of his times.

Zola examined the fabric of nineteenth-century France, tested every strand for strength and color, noted stains and the dirt that had been swept out of sight—and then rewove his own interpretation in the ROUGON-MACQUART series of twenty novels. In this stupendous achievement no aspect of French life escaped his meticulous attention and brilliant powers of characterization and description. The mentality and morals, weaknesses and ambitions of noble families and bourgeoisie were recorded; the drudgery, poverty, courage, and hopelessness of railway workers, masons, prostitutes, and peasants were set vividly and unforgettably before the eyes of readers who were frequently outraged and infuriated.

Zola's work often aroused anger. There is probably no other author who was the object of such vitriolic hatred and violent criticism in his lifetime. He laid bare the acquisitive, narrow, and conformist souls of the middle classes and incurred their enmity. He pinpointed the moral weakness and corruption in the arm—that led to the disastrous defeat by the Prussians—in *La debacle*, which was compared to Tolstoy's *War and Peace* and earned Zola the loathing of St. Cyr and everything it stood for. He went further, and exposed in "J'Accuse" the virulent anti-Semitism that existed in the army. He attacked the Roman Catholic Church in *La faute de l'abbé Mouret* and in *Lourdes* and *Rome*. And in *Nana,* in particular, he shocked the innocent and embarrassed the guilty by his picture of the degradation that lust could bring, the corruption and disease that attended sexual promiscuity. And, by equating the once-beautiful, rotting body of Nana the prostitute with the body politic of France, as Nana lay dying and the crowds in the streets screamed "To Berlin," he struck simultaneously at private sexuality and national pride.

Where do the short stories, especially translated into English for this collection, fit into the pattern of Zola's work, both as chronicler of his times and moral reformer? What have the stories in common with his masterworks? Were they facets of life as lived in nineteenth-century France, aspects of sexuality, or tracts written to illustrate selected themes? Were they written at widely spaced intervals? And what relation do they bear to Zola's life and the mainstream of his work at the time they were written?

A few years ago, while engaged in research on another project, I reread *The Stew Pot* in order to get the atmosphere of the transformation Paris underwent just over a century ago. Narrow, winding streets were being torn down and the wide, straight avenues and boulevards planned by Haussman and familiar to us today rose from a storm of dust and noise. I went on reading Zola's novels for my own pleasure and instruction but I must confess I faltered and gave up when I tackled the three tired and turgid volumes of the unfinished *Quatre Evangiles*, in which the old master had at last ground to a sad and boring halt. But everything he had written, the staggering number of tongues into which his work had been translated, fascinated me, and I discovered that many of his stories, including the many in this volume, were initially published in Russian, thanks to Ivan Turgenev. This came about in the following way.

In 1874, Zola was still a struggling writer. In that year, the fourth volume in the ROUGON-MACQUART series, *The Conquest of Plassans*, was published, but apparently with little success. Flaubert, in a letter to George Sand, said that in six months it had sold only 1,700 copies and had not received a single review. Zola was debt-ridden and lived on a fixed salary paid to him by his publisher in lieu of royalties. This brought him the equivalent of a little less than fifteen dollars a week. Turgenev, who was living in Paris and knew how poor Zola was, arranged with Mikhail Stassyulevich, editor of the St. Petersburg journal *V Yestnik Evropy (The European Herald)*, for Zola to contribute regularly to the paper. From 1874 to 1880, articles and stories by Zola appeared every month. "Shellfish for Monsieur Chabre" was published as "Sea-bathing in France" in September, 1876; "For One Night of Love" as "A Drama in a Country Town" the following month, and in November, 1877, "Round Trip" came out as "The Parisian on Holiday in the Country."

This was the year during which Zola's luck turned and his fame and success began. On February 26, 1877, when he was thirty-seven, *L'Assommoir* was published and went through thirty-eight printings before the end of the year. As a result, his publisher drew up a new contract on a royalty basis. Zola's command of a larger audience also led to publication in French of some of those stories that had first appeared in Russian.

"Pour une nuit d'amour" ("For One Night of Love") was published in 1882 in a collection of stories entitled *Le Capitaine Burle*. It appeared again as a separate book in the *Lotus Bleu* collection in 1896, as a rivulet of type running between broad paper banks down a tiny page and with typically ninety-ish fuzzy illustrations by Georges Picard. The title page has a medallion drawing in pale blue of Thérèse de Marsanne riding on Colombel's back and plying her whip on that youth's masochistic shoulders. There is a pink frontispiece portrait of the imperious and heavy-browed heroine.

"Voyage circulaire" ("Round Trip") first appeared in French in 1929 in a posthumous collection of stories, *Madame Sourdis*; and "Les coquillages de Monsieur Chabre" was published with four other stories in *Naïs Micoulin* in 1884.

In England, Zola's work was first made available through the devoted admiration and zealous energy of Henry Vizetelly who, with the help of his son Ernest, translated nearly everything Zola wrote. In 1888, Vizetelly was sent to prison for three months for publishing, under the title *The Soil*, his rendering into English of *La Terre*, which was condemned as "obscene." In the same year he brought out his own translation of a selection of stories, including the two longer ones in this volume, under the title *A Soldier's Honour*, which appears never to have been reissued. Although he had great courage and enthusiasm, Vizetelly, as Angus Wilson has pointed out in his excellent *Emile Zola: an Introductory Study of His Novels* (revised edition, 1964, Secker and Warburg, London) was "in his approach to his own work as translator, disarmingly modest, for he confessed that most of it was of poor quality, overhurriedly performed to meet debts or the demands of publishers who cared about novelty rather than quality…." But he carried on, even though some of his translations had to be bowdlerized to avoid further prosecution and appear under another imprint because he lacked the money to publish them himself.

This, then, was the background to the first publication and translations of many stories, written before Zola became an international figure. What echoes and similarities are there in his other work?

"For One Night of Love" is a deliberately horrifying story of murder resulting from sexual license. Throughout all his work, Zola's Puritanism led him to denounce the perils of sex, and his sensualism colored the risks he described. In May, 1867, *Thérèse Raquin* was published. This other Thérèse resembled Thérèse de Marsanne in more than name; but whereas Thérèse Raquin's lover Laurent is driven by lust for her to kill her husband Camille, Thérèse de Marsanne, gripped by the fury of her perverted nature, kills her lover with her own hands. Camille is drowned by his wife and her lover in a river; Colombel is tumbled into the Chanteclair as a corpse by his would-be-successor in Thérèse's bed. But while Thérèse Raquin and Laurent are haunted and harried to suicide by consequences of their lustful crime, Thérèse de Marsanne goes scot-free to enter into and arranged and love-less marriage to a "suitable" husband before the eyes of those who admire her maidenly demeanor. By sparing her the retribution she deserved, Zola directed his barbs against her Catholic education, her noble status, and the stupidity of those of all classes who were deceived by her.

Nana appeared in 1880, and there is an interesting parallel—and some equally interesting differences—between the passage in which Nana climbs on the back of her distinguished and aristocratic lover Muffat and rides him across the room, and Thérèse's fetishist mounting of Colombel to spur him through the hidden paths of the garden of the château.

Nana had risen from slum poverty by the shrewd exploitation of her sexual charms to dominate men of political importance and distinction, and displayed in a crude and realistic way the extent of her domination. Thérèse de Marsanne, on the other hand, belonged to a noble family in which there was a streak of madness and perversion. She exercised her sadism on a social and physical inferior until he, the perfect masochistic partner, had suffered sufficiently as her steed to bolt with her, throw her to the ground, and rape her. They now played new and adult roles and were welded into a struggling pair of demoniac lovers. Later, she calculatingly used her sexual allure to attract to her a humble post office employee, to whom she offered her body in return for his disposal of the corpse of her lover. There are therefore both moral and social differences between the prostitute Nana, straddling and straddled by French society, and Thérèse, who uses her humble admirers for the furtherance and concealment of her perverted desires.

"Round Trip," compared with the immense bulk of Zola's detailed and highly colored oil paintings of French society, is an affectionate and gay etching. One can almost see it as a short film in the manner of Renoir or Tati. In fact, Zola's novels and stories are all highly cinematic in conception and execution.

In this story there are the initial thrusts against the cash-conscious mother, for whom centimes and francs have long since taken the place of kisses and love-making, the embodiment of the grasping shopkeeper, and against the train passengers who frown on the young couple's public tokens of affection. There is the father-in-law, also a shopkeeper, but one who is capable, one feels, of a vigorous flirtation on the side despite his enervating talk of the architectural delights of the tour. And there are all the sad-comic (as distinct from sick-comic) touches of the single beds, the too-thin walls in the hotels, ending in the train's momentary halt at a kind of French Adlestrop, which Edward Thomas remembered because "…one afternoon of heat the express-train drew up there unwontedly…."

But this was France, and "un trou adorable de verdure perdu dans les arbres," "an enchanting green arbor hidden by trees," and some forty years before Edward Thomas wrote his poem. The young couple might not have found such a pleasant inn at Adlestrop in which to spend the remainder of their honeymoon in idyllic solitude. IN this story the forceful proselytizing genius of Zola drew up, like the train, unwontedly, at a whistle stop of amused and touching tenderness.

There is also tenderness in "Monsieur Chabre," but of a different kind. This is no etching. This is Zola in action with a full palette, painting the vivid and dramatic Atlantic coastline with giant strokes on the granite cliffs. This background of caves and cliffs, tides and shellfish, with the characters of the plodding, worrying cuckolded husband who so richly deserves his horns, and the handsome, youthful giant who sports with the beautiful and unfulfilled young woman in the sea, pursues her across the damp sands that terrify the timid husband, and eventually mates with her to the sound of the sea while her husband on the cliffs above fortifies his virility with winkles— all this unrolls with the inevitability of a myth or a folk tale. But if there is a legendary quality in the evocation of towering pillars of rock, crystal pools, and waving seaweed, there is at times also something of the comic seaside postcard. Then the aging protagonist with the wife who is part Atalanta and part naiad, becomes "timid, middle-aged party" sweating in the sun while his nubile wife disports herself in the sea with "handsome young local man." It is impossible to resist the idea that a suitable legend for such a postcard would be "cuckolds and muscles."

Edmund Gosse, in his preface to Zola's "Attack on the Mill," which was published in 1892, referred to both "Pour une nuit d'Amour" and "Les Coquillages de Monsieur Chabre," and it is amusing to see what he had to say: "As to 'Pour une nuit d'Amour,' it is not needful to do more than say that it is one of the most repulsive productions ever published by its author, and a vivid exception to the general innocuous character of his short stories... In "Les coquillages de Monsieur Chabre," which I confess I read when it first appeared, and have now reread with amusement, we see the heavy M. Zola endeavoring to sport as gracefully as M. de Maupassant, and in the same style. The impression of buoyant Atlantic seas and hollow caverns is well rendered in this most unedifying story."

Zola never wrote another story in quite the same vein as "Monsieur Chabre." Here the bourgeois husband gets his desserts, adultery goes unpunished. Estelle is depicted as a wholesome and healthy young woman and not as a scheming sensualist. Hector is no sinister seducer, but a fine upstanding young man bearing impeccable manners and gifts of seafood. He and Estelle enjoy each other without arrière pensée or fear of retribution, and Monsieur Chabre gets his long-awaited heir. All ends happily, without either condemnation or catastrophe. Estelle is more fille mal gardée than bartered bride, and what Monsieur Chabre's eye does not see, his heart will not grieve for. Many of Zola's stories show the varying expressions of the faces of love. All are portraits signed with the force and clarity of Emile Zola's artistic genius.

The Complete Short Stories of Émile Zola

Volume III

FOR ONE NIGHT OF LOVE

I

THE little town of P—stands on a hill. Below its ancient walls a deep stream flows between steep banks. It is called the Chanteclair and undoubtedly got its name from the rippling sound of its water. If you come from the south by the Versailles road, you cross the Chanteclair by a single-arch bridge whose low, broad sides are used as seats by the old men of the town. The road from the bridge leads directly into the Rue Beau-Soleil, which goes up to the Place des Quatre-Femmes, where coarse grass grows between the large paving stones and masks them with a meadowy greenness. The houses are wrapped in silence. Every half hour or so, the lagging step of a passer-by starts a dog barking behind a stable door, and the only excitement—twice daily—is the steady tread of the officers who go for their meals to a pension in the Rue Beau-Soleil.

Julien Michon lived in a house on the left-hand side of the street, belonging to a gardener. He rented a big room on the first floor, and as the gardener lived in the other side of the house, overlooking the Rue Catherine, Julien was left to himself, with his own stairway and door. At twenty-five, Julien was as set in his ways as any retired middle-class citizen.

In the old days, the Michons were harness-makers at Alluets near Mantes. After their death—and Julien's parents died when he was very young—an uncle sent Julien to a boarding school. When he too died, Julien had to earn a living and for the past five years had been a clerk in the post office at P—. He earned a very small wage and had no prospect of a raise. Yet he managed to save a little and considered himself lucky.

Julien was tall, big-boned, and very self-conscious of his large hands. He felt that he was ugly, his head too square and like a sculpture left unpolished and roughly finished by an inexperienced sculptor. Therefore he was shy and particularly so toward girls. He remembered with embarrassment that a laundress had once laughingly told him that he was not too bad. He walked with dangling arms, hunched back, and bent head, striding along as though he wanted to catch up with his own shadow. His awkwardness gave him a perpetually alarmed air and an unhealthy wish to bury himself in ordinariness and self-effacement. He seemed resigned to growing older in his own way, without friends and without a girl, like a cloistered monk.

But the existence he led did not seem to weigh on his broad shoulders. Julien was very happy in his own way. His outlook on life was calm and uncomplicated. He went about his daily work, with its set routine, in a straightforward way. He left each morning and applied himself to his job just as he had done the previous day. He lunched on a sandwich, went back to work, later returned home, had his supper, retired to bed, and slept. The following day he did the same things, and so on throughout the week, and for months on end. This routine eventually lulled him into the same way of life as that of oxen dragging carts during the daytime and resting at night in clean straw. He endured with pleasure the monotony of the life he led. After dinner, he often liked to walk down the Rue Beau-Soleil and sit on the bridge until nine o'clock. With his legs dangling over the water, he enjoyed watching the River Chanteclair below and listening to the whisper of its silver ripples. The water reflected the willows overhanging from the banks, and twilight filled the sky with an ashy softness. Julien loved the surrounding calm and felt that the Chanteclair shared his contentment as it flowed ceaselessly and silently along its appointed course. When the stars came out he went home to bed, replete with the freshness of the evening.

Julien had other distractions. On public holidays he went walking for long distances and returned worn out. He made friends with a dumb man, a printer's engraver, with whom he would walk for a whole afternoon without their exchanging even a sign. And sometimes he went to the Café des Voyageurs and played draughts with his dumb friend, games that were both slow and thoughtful. At one time he kept a dog, but it was run over by a carriage, and his affection for it was so deep and lasting that he could never again bring himself to have a pet at home.

His colleagues at the post office used to tease him about a ragged and barefoot little girl of about ten who sold boxes of matches. He gave her money but always left the matches, and took good care to be out of sight when he did so because the others' teasing annoyed him. He had never been seen in the company of a girl on the walks above the town walls. Even the working girls of P—, who were by no means slow in coming forward, decided in the end to leave him in peace, once they had seen him frozen with embarrassment because he took their laughing encouragement for mockery. Some of the townspeople called him stupid, while others maintained that a sharp eye should be kept on such boys, with their gentle airs and solitary habits.

Julien's sole refuge and the only place where he could breathe freely was his room. There he felt safely shut away from people. He could hold up his head, laugh out loud, and, catching sight of himself in his looking glass, be surprised at how young he looked. His room was very big and he had moved into it a large sofa, a round table, two upright chairs, and an armchair. But there was still plenty of space to walk around; his bed stood unseen in a deep alcove, and a walnut dressing chest between two windows looked like a toy. Whether walking around or lying down he never tired of his own company. Once he left his office, he never set pen to paper and decided that reading tired him. The old woman who ran the place he went to for his meals persisted in trying to educate him and lent him novels that he took back to her without being able to remember a thing about plots he found too complicated and, to his way of thinking, lacking in common sense. He used to draw a little, always the same profile of a woman with a stern expression, her braids twisted around her head and pearls wound into her hair. His only passion was music, and for whole evenings at a time he played the flute. This, more than anything, was his great relaxation.

Julien's playing was self-taught. For a long time one of his dearest ambitions had been to buy a flute of yellow wood from a junk dealer in the market place. He had the money but dared not go into the shop for fear of looking ridiculous. At last he plucked up enough courage one evening to buy it, and hurried off with the flute held tight beneath his overcoat. For two years, with doors and windows carefully closed so that he should not be overheard, he went over and over again an old teaching manual that he had picked up in a little bookshop. It was only during the past six months that he had dared play with the window open. He could only play tunes, slow and simple romantic airs, a century old, which were unbearably tender as he played them with the clumsiness of a novice bursting with feeling. During the warm evenings when the neighborhood was asleep, the sound of the flute floated from the big candlelit room like a soft vibrating voice that spoke of love to the lonely night—not daring to do so in the daytime.

If Julien played a tune he knew by heart, he would often blow out the light and play in the dark, so saving on the candles. Passers-by used to look up, wondering whence came this frail, pleasing sound, not unlike the song of a distant nightingale. As the old yellow wood of the flute was slightly cracked, it had a rather muted tone, like the still, innocent voice of an old gentlewoman singing the minuets of her youth. One by one the notes took the air with a fragile, winged sound, as if the melody belonged to night itself, blending with the nocturnal sighs and shadows.

Julien was always afraid that the neighbors might complain. But the inhabitants of small country towns sleep soundly, and the only people whose houses gave on to the Place des Quatre-Femmes were a lawyer named Savournin and Captain Pidoux, a retired police officer. Both neighbors were in bed and asleep by nine o'clock. But Julien was more afraid of the people living in the big private house belonging to the Marsanne family, a house whose gray and dismal façade was directly in front of his windows, austere as a cloister. A flight of stone steps, green with grass, led up to a door with a rounded arch, studded with huge nails. It had only two stories and its ten windows were opened and closed at the same time each day without revealing a glimpse of the rooms that lay hidden behind tight drawn thick curtains. On the left, the tall chestnut trees in the garden threw up a billow of green leaves that foamed to the eaves of the house. When Julien looked at this impressive mansion, with its private grounds, imposing walls, and air of majestic boredom, it seemed to him that the Marsannes only had to say the word to stop his playing the flute.

As Julien leaned on his window sill and looked out at the sprawling grandeur of it all, he had an almost religious feeling about the building and its grounds. The Marsannes' house was famous in the district, and it was said that visitors from far-off places came to see it. There were also stories about the Marsanne fortune. For a long time Julien stared at the old house in an attempt to fathom the mysteries of that all-powerful wealth. But in the hours he spent dreaming at his window, all he could see were the gray walls and the dark spread of the chestnut trees.

Nobody ever walked down the uneven stone steps, and the great mossy door was never opened; it had been closed when the Marsannes took to using a side gate on the Rue Saint-Anne. There was another entrance at the far end of an alley near the town walls. This led into the garden, but Julien could not see it from his room. It seemed to him that the house was as dead as one of those fairy-tale palaces inhabited by invisible people. He could just see, each morning and evening, the arms of a servant who opened and closed the shutters, and then the house lapsed once again into its usual melancholy look of a neglected tomb in a churchyard. The branches of the chestnuts spread so low and thick that they hid the paths in the garden. The impression of being near a hermetically sealed existence, haughty and silent, sharpened the young man's excitement. So that was wealth? A sad kind of peace, which gave you the same sort of religious shivers as a church vault!

He often stayed at his window for an hour at a time after blowing out his candle, in the hope of probing the secrets of the Marsannes. At night the house stood out against the sky as a dark silhouette and the chestnuts cast their inky shadow against it. The curtains must have been very carefully drawn, because no chink of light showed through the shutters. The house even seemed to be without that kind of breathing inhabited houses have, in which the breath of sleeping people can be sensed. It melted completely into the darkness of night; and it was then that Julien took heart to play boldly. He was able to trill away without hindrance and the empty house opposite echoed the pearl-like notes. Slow passages trickled away into the shadows of the garden, where you could have heard a pin drop. The old yellow wood seemed to play its ancient airs before Sleeping Beauty's castle.

One Sunday, when Julien was in the square where the church stood, a colleague from the post office pointed out to him a tall old man and an old woman: the Marquis and Marquise de Marsanne. Julien had never seen them before, since they went out so rarely. He was strangely moved by the thin and solemn couple who walked with measured tread and acknowledged obsequious greetings with a slight nod. Julien's companion told him that they had a daughter, Mademoiselle Thérèse de Marsanne, who was still at convent school. He added that young Colombel, Monsieur Savournin's clerk, was the son of Thérèse's wet nurse. As the old couple turned into the Rue Saint-Anne, Colombel went up to them and the Marquis shook hands with him, an honor he had not granted to anyone else in the street that morning. It cut Julien to the quick because Colombel, a youth of twenty with clever eyes and a peevish mouth, was an old enemy. He used to tease Julien about his shyness and set the laundresses of the Rue Beau-Soleil on him, to such an extent that the two boys fought one day and the lawyer's clerk collected a pair of black eyes.

That Sunday evening, recalling what he had learned in the morning about the Marsannes, Julien played his flute more softly than ever. Yet his preoccupation with the Marsanne house did not upset his daily habits, which were as regular as clockwork. He went to his office, lunched and supped, and took a walk along the bank of the Chanteclair, and eventually the silent house became a part of his quiet life. After two years he had grown so used to the grass in the cracks of the stone steps and the gray wall of the house with the black shutters, that they fell into place with everything and merged with the neighborhood.

Julien had been living in the Place des Quatre-Femmes for five years when something happened one July evening that changed his whole life. It was warm, and the sky was bright with stars. He was playing in the dark without paying much attention to what he was doing, lingering on certain notes and changing tempi, when suddenly a window in the Marsanne house opened and stayed open, lighting up the gray wall. A young girl leaned on the sill, in profile, as if she were listening. Julien trembled and stopped playing. He could not see the girl's face clearly, but only her shoulder-length hair. A soft voice floated over to him out of the silence.

"Did you hear that, Francoise? It sounded like music."

"Perhaps it was just a nightingale, mademoiselle," replied a rough voice from inside the room. "Close the window, and mind the insects don't get in."

When the house was once more shrouded in darkness, Julien sat in his chair, his eyes still seeing the square of light that had appeared in a wall which, until then, had seemed dead. He shivered, wondering whether or not he should be pleased by what he had seen. An hour went by and then he began to play again, very softly, and smiling at the idea that the girl probably thought it was a nightingale singing in the chestnut trees.

II

Next day everyone at the post office was talking about Mademoiselle Thérèse de Marsanne having come home from convent school. Julien did not mention that he had seen her, with her hair hanging loose about her shoulders. He was very perturbed and had a peculiar, indefinable resentment against this girl who would upset his habits. That window opposite, which might open at any moment, was certainly going to be a nuisance. He would no longer feel at home; a man at the window would have been preferable because a woman was always more ready to make fun of you. How could he go on with the flute now? He played too badly for the ears of a young lady who had surely studied music. By evening, after thinking about it all day, he was convinced that he detested Thérèse.

Julien crept home furtively that day and did not light a candle when he went into his room, so that she would not see him. He was so bad tempered that he thought of going to bed at once. But the wish to know what was going on in the house opposite was too strong. The window stayed shut. At about ten o'clock, only a pale gleam showed between the slats of the shutters, and when it went out he was left staring at a dark rectangle.

Each evening, from then on, he took up his reluctant watch. He spied on the house and noticed, as he had done when he first lived there, every puff of breeze that brushed against the silent old stones. Nothing seemed to have changed and the house appeared to be sunk in the same profound sleep as before. Only by straining his eyes and ears could he sense the new life that had entered it. Sometimes it was a light moving behind the windowpanes, the edge of a curtain not tightly drawn, a glimpse of an enormous room. At other times he caught the sound of a light step in the garden, of a distant piano accompanying a voice, or of even fainter noises betraying the presence of youth within the ancient walls. Julien explained his curiosity to himself by pretending that the noises disturbed him. How he missed the old days, when the empty house echoed the music of his flute!

Although he would not admit it to himself, one of his deepest wishes was to see Thérèse again. He saw in his mind's eye a pink face, a mischievous expression, and sparkling eyes. But since he never dared look out his window in the daytime, he merely had a glimpse of her at night, in deep shadow.

One morning, as he was opening his shutters to let in the sun, he saw Thérèse standing in the middle of her room. He stood stock still, not daring to move. She was tall and pale, with regular and beautiful features, and seemed lost in thought. She was so different from the picture he had formed of her that he was almost frightened. Her mouth was wide, with very red lips, and her deep-set eyes, dark and expressionless, gave her a cruel and regal look. She crossed slowly to the window, appearing not to see him, as if he were too far, too remote from her. As she moved away, there was so much grace and strength in the rhythmical swaying of her neck that Julien, despite his broad shoulders, felt as weak as a child by comparison. When he got to know her she alarmed him even more.

Henceforth the young man led a miserable existence. This beautiful girl with her serious and patrician expression, who was living so near him, drove him to despair. She never looked at him, she ignored his presence. But the thought that she might notice him and find him ridiculous made him shudder. His pathological shyness led him to believe that her every movement was calculated to make fun of him. He took to slinking home with his shoulders hunched and, once in his room, he took good care not to move around. Why didn't she look at him? When walked to her window, glanced at the dark stones below, and then turned away without suspecting that he was anxiously watching from the other side of the square. And just as he had once trembled at the idea that she might see him, so now he shivered with the desire to feel her gaze upon him. His every thought was of her.

When Thérèse rose in the morning, Julien, who had always been punctual, forgot about his office. Her pale face and red lips still frightened him, but now he enjoyed the feeling of fear. Hidden behind a curtain, he let himself be filled with the terror she inspired in him until he felt faint and his legs trembled as though he had walked a long way. In his daydreams he imagined that she suddenly noticed him and that his fear vanished because she smiled at him.

He then had the notion of winning her over with music. On warm evenings he began playing again. He left the window wide open and, in the dark, played the oldest tunes he knew—pastorales as simple as the country songs that girls sing. Lingering tremolo notes followed one another like lovesick ladies of another age dancing with their skirts outspread. He played on moonless nights and when the square was in darkness, so that nobody could tell whence came the soft music that brushed the sleeping houses with the gentleness of a night bird's wing. One evening, he had the thrill of seeing Thérèse, dressed in white, lean on her window sill at bedtime, listening to the same music she had heard on the day she returned home.

"Listen to that, Francoise," she said in her deep voice. "It can't be a bird, can it?"

"Oh," replied an elderly woman whose shadow Julien could just see, "it's probably a street musician playing down in the town somewhere."

"Yes, it's very far off," said the young girl after a moment's silence, cooling her arms on the sill in the evening breeze.

After this Julien played louder in the evenings. The fever in his blood rounded the notes and pulsed through the old yellow wood of the flute. Thérèse listened each night and wondered about the elusive music that danced to her ears from rooftop to rooftop once darkness had fallen. One evening the music was so close that it washed over her, and she guessed that it came from one of the old, sleeping houses in the square, Julien played with all the passionate feeling of which he was capable. The dark lent him such courage that he hoped to attract her by the sound of his music. And Thérèse did, in fact, lean out of her window as if she were drawn and won over by it.

"Come inside," said the old woman. "It's stormy and you'll have nightmares."

Julien could not sleep that night. He imagined that Thérèse had guessed his feelings and might even have seen him. As he tossed and turned feverishly in his bed, he wondered if he should show himself at the window the next day. It seemed ridiculous to go on hiding now. But he decided against it and was standing at his window at six the following morning, putting his flute back in its case, when Thérèse's window opened.

Usually Thérèse never rose until eight, but there she was, in a dressing gown and with her hair braided at the nape of her neck, leaning on her window sill. Julien stared stupidly at her, unable to turn away and with his hands fumbling with the flute he was trying to take apart. Thérèse stared back with a steady and imperious look. For a moment she seemed to be taking him in—his great, bony, rough-hewn body that gave him the ugliness of a shy giant. She was longer the excited young girl of whom he had caught a glimpse the previous evening. Now she had a haughty air; she was very pale and her lips were very red. When she had finished studying him with the detached air with which she would have summed up a dog on the footpath, had her opinion been asked, the slight pursing of her lips expressed disapproval and, turning her back on him, she closed the window.

With legs trembling, Julien collapsed into a chair, babbling to himself. "Oh, my God! She doesn't like me! And I love her so much, I'll die!"

He put his head in his hands and sobbed. That was what came of letting himself be seen. When one is awkward and shambling, it is better to keep out of sight and not frighten young girls. He cursed himself, furious at his ugliness. He should have gone on playing the flute in the dark, like a night bird that charms with its song, and never have shown himself in the light of day if he wanted to please her. Then he would have remained for her a soft music, just an old melody of a mysterious love. Then, too, she would have adored him without knowing him, like a kind of Prince Charming come from afar to die of love beneath her window. But he, rough and stupid Julien, had broken the spell. Now that she knew him to be as coarse as an ox, she would nevermore like the music he played.

And indeed, although he went on playing his most tender airs and chose the warm nights filled with the scent of flowers and leaves, Thérèse no longer listened, no longer heard him. She walked back and forth in her room and leaned on her window sill as if he were not there in the house opposite, telling of his love in humble notes. There was even a time when she exclaimed, "Oh, that out-of-tune flute gets on my nerves!"

Julien, in despair, threw the flute into a drawer and gave up playing.

Young Colombel too, jeered at Julien. As he was going to his office one day, he had looked up and seen Julien practicing at his window. Ever since then, Colombel had laughed sarcastically whenever he crossed the square. Julien knew that Colombel was invited to the Marsannes' house; and that was a heart-rending thought—not because Julien was jealous of the little creature, but because he would have given his life's blood to be in his place for just one hour.

Colombel's mother, old Francoise, had been in the household for years. She had suckled Thérèse as a baby and now she was her personal maid. The child of noble family and the little peasant boy had grown up together, and it was quite natural that something of their childhood friendship should have remained. But this did nothing to lessen Julien's suffering when he met Colombel in the street and saw his thin-lipped smile. His antipathy increased from the day he realized that the skinny youth was rather good-looking. He had a face like a cat, delicate, pretty, and devilish, with green eyes and a slight beard curling on his soft chin. If only Julien could have pushed him into a corner of the ramparts, he would have made him pay dearly for his luck in visiting Thérèse at home!

A year went by. Julien was very unhappy. He lived only for Thérèse. His heart was locked in that cold house across the way and he was dying of love and his own clumsiness. Whenever he had a moment to spare, he went to his room and stared across at the gray wall whose every patch of moss he knew by heart. During those long months he had strained both eyes and ears, yet still had no idea of the kind of life that went on in the grim house that had become the prison of his soul. He was thrown into confusion by the slightest sounds and the smallest glimmers of light. What was going on? A celebration or a funeral? He could never tell, because only the front of the house, on the other side, gave any sign of life. According to whether he was sad or happy he daydreamed whatever he wished: the boisterous games played by Thérèse and Colombel, the young girl strolling beneath the branches of the chestnuts, the dancing that placed her in the arms of her partners, her sudden melancholic moods that sent her to her shuttered room to sit and weep. Or perhaps all he heard were the mincing steps of the Marquis and Marquise crossing the old floors like mice. He really knew nothing; all he had before his eyes was Thérèse's window set in that mysterious wall. Every day she came to the window, as silent as the stone itself, and never once did her appearance there give him cause for hope. He was filled with dismay when he thought how unknown and distant she was to him.

Julien's happiest moments were the days when the window remained open. Then he could see every corner of the room while Thérèse was out of it. It took him six months to discover that her bed was in an alcove to the left and that it had pink silk curtains. Then, after a further six months, he saw that opposite the bed was a Louis Quinze chest with a looking glass in a china frame on top of it. There was also a white marble fireplace. The room became Julien's dream paradise.

His love for her was torn in all directions. For weeks on end he hid himself, ashamed of his ugliness. Then, in all his feverish longing, he was rent by anger and the wish to show her his strong limbs and irregular features. Again, for weeks at a time, he went to his window, wearing her down with his steady stare. On two occasions he blew kisses to her, with that roughness of which shy people are capable when they are carried away by a sudden gust of audacity.

Thérèse was not even annoyed. While he watched her from his hiding place, she went to and fro with the same regal expression and, when he came into view, she looked no different, only haughtier and colder. He never caught her in an unguarded moment. If their eyes met, she was in no hurry to turn away. When he heard in the post office that Mademoiselle de Marsanne was very devout and kind, he protested silently. No, she was not religious at all, she was ruled only by the pulsing of her blood and that was why she had bright red lips; the pallor of her face was the result of the contempt with which she treated everyone. Then he would weep because he had insulted her and he begged her forgiveness, as though she were a saint wrapped in the purity of her own wings.

During that first year, the days went by without bringing any change in the situation. When summer came around again, Julien was disturbed by a strange feeling. The same things happened each day, shutters opening in the morning and closing at evening, and her regular appearances. Yet there was the hint of something new from her room. Thérèse was both paler and taller. One day, in a feverish moment, he dared once more to blow a kiss from the tips of his burning fingers. She stared fixedly at him in her disturbing way without leaving her window and it was Julien who turned away with a crimson face.

Toward the end of summer something happened that shook Julien deeply, although it was quite ordinary. Almost every day at twilight Thérèse's window, which had been left ajar, was closed so roughly that both wood and fastener creaked. Each time Julien started violently, racked by doubts and deeply troubled in heart without knowing why. After this sudden clatter, the house relapsed into such a deathly silence that he was afraid. For a long time he was unable to see whose hands closed the window, but one evening he saw Thérèse's pale hands snatch at the fastening with angry impatience. Then, an hour later, when she opened it again, she did so slowly and listlessly, pausing a moment to rest her elbows on the sill. Then she paced slowly throughout her room, with all its virginal purity, preoccupied with the sweet nothings that young girls think about. Julien remained without a thought in his head, but with the creaking of the window latches constantly in his ears.

One autumn evening, when the weather was mild and the sky overcast, he heard the shutter creak more violently than usual. Julien shuddered and tears coursed down his cheeks without his knowing shy, as he sat facing the dismal walls fading into the shadows of twilight. That morning it had rained and the half-bare chestnut trees had a smell of death about them.

Yet Julien waited for the window to open again. And suddenly it did, as abruptly as it had closed. Thérèse stood there. She was very pale, wide-eyed and with her hair falling about her face. She stayed in front of the open window and blew a kiss to Julien, touching her scarlet mouth with the tips of all ten fingers.

In his dismay, he clasped both hands to his chest, as though asking if that kiss were meant for him.

Thérèse thought he was retreating and she leaned farther out, placed her fingers to her lips again, and blew him a second kiss. Then a third—as though she were sending back to Julien the three kisses he had sent to her. He stood open-mouthed, staring at her framed there by her window in the pale twilight.

When she thought she had convinced him, she glanced down into the little square and said in a stifled voice,

"Come."

He went down and walked toward the Marsanne house. As he looked up, a door was opened—that same door that had been bolted for perhaps half a century and the hinges of which were thick with lichen. He walked in a stupor, no longer surprised at anything. The moment he entered the house, the door closed and a small icy hand took his and led him up a flight of stairs, along a corridor, through a room, and into another that he recognized at once. He stood in that dreamed-of paradise, the room with the pink silk bed curtains. The sun was setting slowly. He wanted to fall to his knees but Thérèse stood straight before him, her hands clasped firmly and so resolute that she suppressed the shiver that almost ran through her.

"Do you love me?" she demanded in a low voice.

"Yes, yes," he stammered.

She made a sign with one hand, forbidding him to waste words. She continued in a haughty voice that lent her words a chaste sincerity becoming to the lips of a young girl.

"If I gave myself to you, you would do anything I ask, would you not?"

He was unable to reply, but merely clasped his hands. He would have sold his soul for a single kiss.

"Well, then, I want you to do something for me."

Since he still stood in a daze, she spoke with sudden violence, feeling that she was near the end of her strength and that she might not risk going further.

"Look here, you must swear to me first. I'll keep my side of the bargain. Swear, swear to me now!"

"I promise. Yes, anything you wish," he said with complete abandon.

The scent of her room intoxicated him. The bed curtains were drawn and the mere though of that chaste bed in the soft shadow of the pink hangings filled him with an almost religious ecstasy. Then, with suddenly brutal hands, she tore open the curtains and revealed the alcove lit by the sinister fading light of evening. The bed was in disorder, the sheets trailing, and a pillow on the floor looked as though a hole had been bitten in it. Across the rumpled lace-edge bed-clothes, there sprawled the barefoot body of a man.

"There," she said in a strangled voice, "that man was my lover. I pushed him, he fell, and I don't know what happened. Anyway, he's dead and you've got to get him out of here. Do you understand? That's all there is to it, so there you are."

III

When she was a small girl, Thérèse de Marsanne bullied Colombel. He was barely six months older than she, and Francoise, her wet nurse, had raised her son—with some difficulty—on a nursing bottle. As he grew up in the house, he later found himself in a vague relationship, somewhere between servant and playmate, to the little girl.

Thérèse was a difficult child. She was, however, neither noisy nor a tomboy. Far from it—she was strangely serious in manner and led those visitors to whom she dropped low curtsies into believing she was a model child. But she did odd things. She would suddenly shout incoherently and stamp furiously when she was alone, or lie flat on her back in the middle of a garden path, obstinately refusing to get up despite the slaps she was given.

Nobody knew what went on in her mind. She already veiled any expression in her eyes, and instead of those calm pools in which one sees the souls of little girls, there was an inky darkness in which it was impossible to read anything.

From the age of six, she began torturing Colombel. He was sickly and small for his years. She used to lead him to the foot of the garden to a place under the chestnut trees and, hidden by branches, leap on his back and make him carry her. She would ride him around in a circle for an hour at a time, squeezing his neck, digging her heels into his ribs, without stopping to let him get his breath back. He was the horse and she was the lady rider. When he stumbled and seemed fit to drop, she bit his ear until it bled, gripping him so furiously that her little nails dug into his flesh. And the gallop would begin again, with the cruel little six year-old queen, her hair streaming behind her as they sped between the trees, riding on the back of the small boy, who she treated like a beast of burden.

Later, in the presence of her parents, she pinched him and forbade him to cry out, threatening to have him sent out of the house if he dared mention the games they played. A kind of secret life sprang up between them, a way of being together that changed when they were with other people. If they were alone, she treated him like a toy that she wanted to break to see what was inside. For wasn't she a marquise, used to seeing people at her feet? And as she had been given a little man to play with, she could do whatever she wanted with him. As she got bored with bullying Colombel when they were out of sight, she invented the added pleasure of kicking him or sticking a pin in his arm when they were among others, mesmerizing him to such an extent with her big solemn eyes that he did not even wince.

Colombel endured his martyrdom with a silent rebellion that often made him tremble with the wish to strangle his young mistress, before he could master his feelings and hide them in his downcast eyes. But Colombel, too, had a sly temperament. He did not actually dislike being beaten and even got a bitter kind of pleasure out of it. Sometimes he deliberately allowed himself to be pricked and, trembling violently, waited for the thrust of the pin. And, when its point pierced his flesh, felt a sense of real fulfillment as he gave himself up to the delights of resentment. He began to take his revenge by falling on stones, dragging Thérèse down with him, heedless of the risk of breaking a leg and delighted when she got bruised. If he refused to cry out when she pricked him in front of others, it was so that nobody should come between them. What went on between them was strictly their affair, a struggle from which he felt he would eventually emerge victorious.

The Marquis was concerned about this violent streak in his daughter's character. He said that she took after one of her uncles, who had led a wild and adventurous life until he was murdered in a sordid district. A thread of tragedy ran through the history of the Marsannes, a strange twist through their arrogant and distinguished line, handed on down the ages. It was like a touch of madness or a form of perversion, a faulty streak that looked for a time as though it might be the end of the family. The Marquis therefore assumed that he was doing the right thing when he sent Thérèse to a convent school where she would be subjected to a strict discipline that he hoped would make her more tractable. She stayed at the convent until she was eighteen.

When Thérèse returned home, she was well-behaved and very tall. Her parents were pleased by her apparent piety. In church, she sat with her forehead bent over clasped hands. At home, she radiated innocence and peace. Her only fault was greediness. From morn to night she ate sweets, sucking them avidly and half-closing her eyes at the same time. Nobody would have recognized the sullen and stubborn child who had once come in from the garden with her clothes in tatters, refusing to say how she got into such a mess. The Marquis and Marquise had kept closed house for fifteen years and they now thought about inviting people again. They gave dinners for their aristocratic neighbors and even held a ball now and then. They hoped to find a husband for their daughter, but although she was well-mannered, well-dressed, and danced well, there was something in the expression on her pale face that alarmed the young men who fell in love with her.

Since her return, Thérèse had never once mentioned Colombel. The Marquis had kept an eye on him and placed him in Monsieur Savournin's office after having attended to his education. One day Francoise brought her son to the house and pushed him forward, presenting him to Thérèse and reminding her that they used to be playmates. Colombel smiled, was very neat and clean, and showed no trace of embarrassment. Thérèse stared calmly at him, said that of course he remembered him, and then turned away. But a week later Colombel was back and he soon slipped into his old position in the house. Each evening, after leaving his office, he went there with music and book. Nobody paid very much attention to him and he was given the run of the house as if he were a servant or a poor relation. He was one of the family's responsibilities. And so he was left alone with the young girl without anyone giving it a second thought. Just as they had done when they were children, so now they shut themselves in the large rooms or stayed for hours in shady hidden corners of the garden. But they no longer played the same games. Thérèse sauntered around, her skirts swishing against the grass, and Colombel, dressed like a rich young man about town, walked beside her, prodding the ground now and then with the Malacca cane he always carried.

Yet once more she became queen and he, her slave. True, she no longer bit him, but she had a way of walking at his side that made him seem smaller and smaller, changing him into a court lackey holding his sovereign's train. She tormented him with her capricious moods, talking affectionately and then, as the whim struck her, switching to a stony hardness. For his part, Colombel—once she turned her head—shot glances at her as bright and sharp as the edge of a sword, and his whole twisted personality was coiled as he watched and planned treachery.

One summer evening, after they had been walking for a long time in the shade of the chestnut trees, Thérèse thought for a moment and then said, very seriously, "You know, Colombel, I'm tired. Suppose you carry me like you used to. Remember?"

He laughed lightly and then replied, in the same serious tone, "If you like, Thérèse."

But she began walking again and merely replied, "All right. I just wanted to know."

They continued their stroll. Night fell and the shadows lay dark beneath the branches. They were talking about a woman in the town who had married an officer. As they turned into a narrow path, Colombel was about to step back so that she could pass in front of him when she pushed him violently and made him go first. They both fell silent.

Suddenly Thérèse leaped onto his back with the same agility as when she was a small, wild girl.

"Come on! Get going!" she said in a different voice, chocked with the same violence she had shown as a child.

She snatched his cane and beat his thighs with it. Clutching his shoulders and almost suffocating him with the nerve-tightened grip of a rider's legs, she drove him crazily into the black shadows of the bushes. She went on beating him, guiding his course so that he should go as fast as possible. The sound of his headlong gallop was muted by the grass. He had not said a single word; he panted deeply, bracing himself on his short, slender legs beneath the tall young girl's warm weight around his neck.

But when she cried out "That's enough," he did not stop. He galloped even faster, as though carried on by his own momentum. With his hands clasped behind him, he held her so tightly by the thighs that she could not jump off. Now the horse was running away from its mistress. Suddenly, despite the scourging cane and her searing nails, he careered toward a gardener's tool shed. There he threw her to the ground and raped her on the straw-littered floor. His turn to be master had come at last.

Thérèse grew paler, her lips redder, and the circles around her eyes darker. She continued her pious mode of life. A few days later the same thing happened again: she leaped onto Colombel's back, tried to master him, and finished by being thrown on the straw in the shed. In front of others, her attitude to him was unchanged—she still showed the kindness and condescension of an older sister. He, too, was still calm and smiling. They were once more just as they had been when they were six years old, like vicious animals that, the moment they were turned loose, fell to biting each other. But now, in the stormy moments of lust, it was the male who was the victor.

Their sexual relationship was terrifying. Thérèse let Colombel go to her bedroom. She had given him a key to the little garden door that led into the alley of the town ramparts. To reach her he had to pass through another room at night, the very room, in fact, where his mother slept. But the lovers displayed such calm audacity that they were never surprised. They even took to meeting in broad daylight. Colombel went to her before dinner and Thérèse closed the shutters against the neighbors' eyes. They were driven into each other's company at all hours, not in order to whisper those tender nothings that lovers of twenty exchange, but to continue the struggle between their respective prides. They often fell to quarreling, insulting each other in low voices, trembling with temper the more because they could not give way to their urge to shout and fight aloud.

One evening, as he walked about in Thérèse's room, barefoot and in his shirt sleeves, it occurred to Colombel to pick her up in the way strong men in a fairground grasp their opponents at the start of a wrestling bout. Thérèse tried to free herself and said, "Let me go. You know I'm stronger than you. I'll hurt you."

"Go on then, hurt me," he sniggered.

He always used to shake her to get the better of her. She, fighting back, would cross her arms and thrust back at him. They often did this through an impulse to struggle together. More often than not, it was Colombel who fell backward onto the carpet, choking, limp, and helpless. He was too short and she could pick him up and crush him to her as if she were a giantess.

But on this particular evening, Thérèse slipped to her knees and Colombel, with a rapid movement, knocked her flat and stood triumphantly over her.

"There you are, you see. You're not stronger than I," he sneered.

She turned white with fury. Rising slowly to her feet, she grabbed him without a word but with such trembling anger that he shuddered. She wanted to strangle and get rid of him; to see him stretched out before her, beaten once and for all. For a moment they struggled together in silence, breathing in gasps, their limbs cracking with the strain. It was no longer a game: there was a cold air of murder about them. Colombel's breath began rattling in his throat. Afraid that someone might overhear them,, she pushed him in a final, terrible effort. His temple struck the corner of the dressing table and he slumped to the floor.

Thérèse stood for a moment, getting back her breath. She looked into the glass, smoothed back her hair, and patted the creases out of her skirt, deliberately ignoring her vanquished opponent. Then she prodded him with her foot. When he did not move, she bent over him, a chill prickling at the nape of her neck. She saw Colombel's wax-white face, his glassy eyes and twisted mouth. His right temple was smashed in by the corner of the table. Colombel was dead.

She straightened up, frozen with horror, and spoke aloud in the silence. "Dead! So now he's dead."

The sudden realization of what had happened filled her with searing anguish. For a second, she had certainly wanted to kill him. But it was merely a stupid angry thought. You always want to kill when you fight, but you don't, because having bodies around is too awkward. No, she was not guilty, because she had not intended to kill him. And to think that he was lying dead in her room!

She went on talking brokenly to herself.

"It's done now. He's dead and he won't leave here of his own accord."

After the paralyzing stupor of the first few moments, a feverish feeling coursed like a flame through her whole body. A dead man was lying in her bedroom. She could never explain how he came to be there, with his feet bare, in his shirt sleeves, and with a hole in his temple. She was in a desperate fix.

Thérèse bent and looked at the wound. As she did so she froze with terror. She could hear Francoise, Colombel's mother, in the corridor. And there were other noises in the house, footsteps and voices and the preparations for the reception to be held that very evening. Any minute now someone might call her or come looking for her. The lover she had killed seemed to have reversed their roles and was now weighing her down with their guilt.

Her head reeled and she got up and began walking round and round her room. She sought some corner in which to hide the corpse sprawling across her very future. She peered under the furniture and probed into corners, trembling with fury at her own helplessness. No, there was not a single corner; the alcove was not deep enough, the wardrobes were too shallow— nothing in the whole room was of any use as a hiding place. Yet it was there that they had concealed their kisses! He used to come in with his quiet, cat-like, and viciously stealthy step and leave in the same way. She would never have imagined that he could have become so heavy.

Thérèse stamped and raged around her room with the vibrant anger of a hunted animal, and then she had an inspiration. Suppose she threw Colombel out the window? But then he would be found and they would guess from which window he had fallen. Nevertheless, she had crossed to the window and raised the curtain to look out and suddenly she saw the young man who lived opposite, that idiot who played the flute, leaning on his window sill with a hangdog air. His pale face was well-known to her, since he was always staring at her window. She was tired of that face and its cringing devotion to her. She stopped when she saw Julien, so humble and lovesick. A smile lit her pale face. There lay her salvation. That fool across the way loved her with the passion of a chained dog and would obey her, even to the extent of committing a crime. She had never felt any love toward him because he was too gentle, but she would make love to him and buy his eternal devotion with the gift of her body if he would share with her the blood of her crime. Her tongue flicked over her scarlet lips as if tasting a love spiced with terror that, because it was untasted, attracted her the more.

She snatched up Colombel's body like a bundle of wash and carried it to her bed. Then, opening her window, she blew kisses to Julien.

IV

Julien was plunged into a nightmare. When he recognized Colombel on the bed he was not surprised—he found it quite predictable and natural. Who but Colombel could have been lying there in the alcove, with his temple smashed in and his limbs sprawling in a position of hideous lewdness?

Thérèse had been talking to him for a long time. At first, he did not hear what she was saying and the words she spoke penetrated his stupor only as a confused noise. Then he realized that she was giving him orders and he made an effort to listen to her. He was to stay in the room until midnight, when the house would be dark and the guests gone. Because of the party her mother was giving, it was out of the question to do anything earlier, but the evening's entertainment had its advantages because it meant that everyone was too busy to go up to Thérèse's room. When the right time came, Julien would have to hoist the body onto his back, carry it out of the house, and throw it into the Chanteclair at the end of the Rue Beau-Soleil. According to the calm plan outlined by Thérèse, nothing could be easier.

She stopped talking and, placing her hands on his shoulders, asked, "Do you understand? It's agreed, isn't it?"

He shuddered.

"Yes, yes, anything you wish. I belong to you, body and soul."

With a solemn expression, she leaned toward him and because he did not understand what she wanted of him, she said, "Kiss me."

Trembling, he kissed her on her cold forehead. Neither of them spoke.

Thérèse had drawn the bed curtains. She dropped into the armchair in the shadows to snatch a little rest. After standing for a moment, Julien also sat down. Francoise was no longer in the next room and only muffled sounds reached the quiet and gradually darkening room.

For nearly an hour nothing stirred. The throbbing in Julien's head prevented him from thinking clearly. He was in Thérèse's room and that filled him with bliss. Then, when he suddenly remembered there was a corpse behind the curtains that brushed against him, he thought he would faint. Had she loved that creature? How in God's name was it possible? He forgave her for having killed him, but what enraged him was the sight of Colombel's bare feet lying among the lace-edged bed linen. How pleased he would be to chuck him from the bridge into that dark, deep part of the Chanteclair that he knew so well. Once they were rid of him, they could set about making love. Then, at the thought of the delight of which he would not dared to have dreamed that morning, he imagined himself on the bed instead of that lolling corpse, and the idea of the coldness of that place which he would take filled him with loathing.

Thérèse sat motionless in her deep armchair. All Julien could see of her was the outline of her hair against the pale light of the window. She sat there with her face in her hands and he could only guess at the cause of her exhaustion. Was it just physical relaxation after the terrible ordeal through which she had just gone? Was it crushing remorse, an emptiness left by her lover who was now sleeping his last sleep? Was she calmly working out the details of her plan of salvation, or was she hiding in the shadows the ravages that fear had left on her face: He had no way of telling.

In the silence the clock struck. Thérèse rose slowly to her feet and lit the candles on her dressing table, seeming as calm, poised, and strong as usual. She appeared to have forgotten about the body sprawling behind the pink silk curtains and went about the room with the unhurried step of a girl completely at ease in her own room. As she let her hair down she said, without turning around, "I have to dress this evening. If anyone comes in you'll hide, won't you?"

He sat there, looking at her. She already treated him like a lover, as if the blood-stained complicity between them had created the understanding of a long love affair.

She dressed her hair, her hand raised above her head. He shivered as he watched her, finding her so desirable, with her bare back turned toward him, her elbows moving slowly, her slender hands twisting curls upon her fingers. Did she wish to win him over completely, show him the woman who would be his if he did what she wanted?

When she had put on her shoes, there was a sound outside the door.

"Hide in the alcove," she said in a low voice.

Swiftly she threw over Colombel's stiff body the underclothes she had just removed, still warm and scented by her body.

Francoise came in and said, "They're waiting for you, mademoiselle."

"I'm just coming, Francoise dear," Thérèse replied calmly. "Give me a hand with my dress, will you?

Through a chink in the curtains, Julien could see the two women and he trembled at Thérèse's audacity. His teeth chattered so much that he took his lower jaw in his hand so that he would not be overheard. Beside him, one of Colombel's bare feet peeped out from under a petticoat. Suppose Francoise had opened the curtains and bumped into her son's naked foot!

"Be careful," said Thérèse, "you'll tear the flowers off."

There was not a tremor in her voice. She was smiling, a girl pleased to be going to a dance. Her frock was of white silk printed with wild roses, the white petals of which had a touch of crimson in the center. Standing in the middle of the room, she looked like a bouquet of flowers, white and virginal. Her bare arms and neck blended with the whiteness of her dress.

"Oh, how lovely you look, how lovely," repeated Francoise with deep satisfaction. "One moment, you don't have your garland."

She seemed to be looking for it and stretched out a hand to the curtains as though about to search on the bed. Julien almost cried out aloud in terror. But Thérèse said unhurriedly, smiling at her reflection in the mirror, "It's over there on my dressing table. Give it to me. No, don't touch my bed; all my clothes are there and you'll muddle them up."

Francoise helped her to place the garland of wild roses on her head, like a crown, with one end trailing onto her neck. Thérèse stood for a moment looking at herself with satisfaction. Then she was ready and drew on her gloves.

"Ah!" exclaimed Francoise. "There's not a statue of the Virgin in church that looks as white and pure as you!"

The compliment made Thérèse smile again. She looked at herself once more in the glass and walked toward the door, saying, "Come, let's go down. You may blow out the candles."

In the sudden darkness, Julien heard the door close and the silken swish of Thérèse's dress along the corridor. He sat on the floor at the back of the alcove, not daring to go out. A deep blackness hung like a veil before his eyes, but he sensed the naked foot beside him that seemed to freeze the entire room. He had no idea how long he sat there, his thoughts weighing on his mind like a kind of drowsiness, when the door opened again. He recognized the sound of Thérèse's dress. She did not go up to him, but merely set something down on the dressing table and whispered, "There, you've had no dinner. You must eat, you know."

The silken sound faded away down the corridor again. Julien got up; he could no longer stay suffocating in the alcove with Colombel. The clock struck eight and there were still four hours to go. He tiptoed soundlessly across the room.

By the faint light of the starlit night, he could make out the dark shapes of the furniture. Some corners of the room were buried in darkness. Only the looking glass cast a pale reflection, like that of old silver. He was not easily frightened, but in that somber room sweat ran down his face. All around him the dark shapes of the furniture seemed to move and take on menacing outlines. Three times he thought he heard sighs from the alcove. He halted in his tracks, terrified. Then, as he strained his ears, he heard gay sounds from below, a dance tune, the laughing murmur of a crowd. He closed his eyes and suddenly he was no longer in a dark pit. Bright lights blazed and he saw Thérèse, in a pure white dress, waltzing down a glittering room in the arms of her partner. The whole house echoed to the sound of merry music while he was there in that hideous place, alone and with chattering teeth. At one moment he started back in horror, thinking he had seen a light on a chair. When he plucked up courage to go over and see what it was, he found a white satin bodice. He took it in his hands, buried his face in the material softened by the young girl's breasts, and drugged himself with the smell of her.

There was such delight there that he wanted to forget everything. It was not a deathwatch he was keeping, but a love watch. He pressed his forehead against the windowpane and went over his love story. There, on the other side of the street, he could see his room with the windows still open. From there he had wooed Thérèse during long evenings of playing the flute that had confessed his love with the gentle voice of a shy lover, until she had been won over and smiled at him. The satin he held to his lips belonged to her, satin that had touched her skin and that she had left with him so he would not be impatient. His dream became so real that he left the window and ran to the door, thinking he had heard her.

The chill of the room struck and sobered him and then he remembered everything. Furiously, he made up his mind. He would return to her that very night. She was too beautiful and he loved her too much to wait. Where there is love and a crime had been committed, one must love with body-searing passion. Yes, he would come back, running and without losing a single minute, once the package had been cast in the river. Maddened by a sudden attack of nerves, he rolled his head in the bodice, biting the satin to choke his sobbing lust.

Ten o'clock struck. He listened, feeling he had been there for years, and waited in a daze. His hand touched the bread and fruit on the table and he ate standing up, ravenously and with a hunger he could not stay. He thought that food might give him strength, but once he had eaten, a terrible weariness overcame him. Night seemed to go on forever. From below the music rose louder, now and then the dancing shook the floor beneath his feet, and then carriages began to roll away from the house. His eyes were fixed on the door and he saw a kind of star of light shining through the keyhole. He did not even try to hide. If somebody came in, then that was that.

"No, thank you, Francoise," said Thérèse, coming into the room, candle in hand. "I can manage alone. Go to bed, you must be tired."

She closed the door and locked it. Finger to lips and candlestick in hand, she stood still for a moment. Dancing had not brought the slightest color to her cheeks. She said nothing and, setting down the candle, sat facing Julien. For half an hour they waited, looking at each other.

The downstairs doors finished banging and the house was quiet. Thérèse's greatest worry was that Francoise's room was next door. The old woman moved around in her room for a moment and then her bed creaked as she retired for the night. For a long time she tossed in her bed as though unable to get to sleep, but at last her deep and regular breathing could be heard through the wall.

Thérèse continued to stare seriously at Julien. She said only two words. "Come on."

They drew back the bed hangings and set about dressing little Colombel's corpse, already as stiff as a macabre puppet. When at last they finished, their foreheads ran with sweat.

"Come on," she said again.

Without hesitation and in a single movement, Julien swing Colombel's body across his shoulders, as a butcher carries a calf. His great, bony frame was bent and Colombel's feet swung a yard from the floor.

"I'll lead the way," whispered Thérèse quickly. "I'll hold onto your coat and you just let yourself be guided by me. And go slowly."

First they had to go through Francoise's room. That was the worst part of all. They had crossed it when one of the corpse's legs banged against a chair. The noise woke Francoise. They heard her raise her head from the pillow and mumble to herself. They stood, frozen to the floor, Thérèse near the door and he, weighed down by the body and terrified that the mother would discover them carrying her dead son to the river. It was a horrible moment. Then Francoise seemed to go to sleep again and they went out carefully into the corridor.

There another terror lay in wait for them. Thérèse's mother was still awake and a sliver of light came from her door, which was still ajar. They were too frightened to go either forward or backward. Julien felt that Colombel would slip from off his shoulders if they had to retrace their steps through Francoise's room. For nearly a quarter of an hour they stood stock still and Thérèse found courage enough to hold up the body so that Julien should not tire. At last the light went out and they were able to get down to the ground floor. They were safe at last.

Thérèse opened the old unused door. When Julien found himself in the middle of the Place des Quatre Femmes, with his load on his back, he could see her standing at the top of the steps, her white arms and white evening dress gleaming. She was waiting for him to come back.

V

Julien was as strong as a bull. As a boy, he liked helping the woodsmen in the forest near his home and carried three trunks on his young back. To him

Colombel was no heavier than a feather; the skinny fellow was no more than a bird on his back. He scarcely felt him there and was suddenly filled with a wicked delight at the feeling that Colombel was so light, so thin, like nothing at all, in fact. No longer would he sneer at him as he passed beneath Julien's window when he played the flute, and his sarcastic remarks in the street were over forever. The thought that he carried a rival on his back, stiff and cold, gave Julien a shiver of satisfaction. He hitched the corpse up onto the nape of his neck, gritted his teeth, and walked faster.

The town was in darkness. Yet there was a light at Captain Pidoux's window in the Place des Quatre Femmes. The captain was probably out of sorts and the distorted shadow of his big-bellied form could be seen crossing and recrossing the room behind the curtains. Alarmed at this, Julien was slipping along in the shadow of the houses on the other side when a sudden cough froze his blood. He stopped in a doorway and recognized Madame Savournin, the lawyer's wife, sitting at her window, gazing at the stars and sighing to herself. This was a quirk of fate, because usually at this time the Place des Quatre Femmes was wrapped in slumber. Fortunately, Madame Savournin decided at last to return to the side of her husband, whose deep snoring reverberated through the open window into the street. When the window had been closed, Julien walked quickly across the square, keeping an eye on the undulating and distorted shadow of Captain Pidoux.

Once he got into the narrow alley of the Rue Beau-Soleil, he was less frightened. The houses leaned so close to one another and the cobbled slope was so crooked that the starlight did not reach into the bottom of the trenchlike street filled with a thick stream of shadow. Once there and in shelter, Julien was filled with a mad desire to run, and he set off at a mad gallop. It was both dangerous and stupid. He knew that, but he could not help himself, feeling behind him the starlit square of the Place des Quatre Femmes, with the windows of the lawyer's wife and the captain like two great watching eyes on his back. His shoes made such a clatter on the stones that he thought he was being followed. Suddenly he stopped. From the blonde widow's dining club, thirty yards down the Rue Beau-Soleil, came the voices of the officers gathered there. They were probably drinking a toast to one of their comrades whose promotion had just come through. Julien knew that he was lost if they came back along the street. There was no intersecting street down which he could escape and he would certainly have no time to retrace his steps. Holding his breath until he nearly choked, he listened to the tramp of boots and the clicking noise of scabbards. For a moment he could not tell if the sounds were coming his way or going in the opposite direction. Little by little, the noise died away. He waited for a moment and then went on his way on tiptoe. If he had had time to take his boots off he would have gone barefoot.

At last he reached the town gate. There was neither tollhouse nor sentry and he could go through freely. But the sudden spread of countryside as he came out of the Rue Beau-Soleil terrified him. The landscape was completely blue, a very pale blue. A country freshness was wafted to him and he had the feeling that a vast crowd was waiting for him and breathing into his face. They could see him, and a sudden clamor would root him to the spot.

But the bridge was there. He could see the white road, the parapets on either side, low and gray like granite seats, and he could hear the rippling of the Chanteclair between the tall reeds. At last he plucked up courage to walk on, bent almost double, avoiding the open spaces, afraid of being seen by the thousands of mute witnesses he imagined surrounded him. The most alarming stretch was o the bridge itself, for once he found himself standing there the whole town was spread out behind him like an amphitheater. He wanted to go to the end of the bridge to where he usually sat, swinging his legs and breathing the sweetness of the night air. In a deep pool the Chanteclair seemed to spread like a black, still cloth dimpled with little swirls thrown up by the racing whirlpool beneath. He had often amused himself by throwing stones in, to guess at the depth of water by the bubbles. With a final effort of will, he crossed the bridge.

Yes, that was the place. He recognized the stone, polished by the long hours he had sat there. He leaned over and looked down into the dimpled surface of the pool. This was the spot; he unloaded his burden onto the parapet. He could not resist having a last look at Colombel before throwing him into the water. The eyes of the whole town would not have stopped him. He stayed there for a moment, face to face with the corpse. The hole in Colombel's temple had turned black. Far away in the sleeping countryside the wheels of a cart groaned. Julien hurried about his task and, so as not to make too loud a splash, he raised the body once more and let it down slowly into the water, leaning over with it. Without Julien's knowing quite how it happened, the dead man's arms became locked around his neck and he began to fall, just saving himself by grabbing a ledge. Colombel had wanted to take Julien with him.

When he sat alone once more on the parapet he was completely exhausted, his back bent and his legs hanging limp, as he had so often sat on returning from a long walk. He looked at the still surface of the water with its smiling ripples. One thing was certain: Colombel, although he was dead, had wanted to take him along with him. But it was all over now. Julien breathed deeply, inhaling the fresh smell of the fields. He looked along the silver shimmer of the river between the velvet shadows of the trees, and the countryside seemed to him like a promise of peace, a long rest in perfect and sheltered surroundings.

Then he remembered Thérèse. He was sure she was waiting for him. He could still see her in his mind's eye, standing at the top of the steps in front of that old moss-covered door. She was standing up straight, in her white silk dress with the crimson-centered wild roses. Perhaps she felt the cold. Then she would have gone up to her room to wait for him. She would have left the door ajar and lain down in her bed like a bride on her wedding night.

Ah, what delights awaited him! No woman had waited for him like that. In a few moments he would keep their tryst. But his legs were leaden and he was afraid of falling asleep. Was he a coward? To pull himself together, he thought of Thérèse changing her clothes. He imagined her arms raised above her head, her breasts thrust forward, her elbows and pale hands. He goaded himself with his memories—the smell of her body, her soft skin, the terrifying sensuality that had already intoxicated him in her room. Was he going to give up all that passion which had been offered to him, the foretaste of which still burned his lips? No, even if his legs refused to carry him, he would drag himself there on his knees.

But he had already lost the battle and his love was guttering out. His one desire was to sleep, to sleep forever. In his mind the picture of Thérèse faded and a black wall took its place. Now he would have been unable to lay even a finger on her shoulder without dying. His lust died amid a smell of corpses. Everything had become too impossible; the ceiling would have fallen in on them had he gone back to that room and held Thérèse to him.

To sleep and to sleep forevermore—that was the only thing worthwhile when there was no longer anything to wake up for. He would not go to the post office tomorrow, he would never play the flute again, he would no longer sit at his window. So why not sleep until the end of time? His life had come to an end and he could lie down and sleep. He looked again at the river, trying to see if Colombel were still there. Colombel had been very intelligent and he knew what he was doing when he tried to take Julien with him.

The surface of the pool spread below, dappled with the quick laughter of the whirlpool. There was a musical gentleness about the Chanteclair and the countryside lay in peace. Julien murmured Thérèse's name three times and then let himself fall, toppling over and over like a bundle before throwing up a great cloud of spray. And the Chanteclair went singing on its way between the reeds.

When the two bodies were found, it was assumed there had been a fight and a whole story was woven around it. It was thought that Julien had lain in wait for Colombel, to get back at him for the teasing he had suffered, and that he had thrown himself into the river after killing Colombel by battering in his temple with a stone.

Three months later, Mademoiselle Thérèse de Marsanne was married to young Count de Véteuil. Her wedding dress was white and her beautiful face radiated a calm and chaste pride.

ROUND TRIP

LUCIEN BÉRARD and Hortense Larivière had been married for exactly one week. For thirty years Hortense's mother, the Widow Larivière, had kept the fancy-goods shop in the Rue de la Chaussée d'Antin. Dried-out, vinegary, and tyrannical by nature, she had been unable to stop her daughter from marrying the only son of a neighboring ironmonger but she had every intention of keeping a close eye on the young couple. The shop had been given to Hortense as her dowry and the window retained one room in the house for her own use. In fact, she still ran the business under the pretext of teaching the young couple how to do so.

It was August and very hot. Business was poor and Madame Larivière's temper was even shorter than usual. She never left Lucien and Hortense to themselves for an instant. Hadn't she surprised them one morning kissing at the back of the shop? And already married for a week, if you please! A fine way of carrying on and just the sort of thing that gets a shop a good name. She had never let Monsieur Larivière so much as lay a finger on her in the shop and it would never have entered his mind to try to do so. That was how they had built up their business.

Lucien did not as yet dare fly the flag of revolt openly so he blew kisses to Hortense behind his mother-in-law's back. One day he plucked up courage to say that the two families had agreed, before the wedding, to pay for a honeymoon.

Madame Larivière set her lips in a thin line and replied, "All right, go for a walk in the Bois de Vincennes."

The young couple looked at each other in dismay and Hortense decided that her mother's attitude was becoming thoroughly ridiculous. Even at night, she scarcely had a chance to be alone with her husband. At the slightest sound Madame Larivière would pad barefoot to the door of their room, knock, and ask if they were ill; and when they answered that they were in the best of health she told them, "Well, you ought to be asleep or you'll be nodding over the counter again tomorrow."

It had become unbearable. Lucien talked of tradesmen who went off on jaunts while their parents or a reliable assistant looked after their shops. The man who kept the glove shop at the corner of the Rue La Fayette had gone to Dieppe, the cutler in the Rue Saint-Nicolas had just left for Luchon, and the jeweler near the boulevard had taken his wife to Switzerland. Nowadays everybody who had a little money spent a month in the country.

"Yes, I know they do—and that's the way business goes to the dogs," declared Madame Larivière. "When my husband was alive, we used to go to the Bois de Vincennes on Easter Monday and we were none the worse for going out only once a year. Let me tell you something. Those globe-trotting habits are the surest way of losing trade. Mark my words, the business will go downhill."

"But it was agreed that we should go away," protested Hortense. "Don't you remember, Maman, you promised?"

"Maybe I did—but that was before the wedding and a lot of silly things are said before weddings. Come on now, be sensible."

To avoid a row, Lucien left the house but he would gladly have throttled his mother-in-law. Two hours later he came back in a totally different mood and spoke very mildly to the widow, the hint of a smile on his face.

That evening he asked Hortense, "Have you ever been to Normandy?"

"You know perfectly well," she replied, "that I have never been farther than the Bois de Vincennes."

Then came a bolt from the blue. Lucien's father, known to everyone in that part of Paris as Old Bérard, a man who enjoyed life and was also a shrewd businessman, invited himself to lunch. When coffee was served he said, "I've brought a present for the children"—and brandished triumphantly a couple of railway tickets.

"What's that?" the widow asked in a choked voice.

"Two first-class tickets for a round trip to Normandy. There you are, my dears, a month in the open air for you. You'll come back with roses in your cheeks."

This completely took the wind out of Madame Larivière's sails. She would have liked to protest but wanted at all costs to avoid a quarrel with Old Bérard, because he always had the last word. To cap it all, Bérard talked about whisking the young couple off to the station right away. He would not let them out of his sight until they were safely on the train.

"That's right, take my daughter away from me," said the widow in a blind rage. "I'd much rather have it that way; then they won't be able to go kissing all over the shop and I can keep our good name."

So Hortense and Lucien arrived at the Gare Saint-Lazare, escorted by

Lucien's father, who had given them just time enough to toss a few clothes into a suitcase before they left home. He gave them both smacking kisses on their cheeks and told them to have a good look at everything so that they could tell him all about it when they came home. He'd look forward to that, he said.

Lucien and Hortense hurried down the corridor of the train to try and find an empty compartment. They found one and were just settling in nicely and looking forward to a long talk when, to their dismay, a man climbed in, sat down, and began staring sternly at them from behind his spectacles. As the train moved out of the station, Hortense, bitterly disappointed at this intrusion, turned to the window and pretended to watch the countryside—but she could not even see the trees for the tears in her eyes.

Lucien tried to think up some ingenious way of getting rid of the old man, but the only solutions that came to mind were far too violent to be carried out. At first he hoped that their fellow passenger might get out at Mantes or Vernon, but unfortunately he was going right through to Le Havre. So, in exasperation, Lucien decided to hold Hortense's hand; they were married, after all. The old man's expression became even more stern and it was so obvious that he thoroughly disapproved of this display of feeling in public that Hortense, blushing, withdrew her hand from her husband's. The rest of the journey was spent in silence. Fortunately, they soon reached Rouen.

Before leaving Paris, Lucien had bought himself a guidebook and they went to one of the hotels he had looked up in it. They were immediately pounced on by hotel porters and waiters and could barely get up courage to talk to each other under the stares of other guests in the dining room. When at last dinner came to an end, they went straight up to their room, but the walls were so thin that they could hear the slightest movement in the adjoining rooms and so neither dared stir in bed or even cough.

Next morning Lucien said, "Let's look around the town and then leave as quickly as we can for Le Havre."

They walked around all day, visiting the Cathedral and the Butter Tower, which got its name from the local tax on butter that contributed toward the cost of its construction. They looked at the palace of the bygone Dukes of Normandy, at disused churches turned into storehouses for fodder, at Saint Joan of Arc's Square, the museum, and even the cemetery. They did not miss a single historic building but walked from one to another as though fulfilling a duty. Hortense was bored to tears and so worn out that she fell asleep in the train next day.

A further annoyance awaited them at Le Havre. The beds in the hotel they stayed at were so narrow that they were put in a room with two single beds. Hortense saw a deliberate insult in this and began to weep. To console her, Lucien swore that they would stay in Le Havre just long enough to look around—and once more the mad rush began.

After Le Havre they stayed in turn in each place of importance listed in their itinerary. They saw Honfleur, Pont l'Evêque, Caen, Bayeux, Cherbourg—their minds reeling at the succession of streets and monuments. They muddled up churches and became bemused by the ever-changing cavalcade of sights that did not interest them in the slightest. Nowhere could they find a spot in which to kiss in peace out of range of inquisitive ears. They reached the stage where they no longer looked at anything, but carried out their itinerary to the letter like an unavoidable drudgery. One evening when they were in Cherbourg, Lucien let slip a remark that showed how serious the situation had become: "I think I'd rather put up with your mother than do this."

Next day they left for Granville. Lucien sat solemnly in his corner, glancing with a rather wild look in his eye at the fields unfolding like a fan on either side of the train. Suddenly, as the train stopped at a little station, the name of which he did not even catch, he exclaimed, "Come on, dear, let's go out at once!"

"But this place isn't mentioned in the guidebook!" said Hortense in astonishment.

"Oh, that damned guidebook!" he shouted. "You just wait and see what I do with it. Come on, quickly."

"What about our luggage?"

But Hortense got out and the train pulled away, leaving just the two of them standing there in the middle of a sweet green isolation. The moment they walked out of the station, they were in the heart of the country. The only sounds were the singing of the birds in the trees and the ripple of a little stream through the valley. The first thing Lucien did was to chuck the guidebook into the middle of a pond. They were free at last!

A few hundred yards away, they came to a lonely inn where the landlady rented them a large white-washed room that was as gay as spring itself. The walls were three feet thick and, what is more, there were no other guests. Only the hens looked at them inquisitively.

"Our tickets are good for another week," said Lucien, "so we'll spend it here."

And what a wonderful week that was! Each morning they set off along deserted footpaths running deep into the woods or up to the slopes of a hill, where they spent all day making love in the tall grass. Sometimes they wandered along the bank of the stream and Hortense, like a child playing truant from school, took off her shoes and stockings to paddle and gasped as Lucien suddenly kissed the nape of her neck. Their lack of clean clothes and luggage did not worry them, they were so thrilled to be alone and far away from everyone and everything. Hortense borrowed the landlady's underclothes and the coarse linen tickled her skin and made her giggle. At eight o'clock every evening, when the darkening and silent countryside no longer tempted them, they locked themselves in their cheerful bedroom. They particularly asked never to be awakened in the morning. Sometimes Lucien went down in his slippers and carried upstairs a breakfast of chops and eggs, allowing nobody but himself to go into their room. Those were delicious meals, eaten on the edge of the bed and spun out by kisses as numerous as the mouthfuls of bread.

When their last day came, they were surprised and sad that their stay had come to an end so quickly. They left without even attempting to find out the name of the place in which they had learned to love each other. At least they had enjoyed a quarter of their honeymoon. They only caught up with their luggage in Paris. They got into a muddle when Old Bérard started asking questions about the trip. They had seen the sea at Caen and they shifted the Butter Tower to Le Havre.

"But you haven't even mentioned Cherbourg and the arsenal," said the ironmonger.

"Oh, it's only a small arsenal," replied Lucien blandly. "And there aren't any trees."

At this point Madame Larivière, as grim as ever, shrugged her shoulders and muttered, "Travel's nothing but a waste of time. They don't even remember the monuments of historical interest. Enough of that nonsense—get back to the counter, Hortense."

RENTAFOIL

I

IN Paris, everything's for sale: wise virgins, foolish virgins, truth and lies, tears and smiles.

You must certainly be aware that in such a commercially-minded place, beauty is a commodity and the object of an obnoxious trade. People buy and sell big bright eyes and charming little mouths; noses and chins are all quoted at their exact valuation. A particular dimple or beauty-spot can command a steady income. And since there's always fraud somewhere or other, at times you have to copy nature's handiwork, so that eyebrows drawn with burnt match heads, and false hairpieces fetch better prices than the real article.

This is quite fair and reasonable. We're a civilized people and what's the good of being civilized if it doesn't help us to take other people in and be taken in ourselves, thereby making life less tedious.

But I must confess to being really astonished yesterday when I learnt that old Durandeau, that businessman known to all and sundry, had come up with the astoundingly ingenious idea of finding a market for ugliness.

Selling beauty is something I can understand, even selling false beauty seems perfectly natural, it's a sign of progress. But I think the businessman I mentioned really has deserved well of his country by putting into circulation such a hitherto unsalable article as ugliness. Don't misunderstand me; I'm talking about real ugliness, ugly ugliness, sold on the open market.

I'm sure you've occasionally seen women in couples, walking slowly along the pavement, stopping in front of shop-windows, giggling and swishing their long skirts in a very fetching way. They go along arm-in-arm like good friends, talking as if they have known each other for ages. They're about the same age and both smartly dressed. But one of them is always relatively good looking, not the sort of face you'd write home about or turn round to examine more closely, but had you caught sight of it accidentally, you'd have viewed it without displeasure. The other woman is always hideous, the sort of ugliness that grates on your nerves but which you can't take your eyes off; it forces the passerby to draw comparisons between her and her companion.

Own up; you've sometimes been taken in and started to follow the couple. In isolation, the hideous one would have disgusted you and the moderately good-looking one would have left you cold. But together, the ugliness of the one has magnified the good looks of the other.

Well, let me explain to you that the hideously ugly one, the monstrosity, belongs to Durandeau's agency. She's on the staff of *Rentafoil*. The great Durandeau had hired her out to the ordinary-looking one at five francs an hour.

II

Let me tell you the full story.

Durandeau is an imaginative and original entrepreneur, a multi-millionaire who has succeeded in turning business into an art. For many years he had been bewailing the fact that no one had hitherto been able to make money out of ugly girls. As for pretty ones, trading in them is a tricky matter and I can assure you that the idea of such a thing has never crossed his mind; he's rich enough to be able to afford scruples.

One day he received a sudden illumination from heaven. As with all great inventions, this brainwave sprang quite unexpectedly into his head. He was walking along the boulevard one day when he saw two girls tripping along in front of him. One was pretty and one was ugly and as he looked the realization dawned on him that the ugly one was an adornment worn, as it were, by the pretty one. Just as you buy ribbons and face-powder and false plaits, it was only right and proper, he said to himself, that the pretty one should buy the ugly one as a suitable embellishment, a foil.

Durandeau went home to ponder over the matter. The commercial operation that he had in mind needed to be conducted with great care. He didn't want to launch out rashly into an enterprise which would be a stroke of genius if it succeeded and preposterous if it failed. He spent the night doing his sums and reading up those philosophers who have written most wisely about the stupidity of men and the vanity of women. When dawn came, his mind was made up: his arithmetic had made sense and the philosophers had shown such a low opinion of mankind that he felt able to rely on a large number of prospective clients.

III

If my Muse were more inspired, I'd produce a splendid epic on the creation of Durandeau's agency. It would be farcical and sad, full of tears and full of laughter.

Durandeau had greater difficulty than he had anticipated in acquiring his stock-in-trade. At first, using the direct approach, he had little handwritten notices stuck on rainwater-pipes, on trees and in out-of-the-way corners. These notices read as follows: 'Ugly girls required. Undemanding work.'

He waited a week and not a single ugly girl came forward. Five or six pretty ones turned up who were facing the desperate alternative of starving to death or a life of vice but still hoping to find work to rescue themselves. Durandeau was dreadfully embarrassed and assured them repeatedly that they were pretty and of no use to him. They insisted that they were ugly and that it was pure gallantry and callousness on his part to describe them as anything else. Since they were unable to sell their non-existent ugliness, I expect by now they'll have found buyers for their undoubted beauty.

By now Durandeau had realized that only pretty women have the courage to make a false confession of ugliness. The ugly ones would never admit of their own free will that their mouths were too big and their eyes ludicrously small. You could put up notices all over Paris offering ten francs to every ugly woman who cared to apply without the slightest risk of becoming impoverished.

So Durandeau gave up his idea of notices and commissioned half-a-dozen agents to scour the city in search of female monstrosities: a general mobilization of the ugly women of Paris. The agents—men of tact and taste—had a tricky assignment, needing to take into account temperament and situation. Thus, when the person concerned needed money urgently, they didn't beat about the bush; when they were dealing with girls not yet on the point of starving, they had to show greater subtlety. It's not easy for someone polite to go up to a woman and say, "Madame, you're ugly; I'll pay you so much per day for your ugliness."

This hunt for girls who dare not face their mirrors without bursting into tears led to many memorable moments. Sometimes the agents would see passing in the street an ideally ugly woman and were so keen to show her to Durandeau that they could barely restrain themselves. Indeed, some of them stopped at nothing.

Every morning Durandeau held court to inspect the goods that had been rounded up the day before. Sprawling in his armchair in a yellow dressing-gown and black satin skull cap, he had the new recruits parade in front of him, each accompanied by her agent. He would lean back and scrutinize them through half-closed eyes, with the air of a satisfied or disappointed connoisseur; he would slowly take a pinch of snuff and reflect; then, to get a better look, he'd make the article turn round and examine it from every angle; sometimes he would even stand up and feel the hair or peep into the face like a tailor stroking a piece of cloth or a grocer checking the quality of a lump of tallow or some pepper. When the ugliness was blatant, when the face was stupid and heavy, Durandeau would rub his hands together and congratulate the agent. He would almost have liked to embrace the monstrosity herself. But he mistrusted any signs of singularity in a woman: eyes that were bright or lips with an ironical twist would make him scowl and he would say to himself that an ugly woman like that might not excite love but could well excite passion. He would give the agent a black look and tell the woman to come back again later—when she was old.

It's not as easy as you might think to be an expert in ugliness and gather a collection of really ugly women unlikely to spoil the chances of pretty ones. Durandeau's deep knowledge of the human heart and its passions made him a collector of genius. For him, the expression was the essential, and he chose only faces that were intimidating by reason of their appalling dullness and stupidity.

The day he felt in a position to offer beautiful women past their prime a full selection of ugly ones to match their coloring and their particular brand of beauty, he opened his agency with the following prospectus:

RENTAFOIL
L. DurandeauParis, May 1st, 18..
18, Rue M…
Paris
Office hours: 10 a.m. to 4 p.m.

Dear Madame,

I have the honor to inform you that I have recently established a firm with the express purpose of providing a unique service for the preservation of a lady's beauty. I have invented an article of fashion which will add new luster to your own natural beauty.

Hitherto the means of enhancing a lady's beauty have been painfully obvious. Jewels and other finery are clearly visible and it is also well known that false hairpieces exist and rosy cheeks come out of a box.

I have endeavored to confront this apparently insoluble problem of making ladies even lovelier while hiding from any indiscreet eye the origin of their adornment. The question was this: could we find some infallible method of ensuring that she should attract favorable attention and avoid wasteful expenditure of time and energy without recourse to one single extra ribbon or facial adornment.

I think that I may flatter myself that I have completely mastered this thorny problem.

Today, any lady prepared to honor me with her patronage will, for a derisory sum, attract the eyes of an admiring public. My article of fashion is extremely simple and its effect is guaranteed. I need only describe it to you, Madame, for you to understand immediately how it operates.

Have you not ever seen a beggar-woman being given alms from elegantly gloved hand of a fine lady dressed in silk and other finery? Did you not notice how splendid the sheen of her silk looked against the beggar-woman's rags and how her wealth stood out with even greater elegance by comparison with the other's poverty?

Madame, I have the pleasure and privilege of providing your lovely countenance with the richest collection of ugly faces to be found anywhere. Tattered rags emphasize the chic of new clothes: my ugly faces bring out the full charm of pretty ones.

Away with false teeth, false hair, false busts! Away with expensive cosmetics and costly toiletries, away with make-up and lace! Simply *Foils* whose arm you can take, with whom you can walk through the streets to bring out your beauty and attract the fond gaze of the gentlemen!

I invite you, Madame, to honor me with your custom. You will find in my agency the greatest possible variety of ugly creations. You will be able to select the exact type of ugliness most suitable to your particular style of beauty.

My charge for this unique service is a paltry five francs an hour or fifty francs for the whole day.

I remain, Madame, your humble and devoted servant.
Durandeau

N.B. My agency also has a stock of Mothers and Fathers, Uncles and Aunts at extremely reasonable prices.

IV

The venture was a great success. When the agency opened the very next morning, the office was crowded with female customers each choosing her own foil and carrying it off with a tigerish delight. You can't imagine the pleasure of a pretty woman leaning on the arm of an ugly one. Not only was she enhancing her own beauty, she was enjoying someone else's ugliness. Durandeau is a great philosopher.

However, don't imagine that organizing this service was an easy matter. There were innumerable hitches. It had been difficult enough to organize the supply; it was far worse trying to satisfy the demand.

When one lady appeared and asked for a foil, they displayed the goods and invited her to make her choice, contenting themselves merely with offering a few helpful hints. The lady then went disdainfully from one foil to the next, finding all the poor girls either too ugly or not ugly enough, on the grounds that not one of them had the right kind of ugliness to suit her own special sort of beauty. The assistants did their best by pointing out a splendidly crooked nose here, an enormous slit of a mouth there: they might have saved their breath.

At other times the lady herself was appallingly ugly and if he happened to be present, Durandeau would be itching to take her on to his staff at any price. This lady wanted a foil to set off her beauty, she declared; she wanted a young one, not too ugly, since her beauty needed little embellishment. The despairing assistants placed her in front of a large mirror and paraded their whole stock beside her. She still took the prize for ugliness and flounced off indignantly, furious that they had dared to offer her such inferior articles.

Gradually, however, a regular clientele became established and each foil had her regular customers. Durandeau was able to relax with the inner satisfaction of having achieved a new breakthrough in civilization.

I don't know if you can realize what it is like to be a foil; they have their joys and public triumphs but they also have their very private sorrows.

Foils are ugly; they're slaves and they suffer since their money comes from being slaves and ugly. On the other hand, they're well-dressed, they wear jewelry, they walk arm-in-arm with the upper crust of the ladies of the town, go everywhere by carriage, eat in the best restaurants and spend their evenings at the theatre. They're on familiar terms with fashionable cocottes and the simple-minded think they belong to the high society of race-goers and first-nighters.

They spend all day in a whirl of gaiety. At night, they fret and fume and sob. They've had to take off their fine dress which belongs to the agency, they're all alone in their attic, sitting in front of a bit of broken mirror which tells them the truth. Their ugliness is staring them mercilessly in the face and they're quite aware that nobody will ever love them. They may help to excite desire but never will they know the joy of being kissed themselves.

VI

I've tried to tell you here the story of the creation of Durandeau's agency and make his name known to posterity. Such men have their special niche in the hall of fame.

One day I may write the *Secret Memoirs of a Foil.* I knew one such unfortunate girl whose sad tale was heartrending. Her customers were ladies of the town known to everyone in Paris and they treated her quite shamefully. Please, ladies, don't misuse your foils, be kind towards the ugly ducklings without whose help you wouldn't even be pretty at all!

This foil I knew was an emotional sort of girl whom I suspect of reading too much Walter Scott. I know nothing sadder than a hunchback in love or an ugly woman full of romantic ideals. The wretched girl kept falling in love with all the young men whose eyes were caught by her unfortunate face, which then led their attention on to her employer. It was like a mirror being in love with the larks which it lures down within the range of the huntsman's gun.

She had many harrowing experiences. She was terribly jealous of those women who bought her like a skin-cream or a pair of boots. She was an object hired for so much an hour and it so happened that this object had feelings. Can you imagine her resentment while she had to smile and joke familiarly with the women who were depriving her of her share of love? Those professional Beauties who took malicious pleasure in using honeyed words in public and treating her like a whore in private, whom they would have smashed with no more concern than they would have broken a china figure in their display-cabinet.

But what importance has a tormented soul when progress is at stake? Mankind marches on. Durandeau will be blessed by future generations because he has created a market for a hitherto unsalable commodity and invented a fashion article which makes love easier.

THREE WARS

War! In France, to men of my generation, men who have passed their fifti-
eth year, this terrible word awakens three special memories, the memory
of the Crimean expedition, of the campaign in Italy, and of our disasters
in 1870. What victories, what defeats, and what a lesson! Assuredly, war is
accursed. It is a horrible thing that nations should cut each other's throats.
According to our progressive humanitarian ideas, war must disappear on the
day when nations come to exchange a kiss of peace. There are exalted
minds which, beyond their native country, behold humanity, and prophesy
universal concord. But how these theories fall to pieces on the day when the
country is threatened! The philosophers themselves snatch a gun and shoot.
All declarations of fraternity are over; and only a cry for extermination rises
from the breast of the whole nation. For war is a dark necessity, like death.
It may be that we must have something of a dung heap to keep civilization
in flower. It is necessary that death should affirm life; and war is like those
cataclysms of the antediluvian world which prepared the world of man.

We have grown tender; we make moan over every existence that passes
away. And yet, do we know how many existences, more or less, are needed
to balance the life of the earth? We yield to the idea that an existence is sacred. Perhaps the fatalism of the ancients, which could behold the mas-
sacres of old without leaping to a Utopia of universal brotherhood, had a
truer greatness. To keep ourselves manly, to accept the dark work wrought
by death in that night wherein none of us can read, to tell ourselves that,
after all, people die, and that there are merely hours in which they die more
—this, when all is said, is the wise man's attitude. Those who are angry with
war should be angry with all human infirmities.

The soft-hearted philosophers who have been loudest in their curses of
war, have been obliged to perceive that war will be the weapon of progress
until the day when, ideal civilization being attained, all nations join in the
festival of universal peace. But that ideal civilization lies so remote in the
blue future, that there will assuredly be fighting for centuries yet. It is the
fashionable thing, just now, to consider war as an old remnant of barbarism,
from which the Republic will one day set us free. To declaim against war is
one way of setting up as a progressive person. But let a single cry of alarm

arise upon the frontier, let a trumpet sound in the street, and we shall all be shouting for arms. War is in the blood of man.

Victor Hugo wrote that only kings desired war, that nations desired only to exchange marks of affection. Alas! That was but a poetic aspiration. The poet has been the high- priest of that dream-peace of which I spoke; he celebrated the United States of Europe, he put forward the brotherhood of nations, and prophesied the new golden age. Nothing could be sweeter or larger. But to be brothers is a trifle; the first thing is to love one another, and the nations do not love one another at all. A falsehood is bad, merely in that it is a falsehood.

Undoubtedly, a sovereign, when he sees himself in danger, may try the fortune of war against a neighbor, in the hope of consolidating his throne by victory. But after the first victory, or the first defeat, the nation makes the war its own, and fights for itself. If it were not fighting for itself, it would not go on fighting. And what shall we say of really national wars? Let us suppose that France and Germany some day again find themselves face to face. Republic, empire, or kingdom, the Government will count for nothing; it will be the whole nation which will rise. A great thrill will run from end to end of the land. The bugles will sound of themselves to call the people together. There has been war germinating in our midst, in spite of ourselves, these twenty years, and if ever the hour strikes, it will rise, an overflowing harvest, in every furrow.

Three times in my life, I repeat, have I felt the passage of war over France; and never shall I forget the particular sound made by her wings. First of all comes a far-off murmur, heralding the approach of a great wind. The murmur grows, the tumult bursts, every heart beats: a dizzy enthusiasm, a need of killing and conquering takes hold of the nation. Then, when the men are gone and the noise has sunk, an anxious silence reigns, and every ear is on the stretch for the first cry from the army. Will it be a cry of triumph or of defeat? It is a terrible moment. Contradictory news comes; every tiniest indication is seized, every word is pondered and discussed until the hour when the truth is known. And what an hour that is, of delirious joy or horrible despair!

I

I WAS fourteen at the time of the Crimean war. I was a pupil in the College of Aix, shut up with two or three hundred other urchins in an old

Benedictine convent, whose long corridors and vast halls retained a great dreariness. But the two courts were cheerful under the spreading blue immensity of that glorious Southern sky. It is a tender memory that I keep of that college, in spite of the sufferings that I endured there.

I was fourteen then; I was no longer a small boy, and yet I feel to-day how complete was the ignorance of the world in which we were living. In that forgotten corner, even the echo of great events hardly reached us. The town, a sad, old, dead capital, slumbered in the midst of its arid landscape; and the college, close to the ramparts, in the deserted quarter of the town, slumbered even more deeply. I do not remember any political catastrophe ever passing its walls while I was cloistered there. The Crimean war alone moved us, and even as to that it is probable that weeks elapsed before the fame of it reached us.

When I recall my memories of that time, I smile to think what war was to us country school-boys. In the first place, everything was extremely vague. The theatre of the struggle was so distant, so lost in a strange and savage country, that we seemed to be looking on at a story come true out of the "Arabian Nights." We did not clearly know where the fighting was; and I do not remember that we had at any time curiosity enough to consult the atlases in our hands. It must be said that our teachers kept us in absolute ignorance of modern life. They themselves read the papers and learned the news; but they never opened their mouths to us about such things, and if we had questioned them, they would have dismissed us sternly to our exercises and essays. We knew nothing precise, except that France was fighting in the East, for reasons not within our ken.

Certain points, however, stood out clear. We repeated the classic jokes about the Cossacks. We knew the names of two or three Russian generals, and we were not far from attributing to these generals the heads of child - devouring monsters. Moreover, we did not for one moment admit the possibility that the French could be beaten. That would have appeared to us contrary to the laws of nature. Then there were gaps. As the campaign was prolonged, we would forget, for months at a time, that there was any fighting, until some day some report came to arouse our attention again. I cannot tell whether we knew of the battles as they happened, or whether we felt the thrill which the fall of Sebastopol gave to France. All these things were confused. Virgil and Homer were realities which caused us more concern than the contemporary quarrels of nations.

I only remember that for a time there was a game greatly in favor in our playgrounds. We divided ourselves into two camps. We drew two lines on the ground, and proceeded to fight. It was "prisoners' base" simplified. One camp represented the Russian and one the French army. Naturally, the Russians ought to have been defeated, but the contrary sometimes occurred; the fury was extraordinary and the riot frightful. At the end of a week the superintendent was obliged to forbid this delightful game: two boys had had to be put on the sick list, with broken heads.

Among the most distinguished in these conflicts was a tall, fair lad, who always got chosen General. Louis, who belonged to an old Breton family that had come to live in the South, assumed victorious airs. I can see him yet, with a handkerchief tied on his forehead by way of plume, a leather belt girded round him, leading on his soldiers with a wave of the hand as if it were the great wave of a sword. He filled us with admiration; we even felt a sort of respect for him. Strangely enough he had a twin-brother, Julien, who was much smaller, frail and delicate, and who greatly disliked these violent games. When we divided into two camps, he would go apart, sit down on a stone bench, and thence watch us with his sad and rather frightened eyes. One day, Louis, hustled and attacked by a whole band, fell under their blows, and Julien gave a cry, pallid, trembling, half-fainting like a woman. The two brothers adored each other, and none of us would have dared to laugh at the little one about his want of courage, for fear of the big one.

The memory of these twins is closely involved for me in the memory of that time.

Towards the spring, I became a day-boarder, and no longer slept at the college, but came in the morning for the seven o'clock lessons. The two brothers, also, were day-boarders. The three of us were inseparable. As we lived in the same street we used to wait to go in to college together. Louis, who was very precocious and dreamed of adventures, seduced us. We agreed to leave home at six, so as to have a whole hour of freedom in which we could be men. For us "to be men" meant to smoke cigars and to go and have drinks at a shabby wine-shop, which Louis had discovered in an out-of-the-way street. The cigars and the drinks made us frightfully ill ; but, then, what an emotion it was to step into the wine-shop, casting glances to right and left, and in terror of being observed.

These fine doings occurred towards the close of the winter. I remember there were mornings when the rain fell in torrents. We waded through, and arrived drenched. After that, the mornings became mild and fair, and then a mania took hold of us — that of going to see off the soldiers. Aix is on the road to Marseilles. Regiments came into the town by the road from Avignon, slept one night, and started off on the morrow by the road to Marseilles. At that time, fresh troops, especially cavalry and artillery, were being sent to the Crimea. Not a week elapsed without troops passing. A local paper even announced these movements before-hand, for the benefit of the inhabitants with whom the men lodged. Only we did not read the paper, and we were much concerned to know overnight whether there would be soldiers leaving in the morning. As the departure occurred at five in the morning, we were obliged to get up very early, often to no purpose.

What a happy time it was! Louis and Julien would come and call me from the middle of the street, where not a person was yet to be seen. I hurried down. It would be chilly, not-withstanding the spring-time mildness of the days, and we three would cross the empty town.

When a regiment was leaving, the soldiers would be assembling on the Cours, before a hotel where the colonel generally stayed. Therefore, the moment that we turned into the Course, our necks were stretched out eagerly. If the Course was empty, what a blow! And it was often empty. On these mornings, though we did not say so, we regretted our beds, and cooled our heels till seven o'clock, not knowing what to do with our freedom. But, then, what joy it was, when we turned the street and saw the Course full of men and horses! An amazing commotion arose in the slight morning chill. Soldiers came in from every direction, while the drums beat and the bugles called. The officers had great difficulty in forming them on this esplanade. However, order was established,

little by little, the ranks closed up, while we talked to the men and slipped under the horses' legs, at the risk of being crushed. Nor were we the only people to enjoy this scene. Small proprietors appeared one by one, early towns-folk, and all that part of the population which rises betimes. Soon there were crowds. The sun rose. The gold and steel of the uniforms shone in the clear morning light.

We thus beheld, on the Course of that peaceful and still drowsy town, Dragoons, Cavalry Chasseurs, Lancers, and, in fact, all branches of light and heavy cavalry. But our favorites, those who aroused our keenest enthusiasm, were the Cuirassiers. They dazzled us as they sat square on their stout horses, with the glowing star of their breastplates before them. Their helmets took fire in the rising sun; their ranks were like rows of suns, whose rays shone on the neighboring houses. When we knew that there were Cuirassiers going, we got up at four, so eager were we to fill our eyes with their glories.

At last, however, the colonel would appear. The colors, which had passed the night with him, were displayed. And all at once, after two or three words of command cried aloud, the regiment gave way. It went down the Course, and with the first fall of the hoofs on the dry earth, rose a beat of drums which made our hearts leap within us. We ran to keep at the head of the column, abreast of the band, which was greeting the town, as it went at a double. First there came three shrill bugle notes as a summons to the players, then the trumpet call broke out, and covered everything with its sounds. Outside the gates the "double" was ended in the open, where the last notes died away. Then there was a turn to the left along the Marseilles road, a fine road planted with elms hundreds of years old. The horses went at a foot pace, in rather open order, on the wide highway, white with dust. We felt as if we were going, too. The town was remote, college was forgotten; we ran and ran, delighted with our outbreak. It was like setting out to war ourselves every week.

Ah, those lovely mornings! It was six o'clock, the sun, already high, lighted the country with great sloping rays. A milder warmth breathed through the little chill breeze of morning. Groups of birds flew up from the hedges. Far off the meadows were bathed in pink mist; and amid this smiling landscape these beautiful soldiers, the Cuirassiers shining like stars, passed with their glowing breasts. The road turned suddenly at the dip of a deep valley. The curious townsfolk never went farther; soon we were the only ones persisting. We went down the slope and reached the bridge crossing the river at the very bottom. It was only there that uneasiness would fall on us. It must be nearly seven; we had only just time to run home, if we did not wish to miss college. Often we suffered ourselves to be carried away; we pushed on farther still; and on those day s we played truant, roaming about till noon, hiding ourselves in the grassy holes at the edge of the waterfall. At other times we stopped at the bridge, sitting on the stone parapet, and never losing sight of the regiment, as it went up the opposite slope of the valley before us. It was a moving spectacle. The road went up the hillside in a straight line for rather more than a mile. The horses slackened their pace yet more, the men grew smaller with the rhythmic swaying of their steeds. At first, each breastplate and each helmet was like a sun. Then the suns dwindled, and soon there was only an army of stars on the march. Finally the last man disappeared and the road was bare. Nothing was left of the beautiful regiment that had passed by, except a memory.

We were only children; but, all the same, that spectacle made us grave. As the regiment slowly mounted the steep, we would be taken by a great silence, our eyes fixed upon the troop, in despair at the thought of losing it, and when it had disappeared, something tightened in our throats, and for a moment or two we still watched the distant rock behind which it had just vanished. Would it ever come back? Would it some day come down this hillside again? These questions, stirring sadly within us, made us sad. Good-bye, beautiful regiment.

Julien, in particular, always came home very tired. He only came so far in order not to leave his brother. These excursions knocked him up, and he had a mortal terror of the horses. I remember that one day we had lingered in the train of an artillery regiment, and spent the day in the open fields. Louis was wild with enthusiasm. When we had breakfasted on an omelet, in a village, he took us to a bend of the river, where lie was set upon bathing. Then he talked of going for a soldier as soon as he was old enough.

"No, no!" cried Julien, flinging his arms round his neck. He was quite pale. His

brother laughed, and called him a great stupid. But he repeated: "You would be killed, I know you would."

On that day, Julien, excited, and jeered at by us, spoke his mind. He thought the soldiers horrid, he did not see what there was in them to attract us. It was all the soldiers' fault, because if there were not any soldiers, there would not be any fighting. In fact, he hated war ; it terrified him, and, later on, he would find some way to prevent his brother from going. It was a sort of morbid, unconquerable aversion which he felt. Weeks and months went by. We had got tired of the regiments; we had found out another sport, which was to go fishing, of a morning, for the little fresh-water fish, and to eat what we caught in a third-rate tavern. The water was icy. Julien got a cold on the chest, of which he nearly died. In college, war was no longer talked about. We had fallen back deeper than ever into Homer and Virgil. All at once, we learned that the French had conquered, which seemed to us quite natural. Then, regiments again began to pass, but in the other direction. They no longer interested us; still, we did see two or three. They did not seem to us so fine, diminished as they were by half—and the rest is lost in a mist. Such was the Crimean war, in France, for schoolboys shut up in a country college.

II

In 1859 I was in Paris, finishing my studies at the Lycée St. Louis. As it happened, I was there with my two school-fellows from Aix, Louis and Julien. Louis was preparing for his entrance examination to the Ecole Polytechnique ; Julien had decided to go in for law. We were all out-students. By this time we had ceased to be savages, entirely ignorant of the contemporary world. Paris had ripened us. Thus, when the war with Italy broke out, we were abreast of the stream of political events which had led to it.

We even discussed the war in the character of politicians and military adepts. It was the fashion at college to take interest in the campaign, and to follow the movements of the troops on the map. During our college hours we used to mark our positions with pins and fight and lose battles. In order to be well up to date, we devoured an enormous supply of newspapers. It was the mission of us out-students to bring them in. We used to arrive with our pockets stuffed, with thicknesses of paper under our coats, enclosed from head to foot in an armor of newspapers. And while lectures were going on these papers were circulated; lessons and studies were neglected; we drank our fill of news, shielded by the back of a neighbor. In order to conceal the big sheets we used to cut them in four, and open them inside our books. The professors were not always blind, but they let us go our own way with the tolerance of men resigned to let the idler bear the burden of his idleness.

At first, Julien shrugged his shoulders. He was possessed by a fine adoration of the poets of 1830, and there was always a volume of Musset or Hugo in his pocket which he used to read at lecture. So when anyone handed him a news-paper he used to pass it on scornfully without even condescending to look at it, and would continue reading the poem which he had begun. To him it seemed monstrous that anybody could care about men who were fighting one another. But a catastrophe which changed the whole course of his life caused him to alter his opinion. One fine day Louis, who had just failed in his examination, enlisted. It was a rash step which had long been in his mind. He had an uncle who was a general, and he thought himself sure of making his way without passing through the military schools. Besides, when the war was over, he could still try Saint-Cyr. When

Julien heard this news, it came upon him like a thunderbolt. He was no longer the boy declaiming against war with girlish arguments, but he still had an unconquerable aversion. He wished to show himself a hardened man; and he succeeded in not shedding tears before' us. But from the time his brother went, he became one of the most eager devourers of newspapers. We came and went from college together; and our conversations turned on nothing but possible battles. I remember that he used to drag me almost every day to the Luxembourg Gardens. He would lay his books on a bench and trace a whole map of Northern Italy in the sand. That kept his thoughts with his brother. In the depths of his heart he was full of terror at the idea that he might be killed. Even now, when I inquire of my memory, I find it difficult to make clear the elements of this horror of war on Julien's part. He was by no means a coward. He merely had a distaste for bodily exercises, to which he reckoned abstract mental speculations far superior. To live the life of a learned man or a poet, shut into a quiet room, seemed to him the real end of man on this earth : while the turmoils of the street, battles, whether with fist or sword, and every-thing which develops the muscles seemed to him only fit for a nation of savages. He despised athletes and ac-robats and wild beast tamers. I must add that he had no patriotism. On this subject we heaped contempt upon him, and I can still see the smile and shrug of the shoulders with which he answered us.

One of the most vivid memories of that time which remains with me is the memory of the fine summer day on which the news of the victory of Magenta became known in Paris. It was June — a splendid June, such as we seldom have in France. It was Sunday. Julien and I had planned the evening before to take a walk in the Champs Élysées. He was very uneasy about his brother, from whom he had had no letter, and I wanted to dis-tract his thoughts. I called for him at one o'clock, and we strolled down to-wards the Seine at the idle pace of school-boys with no usher behind them. Paris on a holiday in very hot weather is something that deserves knowing. The black shadow of the houses cuts the white pavement sharply. Between the shuttered, drowsy house fronts is visible but a strip of sky of a hard blue. I do not know any place in the world where, when it is hot, it is hot-ter than in Paris : it is a furnace, suffocating, asphyxiating. Some corners of Paris are deserted, among others the quays, whence the loungers have fled to suburban copses. And yet, what a delightful wall it is, along the wide, quiet quays, with their row of little thick trees, and below, the magnificent rush of the river all alive with its moving populace of vessels.

Well, we had come to the Seine and were walking along the quays in the shadow of the trees. Slight sounds came up from the river, whose waters quivered in the sun and were marked out as with lines of silver into large wavering patterns. There was something special in the holiday air of this fine Sunday. Paris was positively being filled already by the news of which everybody, and even the very houses, seemed expectant. The Italian campaign, which was, as everybody knows, so rapid, had opened with successes; but so far there had been no important battle, and it was this battle which

Paris had for two days been feeling. The great city held her breath and heard the distant cannon.

I have retained the memory of this impression very clearly. I had just confided to Julien the strange sensation which I felt, by saying to him that Paris "looked queer," when, as we came to the Quai Voltaire, we saw, afar off, in front of the printing-office of the Monteury a little knot of people, standing to read a notice. There were not more than seven or eight persons. From the pavement where we stood, we could see them gesticulating, laughing, calling out. We crossed the road quickly. The notice was a telegram, written, not printed ; it announced the victory of Magenta, in four lines. The wafers which fixed it to the wall were not yet dry. Evidently we were the first to know in all this great Paris, that Sunday. People came running, and their enthusiasm was a sight to see. They fraternized at once, strangers shook hands with each other. A gentleman, with a ribbon at his button-hole, explained to a workman how the battle must have occurred; women were laughing with a pretty laughter and looking as if they were inclined to throw themselves into the arms of the bystanders. Little by little the crowd grew; passers-by were beckoned; coachmen stopped their vehicles and came down from their seats. When we came away there were more than a thousand people there.

After that it was a glorious day. In a few minutes the news had spread to the whole town. We thought to bear it with us, but it out-stripped us, for we could not turn a corner or pass along a street without at once understanding by the joy on every face that the thing was known. It floated in the sunshine; it came on the wind. In half-an-hour the aspect of Paris was changed; solemn expectancy had given place to an out-burst of triumph. We sauntered for a couple of hours in the Champs Élysées among crowds who laughed for joy. The eyes of the women had a special tenderness. And the word "Magenta" was in every mouth. But Julien was still very pale; he was much disturbed and I knew what was his secret terror, when he murmured:—"They laugh today, but how many will be crying tomorrow?" He was thinking of his brother. I made jokes to try and reassure him, and told him that Louis was sure to come back a captain. "If really he does come back," he answered, shaking his head.

As soon as night fell, Paris was illuminated. Venetian lanterns swung at all the windows. The poorest persons had lighted candles ; I even saw some rooms whose tenants had merely pushed a table to the window and set their lamp on it. The night was exquisite, and all Paris was in the streets. There were people sitting all along upon the doorsteps as if they were waiting for a procession. Crowds were standing in the squares, the cafes and the wine-shops were thronged, and the urchins were letting off crackers which scented the air with a fine smell of powder. I repeat I never saw Paris so beautiful. That day, all joys were united, sunshine, a Sunday, and a victory. Afterwards, when Paris heard of the decisive battle of Solferino, there was not the same enthusiasm, even though it brought the immediate conclusion of the war. On the day when the troops made their entry, the demonstration was more solemn, but it lacked that spontaneous popular joy. We got a two days' holiday from Magenta.

We grew even more eager about the war, and were among those who thought that peace had been made too hastily. The school year was drawing to its end. The holidays were coming, bringing the feverish excitement of liberty; and Italy, the army, and the victories, all disappeared in the general setting free of the prize distribution. I remember that I was to go and spend my holidays in the South that year. When I was just about to start, in the beginning of August, Julien begged me to stay till the 14th, the date fixed for the triumphal entry of the troops. He was full of joy. Louis was coming back with the rank of sergeant, and he wished me to be present at his brother's triumph. I promised to stay.

Great preparations were made for the reception of the army which bad for some days been encamped in the immediate neighborhood of Paris. It was to enter by the Place de la Bastille, to follow the line of the Boulevards, to go down the Rue de la Paix, and cross the Place Vendôme. The Boulevards were decorated with flags. On the Place Vendôme, immense stands had been erected for the members of the Government and their guests. The weather was splendid. When the troops came into sight along the boulevards, vast applause burst forth. The crowd thronged on both sides of the pavement. Heads rose above heads at windows. Women waved their handkerchiefs and threw down the flowers from their dresses to the soldiers. All the while, the soldiers kept on passing with their regular step, in the midst of frantic hurrahs. The bands played; the colors fluttered in the sun. Several, which had been pierced by balls, received applause, and one in particular, which was in rags, and crowned. At the corner of the Rue du Temple an old woman flung herself headlong into the ranks and embraced a corporal, her son, no doubt. They came near to carrying that happy mother in triumph.

The official ceremony took place in the Place Vendôme. There ladies in full dress, magistrates in their robes, and officials in uniform applauded with more gravity. In the evening, the Emperor gave a banquet to three hundred persons at the Louvre, in the Salle des Etats. As he was proposing a toast, which has remained historic, he exclaimed: "If France has done so much for a friendly people what would she not do for her own independence?" An imprudent speech which he must have regretted later. Julien and I had seen the march past from a window in the Boulevard Poissoniere. He had been to the camp the night before and had told Louis where we should be. Thus when his regiment passed Louis lifted his head to greet us. He was much older, and his face was brown and thin. I could hardly recognize him. He looked like a man, compared with us who were still children, slender and pale like women. Julien followed him with his eyes as long as he could, and I heard him murmur, with tears in his eyes, while a nervous emotion shook him," It is beautiful after all — it is beautiful."

In the evening I met them both again in a little cafe of the Quartier Latin. It was a small place at the end of an alley where we generally went, because we were alone there and could talk at our ease. When I arrived, Julien, with both elbows on the table, was already listening to Louis, who was telling him about Solferino. He said that no battle had ever been less foreseen. The Austrians were thought to be in retreat and the allied armies were advancing when suddenly, about five in the morning, on the 24th, they had heard guns it was the Austrians who had turned and were attacking us. Then a series of fights had begun, each division taking its turn. All day long, the different generals had fought separately, without having any clear idea of the total form of the struggle. Louis had taken part in a terrible hand-to-hand conflict in a cemetery, in the midst of graves; and that was about all he had seen. He also spoke of the terrible storm which had broken out towards the evening. The heavens took part and the thunder silenced the guns. The Austrians had to give up the field in a veritable deluge. They had been firing on each other for sixteen hours, and the night which followed was full of terrors, for the soldiers did not exactly know which way the victory had gone, and at every sound in the darkness they thought that the battle was beginning again.

During this tale Julien kept on looking at his brother. Perhaps he was not even listening, but was happy in merely having him before his eyes. I shall never forget the evening spent thus in that obscure and peaceful cafe, whence we heard the murmur of festival Paris, while Louis was leading us across the bloody fields of Solferino. When he had finished Julien said quietly, "Anyway, you are here and what does anything else matter?"

III

Eleven years later, in 1870, we were grown men. Louis had reached the rank of captain. Julien, after various beginnings, had settled down to the idle, ever-occupied life of those wealthy Parisians who frequent literary' and artistic society without themselves ever touching pen or paint brush. There was great excitement at the first report of a war with Germany. People's brains were fevered: there was talk about our natural frontier on the Rhine, and about avenging Waterloo, which had remained a weight on our hearts. If the campaign had been opened by a victory, France would certainly have blessed this war which she ought to have cursed. Paris certainly would have felt disappointed if peace had been maintained, after the stormy sittings of the Legislative Corps. On the day when conflict became inevitable, all hearts beat high. I am not speaking now of the scenes which took place in the evenings on the boulevards, of the shrieking crowds, or the shouts of men who may have been paid, as, later on, it was declared that they had been. I only say that, among sober citizens, the greater number were marking out on maps the different stages of our army as far as Berlin. The Prussians were to be driven back with the butt end of the rifle. This absolute confidence of victory was our inheritance from the days in which our soldiers had passed, always conquering, from one end of Europe to the other. Nowadays we are thoroughly cured of that very dangerous patriotic vanity.

One evening when I was on the Boulevard des Capuchins, watching hordes of men in blouses who passed along, yelling, "A Berlin ! A Berlin" I felt someone touch me on the shoulder. It was Julien. He was very gloomy.

I reproached him with his lack of enthusiasm. "We shall be beaten," said he, quietly. I protested, but he shook his head, without giving any reasons. He felt it, he said. I spoke of his brother. Louis was already at Metz with his regiment, and Julien showed me a letter which he had received the night before, a letter full of gaiety, in which the captain declared that he should have died of barrack-life if the war had not come to lift him out of it. He vowed that he would come home a colonel, with a medal. But when I tried to use this letter as an argument against Julien's dark prognostications, he merely repeated: "We shall be beaten."

Paris's time of anxiety began once more. I knew that solemn silence of the great city; I had witnessed it in 1859 before the first hostilities of the Italian campaign. But this time the silence seemed more tremulous. No one seemed in doubt about the victory; yet sinister rumors were current, coming no one knew whence. Surprise was felt that our army had not taken the initiative and carried the war at once into the enemy's territory.

One afternoon on the Exchange a great piece of news broke forth; we had gained an immense victory, taken a considerable number of cannons, and made prisoners a whole division. Houses were actually beginning to be decorated, people were embracing one another in the street, when the falsehood of the news had to be acknowledged. There had been no battle. The victory had not seemed natural in the expected order of events, but the sudden contradiction, the trick played on a populace that had been too ready with its rejoicings and had to put off its enthusiasm to another day, struck a chill to my heart. All at once I felt an immense sadness, I felt the quivering wing of some unexampled disaster passing over us. I shall always remember that ill-omened Sunday. It was a Sunday again, and many people must have remembered the radiant Sunday of Magenta. It was early in August; the sunshine had not the young brightness of June. The weather was heavy, great flags of storm-cloud weighed upon the city. I was returning from a little town in Normandy, and I was particularly struck by the funereal aspect of Paris. On the boulevards, people were standing about in groups of three or four, and talking in low tones.

At last I heard the horrible news: we had been defeated at Worth, and the torrent of invasion was flowing into France. I never beheld such deep consternation. All Paris was stupefied. "What? Was it possible?" We were conquered ! The defeat seemed to us unjust and monstrous. It not only struck a blow at our patriotism; it destroyed a religion in us.

We could not yet measure all the disastrous consequences of this reverse, we still hoped that our soldiers might avenge it; and yet we remained as it were annihilated. The despairing silence of the town was full of a great shame. That day and that evening were frightful. The public gaiety of victorious days was not. Women no longer wore that tender smile, nor did people pass from group to group making friends. Night fell black on this despairing populace. Not a firework in the street; not a lamp at a window. Early on the morrow I saw a regiment going down the boulevard. People were pausing with sad faces, and the soldiers passed, hanging their heads, as if they had had their share in the defeat. Nothing saddened me so much as that regiment, applauded by no one, passing over the same ground where I had seen the army from Italy marching past amid rejoicings that shook the houses.

Then began the days cursed with suspense. Every two or three hours I used to go to the door of the Mairie in the ninth arrondissement, which is in the Rue Drouot, where the telegrams were put up. There were always people gathered there, waiting, to the number of a hundred or so. Often the crowd would extend right to the boulevard. There was nothing noisy about these crowds. People spoke in low tones, as if they were in a sick-room. Directly a clerk appeared to put a telegram on the board, there was a rush. Soon the news ran from mouth to mouth. But the news had long been persistently bad, and public consternation grew. Even today I cannot pass along the Rue Drouot without thinking of those days of mourning. There, on that pavement, the people of Paris had to undergo the most awful of torments. From hour to hour we could hear the gallop of the German armies drawing nearer to Paris.

I saw Julien very often. He did not boast to me of having foreseen the defeat. He only seemed to think what had happened was natural and in the order of things. Many Parisians shrugged their shoulders when they heard talk of a siege of Paris. Could there be a siege of Paris." And others would demonstrate mathematically that Paris could not be invested. Julien, by a sort of foreknowledge, which struck me later, declared that we should be surrounded on September 15th. He was still the schoolboy to whom physical exercises were strangely repulsive. All this war, upsetting all his customary ways, put him beside himself. Why, in the name of God, did people want to fight? And he would lift up his hands with a gesture of supreme protestation. Yet he read the telegrams greedily. "If Louis were not out there," he would repeat. "I might make verses while we are waiting for the end of the commotion."

At long intervals letters came to him from Louis. The news was terrible, the army was getting discouraged. On the day when we heard of the battle of Borny, I met Julien at the corner of the Rue Drouot. Paris had a gleam of hope that day. There was talk of a success. He, on the other hand, seemed to me gloomier than usual. He had read, somewhere, that his brother's regiment had done heroically, and that its losses had been severe.

Three days later a common friend came to tell me the terrible news. A letter had brought word to Julien the night before of his brother's death. He had been killed at Borny by the bursting of a shell. I immediately hurried to go to the poor fellow, but I found no one at his lodging. The next morning, while I was still in bed, a young man came in dressed as a priest. It was Julien. At first I hardly knew him. Then I folded him in my arms and embraced him heartily, while my eyes were full of tears. He did not weep. He sat down for a moment and made a sign to stop my condolences. "There," said he, quietly, "I wanted to say 'good-bye' to you. Now that I am alone I could not endure to do nothing so as I found that a company of priests was going, I joined yesterday. That will give me something to do," "When do you leave Paris?"

I asked him. "Why, in a couple of hours. Good-bye." He embraced me in his turn. I did not dare to ask him anymore questions. He went, and the thought of him was always with me. After the catastrophe of Sedan, some days before the surrounding of Paris, I had news of him. One of his comrades came to tell me that this young fellow, so pale and slender, fought like a wolf. He kept up a savage warfare against the Prussians, watching them from behind a hedge, using a knife rather than his gun. Whole nights long he would be on the hunt, watching for men as for his prey, and cutting the throat of anyone who came within his reach. I was stupefied. I could not think that this was Julien ; I asked myself whether it was possible that the nervous poet could have become a butcher.

Then Paris was isolated from the rest of the world, and the siege began with all its fits of sleepiness and of fever. I could not go out without remembering Aix on a winter evening. The streets were dark and empty, the houses were shut up early. There were, indeed, distant sounds of cannon and of shots, but the sounds seemed to get lost in the dull silence of the vast town. Some days, breaths of hope would come over, and then the whole population would awake, forgetful of the long standing at the baker's door, the rations, the cold chimneys, the shells showering upon some districts of the left side of the river. Then the crowd would be struck dumb by some disaster, and the silence began again — the silence of a capital in the death agony. Yet, in the course of this long siege, I saw little glimpses of quiet happiness; people who had a little to live on, who kept up their daily "constitutional" in the pale wintry sunshine, lovers smiling at each other in some out of the way nook and never hearing the cannonade. We lived from day to day. All our illusions had fallen; we counted on some miracle, help from the provincial armies, or a sortie of the whole populace, or some prodigious intervention to arise in its due time. I was at one of the outposts, one day, when a man was brought in, who had been found in a trench. I recognized Julien. He insisted on being taken to a general and gave him sundry pieces of information. I stayed with him, and we spent the night together. Since September he had never slept in a bed, but had given himself up obstinately to his vocation as a cut throat. He seemed chary of details, shrugged his shoulders, and told me that all expeditions were alike; he killed as many Prussians as he could, and killed them how he could: with a gun or with a knife. According to him it was after all a very monotonous life, and much less dangerous than people thought. He had run no real danger, except once when the French took him for a spy and wanted to shoot him. The next day he talked of going off again, across fields and woods. I entreated him to stay in Paris. He was sitting beside me, but did not seem to listen to me. Then he said, all at once, "You are right, it is enough. I have killed my share." Two days later he announced that he had enlisted in the Infantry. I was stupefied. Had he not avenged his brother enough? Had the idea of his country awakened in him? And, as I smiled in looking at him, he said quietly, "I take Louis' place. I cannot be anything but a soldier. Oh, gun powder intoxicates! And one's country, you see, is the earth where they lie, whom we loved."

CAPTAIN BURLE or
The Honor of the Army

CHAPTER I
THE SWINDLE

It was nine o'clock. The little town of Vauchamp, dark and silent, had just retired to bed amid a chilly November rain. In the Rue des Recollets, one of the narrowest and most deserted streets of the district of Saint-Jean, a single window was still alight on the third floor of an old house, from whose damaged gutters torrents of water were falling into the street. Mrs. Burle was sitting up before a meager fire of vine stocks, while her little grandson Charles pored over his lessons by the pale light of a lamp.

The apartment, rented at one hundred and sixty francs per annum, consisted of four large rooms which it was absolutely impossible to keep warm during the winter. Mrs. Burle slept in the largest chamber, her son Captain and Quartermaster Burle occupying a somewhat smaller one overlooking the street, while little Charles had his iron cot at the farther end of a spacious drawing room with mildewed hangings, which was never used. The few pieces of furniture belonging to the captain and his mother, furniture of the massive style of the First Empire, dented and worn by continuous transit from one garrison town to another, almost disappeared from view beneath the lofty ceilings whence darkness fell. The flooring of red-colored tiles was cold and hard to the feet; before the chairs there were merely a few threadbare little rugs of poverty-stricken aspect, and athwart this desert all the winds of heaven blew through the disjointed doors and windows.

Near the fireplace sat Mrs. Burle, leaning back in her old yellow velvet armchair and watching the last vine branch smoke, with that stolid, blank stare of the aged who live within themselves. She would sit thus for whole days together, with her tall figure, her long stern face and her thin lips that never smiled. The widow of a colonel who had died just as he was on the point of becoming a general, the mother of a captain whom she had followed even in his campaigns, she had acquired a military stiffness of bearing and formed for herself a code of honor, duty and patriotism which kept her rigid, desiccated, as it were, by the stern application of discipline. She seldom, if ever, complained. When her son had become a widower after five years of married life she had undertaken the education of little Charles as a matter of course, performing her duties with the severity of a sergeant drilling recruits. She watched over the child, never tolerating the slightest waywardness or irregularity, but compelling him to sit up till midnight when his exercises were not finished, and sitting up herself until he had completed them. Under such implacable despotism Charles, whose constitution was delicate, grew up pale and thin, with beautiful eyes, inordinately large and clear, shining in his white, pinched face.

During the long hours of silence Mrs. Burle dwelt continuously upon one and the same idea: she had been disappointed in her son. This thought sufficed to occupy her mind, and under its influence she would live her whole life over again, from the birth of her son, whom she had pictured rising amid glory to the highest rank, till she came down to mean and narrow garrison life, the dull, monotonous existence of nowadays, that stranding in the post of a quartermaster, from which Burle would never rise and in which he seemed to sink more and more heavily. And yet his first efforts had filled her with pride, and she had hoped to see her dreams realized. Burle had only just left Saint-Cyr when he distinguished himself at the battle of Solferino, where he had captured a whole battery of the enemy's artillery with merely a handful of men. For this feat he had won the cross; the papers had recorded his heroism, and he had become known as one of the bravest soldiers in the army. But gradually the hero had grown stout, embedded in flesh, timorous, lazy and satisfied. In 1870, still a captain, he had been made a prisoner in the first encounter, and he returned from Germany quite furious, swearing that he would never be caught fighting again, for it was too absurd. Being prevented from leaving the army, as he was incapable of embracing any other profession, he applied for and obtained the position of captain quartermaster, "a kennel," as he called it, "in which he would be left to kick the bucket in peace." That day Mrs. Burle experienced a great internal disruption. She felt that it was all over, and she ever afterward preserved a rigid attitude with tightened lips.

A blast of wind shook the Rue des Recollets and drove the rain angrily against the windowpanes. The old lady lifted her eyes from the smoking vine roots now dying out, to make sure that Charles was not falling asleep over his Latin exercise. This lad, twelve years of age, had become the old lady's supreme hope, the one human being in whom she centered her obstinate yearning for glory. At first she had hated him with all the loathing she had felt for his mother, a weak and pretty young lacemaker whom the captain had been foolish enough to marry when he found out that she would not listen to his passionate addresses on any other condition. Later on, when the mother had died and the father had begun to wallow in vice, Mrs. Burle dreamed again in presence of that little ailing child whom she found it so hard to rear. She wanted to see him robust, so that he might grow into the hero that Burle had declined to be, and for all her cold ruggedness she watched him anxiously, feeling his limbs and instilling courage into his soul. By degrees, blinded by her passionate desires, she imagined that she had at last found the man of the family. The boy, whose temperament was of a gentle, dreamy character, had a physical horror of soldiering, but as he lived in mortal dread of his grandmother and was extremely shy and submissive, he would echo all she said and resignedly express his intention of entering the army when he grew up.

Mrs. Burle observed that the exercise was not progressing. In fact, little Charles, overcome by the deafening noise of the storm, was dozing, albeit his pen was between his fingers and his eyes were staring at the paper. The old lady at once struck the edge of the table with her bony hand; whereupon the lad started, opened his dictionary and hurriedly began to turn over the leaves. Then, still preserving silence, his grandmother drew the vine roots together on the hearth and unsuccessfully attempted to rekindle the fire.

At the time when she had still believed in her son she had sacrificed her small income, which he had squandered in pursuits she dared not investigate. Even now he drained the household; all its resources went to the streets, and it was through him that she lived in penury, with empty rooms and cold kitchen. She never spoke to him of all those things, for with her sense of discipline he remained the master. Only at times she shuddered at the sudden fear that Burle might someday commit some foolish misdeed which would prevent Charles from entering the army.

She was rising up to fetch a fresh piece of wood in the kitchen when a fearful hurricane fell upon the house, making the doors rattle, tearing off a shutter and whirling the water in the broken gutters like a spout against the window. In the midst of the uproar a ring at the bell startled the old lady.

Who could it be at such an hour and in such weather? Burle never returned till after midnight, if he came home at all. However, she went to the door. An officer stood before her, dripping with rain and swearing savagely.

"Hell and thunder!" he growled. "What cursed weather!"

It was Major Laguitte, a brave old soldier who had served under Colonel Burle during Mrs. Burle's salad days. He had started in life as a drummer boy and, thanks to his courage rather than his intellect, had attained to the command of a battalion, when a painful infirmity—the contraction of the muscles of one of his thighs, due to a wound—obliged him to accept the post of major. He was slightly lame, but it would have been imprudent to tell him so, as he refused to own it.

"What, you, Major?" said Mrs. Burle with growing astonishment.

"Yes, thunder," grumbled Laguitte, "and I must be confoundedly fond of you to roam the streets on such a night as this. One would think twice before sending even a parson out."

He shook himself, and little rivulets fell from his huge boots onto the floor. Then he looked round him.

"I particularly want to see Burle. Is the lazy beggar already in bed?"

"No, he is not in yet," said the old woman in her harsh voice.

The major looked furious, and, raising his voice, he shouted: "What, not at home? But in that case they hoaxed me at the cafe, Melanie's establishment, you know. I went there, and a maid grinned at me, saying that the captain had gone home to bed. Curse the girl! I suspected as much and felt like pulling her ears!"

After this outburst he became somewhat calmer, stamping about the room in an undecided way, withal seeming greatly disturbed. Mrs. Burle looked at him attentively.

"Is it the captain personally whom you want to see?" she said at last.

"Yes," he answered.

"Can I not tell him what you have to say?"

"No."

She did not insist but remained standing without taking her eyes off the major, who did not seem able to make up his mind to leave. Finally in a fresh burst of rage he exclaimed with an oath: "It can't be helped. As I am here you may as well know—after all, it is, perhaps, best."

He sat down before the chimney piece, stretching out his muddy boots as if a bright fire had been burning. Mrs. Burle was about to resume her own seat when she remarked that Charles, overcome by fatigue, had dropped his head between the open pages of his dictionary. The arrival of the major had at first interested him, but, seeing that he remained unnoticed, he had been unable to struggle against his sleepiness. His grandmother turned toward the table to slap his frail little hands, whitening in the lamplight, when Laguitte stopped her.

"No—no!" he said. "Let the poor little man sleep. I haven't got anything funny to say. There's no need for him to hear me."

The old lady sat down in her armchair; deep silence reigned, and they looked at one another.

"Well, yes," said the major at last, punctuating his words with an angry motion of his chin, "he has been and done it; that hound Burle has been and done it!"

Not a muscle of Mrs. Burle's face moved, but she became livid, and her figure stiffened. Then the major continued: "I had my doubts. I had intended mentioning the subject to you. Burle was spending too much money, and he had an idiotic look which I did not fancy. Thunder and lightning! What a fool a man must be to behave so filthily!"

Then he thumped his knee furiously with his clenched fist and seemed to choke with indignation. The old woman put the straightforward question, "He has stolen?"

"You can't have an idea of it. You see, I never examined his accounts; I approved and signed them. You know how those things are managed. However, just before the inspection—as the colonel is a crotchety old maniac—I said to Burle: 'I say, old man, look to your accounts; I am answerable, you know,' and then I felt perfectly secure. Well, about a month ago, as he seemed queer and some nasty stories were circulating, I peered a little closer into the books and pottered over the entries. I thought everything looked straight and very well kept."

At this point he stopped, convulsed by such a fit of rage that he had to relieve himself by a volley of appalling oaths. Finally he resumed: "It isn't the swindle that angers me; it is his disgusting behavior to me. He has gammoned me, Madame Burle. By God! Does he take me for an old fool?"

"So he stole?" the mother again questioned.

"This evening," continued the major more quietly, "I had just finished my dinner when Gagneux came in—you know Gagneux, the butcher at the corner of the Place aux Herbes? Another dirty beast who got the meat contract and makes our men eat all the diseased cow flesh in the neighbor-hood! Well, I received him like a dog, and then he let it all out—blurted out the whole thing, and a pretty mess it is! It appears that Burle only paid him in driblets and had got himself into a muddle—a confusion of figures which the devil himself couldn't disentangle. In short, Burle owes the butcher two thousand francs, and Gagneux threatens that he'll inform the colonel if he is not paid. To make matters worse, Burle, just to blind me, handed me every week a forged receipt which he had squarely signed with Gagneux's name. To think he did that to me, his old friend! Ah, curse him!"

With increasing profanity the major rose to his feet, shook his fist at the ceiling and then fell back in his chair. Mrs. Burle again repeated:

"He has stolen. It was inevitable."

Then without a word of judgment or condemnation she added simply: "Two thousand francs—we have not got them. There are barely thirty francs in the house."

"I expected as much," said Laguitte. "And do you know where all the money goes? Why, Melanie gets it—yes, Melanie, a creature who has turned Burle into a perfect fool. Ah, those women! Those fiendish women! I always said they would do for him! I cannot conceive what he is made of! He is only five years younger than I am, and yet he is as mad as ever. What a woman hunter he is!"

Another long silence followed. Outside the rain was increasing in vio-lence, and throughout the sleepy little town one could hear the crashing of slates and chimney pots as they were dashed by the blast onto the pave-ments of the streets.

"Come," suddenly said the major, rising, "my stopping here won't mend matters. I have warned you—and now I'm off."

"What is to be done? To whom can we apply?" muttered the old woman drearily.

"Don't give way—we must consider. If I only had the two thousand francs—but you know that I am not rich."

The major stopped short in confusion. This old bachelor, wifeless and childless, spent his pay in drink and gambled away at cards whatever money his cognac and absinthe left in his pocket. Despite that, however, he was scrupulously honest from a sense of discipline.

"Never mind," he added as he reached the threshold. "I'll begin by stir-ring him up. I shall move heaven and earth! What! Burle, Colonel Burle's son, condemned for theft! That cannot be! I would sooner burn down the town. Now, thunder and lightning, don't worry; it is far more annoying for me than for you."

He shook the old lady's hand roughly and vanished into the shadows of the staircase, while she held the lamp aloft to light the way. When she returned and replaced the lamp on the table she stood for a moment motionless in front of Charles, who was still asleep with his face lying on the dictionary. His pale cheeks and long fair hair made him look like a girl, and she gazed at him dreamily, a shade of tenderness passing over her harsh countenance. But it was only a passing emotion; her features regained their look of cold, obstinate determination, and, giving the youngster a sharp rap on his little hand, she said, "Charles—your lessons."

The boy awoke, dazed and shivering, and again rapidly turned over the leaves. At the same moment Major Laguitte, slamming the house door behind him, received on his head a quantity of water falling from the gutters above, whereupon he began to swear in so loud a voice that he could be heard above the storm. And after that no sound broke upon the pelting downpour save the slight rustle of the boy's pen traveling over the paper. Mrs. Burle had resumed her seat near the chimney piece, still rigid, with her eyes fixed on the dead embers, preserving, indeed, her habitual attitude and absorbed in her one idea.

CHAPTER II
THE CAFE

The Cafe de Paris, kept by Melanie Cartier, a widow, was situated on the Place du Palais, a large irregular square planted with meager, dusty elm trees. The place was so well known in Vauchamp that it was customary to say, "Are you coming to Melanie's?" At the farther end of the first room, which was a spacious one, there was another called "the divan," a narrow apartment having sham leather benches placed against the walls, while at each corner there stood a marble-topped table. The widow, deserting her seat in the front room, where she left her little servant Phrosine, spent her evenings in the inner apartment, ministering to a few customers, the usual frequenters of the place, those who were currently styled "the gentlemen of the divan." When a man belonged to that set it was as if he had a label on his back; he was spoken of with smiles of mingled contempt and envy.

Mrs. Cartier had become a widow when she was five and twenty. Her husband, a wheelwright, who on the death of an uncle had amazed Vauchamp by taking the Cafe de Paris, had one fine day brought her back with him from Montpellier, where he was wont to repair twice a year to purchase liqueurs. As he was stocking his establishment he selected, together with divers beverages, a woman of the sort he wanted—of an engaging aspect and apt to stimulate the trade of the house. It was never known where he had picked her up, but he married her after trying her in the cafe during six months or so. Opinions were divided in Vauchamp as to her merits, some folks declaring that she was superb, while others asserted that she looked like a drum-major. She was a tall woman with large features and coarse hair falling low over her forehead. However, everyone agreed that she knew very well how to fool the sterner sex. She had fine eyes and was wont to fix them with a bold stare on the gentlemen of the divan, who colored and became like wax in her hands. She also had the reputation of possessing a wonderfully fine figure, and southerners appreciate a statuesque style of beauty.

Cartier had died in a singular way. Rumor hinted at a conjugal quarrel, a kick, producing some internal tumor. Whatever may have been the truth, Melanie found herself encumbered with the cafe, which was far from doing a prosperous business. Her husband had wasted his uncle's inheritance in drinking his own absinthe and wearing out the cloth of his own billiard table. For a while it was believed that the widow would have to sell out, but she liked the life and the establishment just as it was. If she could secure a few customers the bigger room might remain deserted. So she limited herself to repapering the divan in white and gold and recovering the benches. She began by entertaining a chemist. Then a vermicelli maker, a lawyer and a retired magistrate put in an appearance; and thus it was that the cafe remained open, although the waiter did not receive twenty orders a day. No objections were raised by the authorities, as appearances were kept up; and, indeed, it was not deemed advisable to interfere, for some respectable folks might have been worried.

Of an evening five or six well-to-do citizens would enter the front room and play at dominoes there. Although Cartier was dead and the Cafe de Paris had got a queer name, they saw nothing and kept up their old habits. In course of time, the waiter having nothing to do, Melanie dismissed him and made Phrosine light the solitary gas burner in the corner where the domino players congregated. Occasionally a party of young men, attracted by the gossip that circulated through the town, would come in, wildly excited and laughing loudly and awkwardly. But they were received there with icy dignity. As a rule they did not even see the widow, and even if she happened to be present she treated them with withering disdain, so that they withdrew, stammering and confused. Melanie was too astute to indulge in any compromising whims. While the front room remained obscure, save in the corner where the few townsfolk rattled their dominoes, she personally waited on the gentlemen of the divan, showing herself amiable without being free, merely venturing in moments of familiarity to lean on the shoulder of one or another of them, the better to watch a skillfully played game of cards.

One evening the gentlemen of the divan, who had ended by tolerating each other's presence, experienced a disagreeable surprise on finding Captain Burle at home there. He had casually entered the cafe that same morning to get a glass of vermouth, so it seemed, and he had found Melanie there. They had conversed, and in the evening when he returned Phrosine immediately showed him to the inner room.

Two days later Burle reigned there supreme; still he had not frightened the chemist, the vermicelli maker, the lawyer or the retired magistrate away. The captain, who was short and dumpy, worshiped tall, plump women. In his regiment he had been nicknamed "Petticoat Burle" on account of his constant philandering. Whenever the officers, and even the privates, met some monstrous-looking creature, some giantess puffed out with fat, whether she were in velvet or in rags, they would invariably exclaim, "There goes one to Petticoat Burle's taste!" Thus Melanie, with her opulent presence, quite conquered him. He was lost—quite wrecked. In less than a fortnight he had fallen to vacuous imbecility. With much the expression of a whipped hound in the tiny sunken eyes which lighted up his bloated face, he was incessantly watching the widow in mute adoration before her masculine features and stubby hair. For fear that he might be dismissed, he put up with the presence of the other gentlemen of the divan and spent his pay in the place down to the last copper. A sergeant reviewed the situation in one sentence: "Petticoat Burle is done for; he's a buried man!"

It was nearly ten o'clock when Major Laguitte furiously flung the door of the cafe open. For a moment those inside could see the deluged square transformed into a dark sea of liquid mud, bubbling under the terrible downpour. The major, now soaked to the skin and leaving a stream behind him, strode up to the small counter where Phrosine was reading a novel.

"You little wretch," he yelled, "you have dared to gammon an officer; you deserve—"

And then he lifted his hand as if to deal a blow such as would have felled an ox. The little maid shrank back, terrified, while the amazed domino players looked, openmouthed. However, the major did not linger there— he pushed the divan door open and appeared before Melanie and Burle just as the widow was playfully making the captain sip his grog in small spoonfuls, as if she were feeding a pet canary. Only the ex-magistrate and the chemist had come that evening, and they had retired early in a melancholy frame of mind. Then Melanie, being in want of three hundred francs for the morrow, had taken advantage of the opportunity to cajole the captain.

"Come." she said, "open your mouth; ain't it nice, you greedy piggy-wiggy?"

Burle, flushing scarlet, with glazed eyes and sunken figure, was sucking the spoon with an air of intense enjoyment.

"Good heavens!" roared the major from the threshold. "You now play tricks on me, do you? I'm sent to the roundabout and told that you never came here, and yet all the while here you are, addling your silly brains."

Burle shuddered, pushing the grog away, while Melanie stepped angrily in front of him as if to shield him with her portly figure, but Laguitte looked at her with that quiet, resolute expression well known to women who are familiar with bodily chastisement.

"Leave us," he said curtly.

She hesitated for the space of a second. She almost felt the gust of the expected blow, and then, white with rage, she joined Phrosine in the outer room.

When the two men were alone Major Laguitte walked up to Burle, looked at him and, slightly stooping, yelled into his face these two words: "You pig!"

The captain, quite dazed, endeavored to retort, but he had not time to do so.

"Silence!" resumed the major. "You have bamboozled a friend. You palmed off on me a lot of forged receipts which might have sent both of us to the gallows. Do you call that proper behavior? Is that the sort of trick to play a friend of thirty years' standing?"

Burle, who had fallen back in his chair, was livid; his limbs shook as if with ague. Meanwhile the major, striding up and down and striking the tables wildly with his fists, continued: "So you have become a thief like the worst scribbling cur of a clerk, and all for the sake of that creature here! If at least you had stolen for your mother's sake it would have been honorable! But, curse it, to play tricks and bring the money into this shanty is what I cannot understand! Tell me—what are you made of at your age to go to the dogs as you are going all for the sake of a creature like a grenadier!"

"YOU gamble?" stammered the captain.

"Yes, I do—curse it!" thundered the major, lashed into still greater fury by this remark. "And I am a pitiful rogue to do so, because it swallows up all my pay and doesn't redound to the honor of the French army. However, I don't steal. Kill yourself, if it pleases you; starve your mother and the boy, but respect the regimental cashbox and don't drag your friends down with you."

He stopped. Burle was sitting there with fixed eyes and a stupid air.

Nothing was heard for a moment save the clatter of the major's heels.

"And not a single copper," he continued aggressively. "Can you picture yourself between two gendarmes, eh?"

He then grew a little calmer, caught hold of Burle's wrists and forced him to rise.

"Come!" he said gruffly. "Something must be done at once, for I cannot go to bed with this affair on my mind—I have an idea."

In the front room Melanie and Phrosine were talking eagerly in low voices. When the widow saw the two men leaving the divan she moved toward Burle and said coaxingly: "What, are you going already, Captain?"

"Yes, he's going," brutally answered Laguitte, "and I don't intend to let him set foot here again."

The little maid felt frightened and pulled her mistress back by the skirt of her dress; in doing so she imprudently murmured the word "drunkard" and thereby brought down the slap which the major's hand had been itching to deal for some time past. Both women having stooped, however, the blow only fell on Phrosine's back hair, flattening her cap and breaking her comb. The domino players were indignant.

"Let's cut it," shouted Laguitte, and he pushed Burle on the pavement.

"If I remained I should smash everyone in the place."

To cross the square they had to wade up to their ankles in mud. The rain, driven by the wind, poured off their faces. The captain walked on in silence, while the major kept on reproaching him with his cowardice and its disastrous consequences. Wasn't it sweet weather for tramping the streets? If he hadn't been such an idiot they would both be warmly tucked in bed instead of paddling about in the mud. Then he spoke of Gagneux—a scoundrel whose diseased meat had on three separate occasions made the whole regiment ill. In a week, however, the contract would come to an end, and the fiend himself would not get it renewed.

"It rests with me," the major grumbled. "I can select whomsoever I choose, and I'd rather cut off my right arm than put that poisoner in the way of earning another copper."

Just then he slipped into a gutter and, half choked by a string of oaths, he gasped:

"You understand—I am going to rout up Gagneux. You must stop outside while I go in. I must know what the rascal is up to and if he'll dare to carry out his threat of informing the colonel tomorrow. A butcher—curse him! The idea of compromising oneself with a butcher! Ah, you aren't overproud, and I shall never forgive you for all this."

They had now reached the Place aux Herbes. Gagneux's house was quite dark, but Laguitte knocked so loudly that he was eventually admitted. Burle remained alone in the dense obscurity and did not even attempt to seek any shelter. He stood at a corner of the market under the pelting rain, his head filled with a loud buzzing noise which prevented him from thinking. He did not feel impatient, for he was unconscious of the flight of time. He stood there looking at the house, which, with its closed door and windows, seemed quite lifeless. When at the end of an hour the major came out again it appeared to the captain as if he had only just gone in.

Laguitte was so grimly mute that Burle did not venture to question him. For a moment they sought each other, groping about in the dark; then they resumed their walk through the somber streets, where the water rolled as in the bed of a torrent. They moved on in silence side by side, the major being so abstracted that he even forgot to swear.

However, as they again crossed the Place du Palais, at the sight of the Cafe de Paris, which was still lit up, he dropped his hand on Burle's shoulder and said, "If you ever re-enter that hole I—"

"No fear!" answered the captain without letting his friend finish his sentence.

Then he stretched out his hand.

"No, no," said Laguitte, "I'll see you home; I'll at least make sure that you'll sleep in your bed tonight."

They went on, and as they ascended the Rue des Recollets they slackened their pace. When the captain's door was reached and Burle had taken out his latchkey he ventured to ask, "Well?"

"Well," answered the major gruffly, "I am as dirty a rogue as you are. Yes! I have done a scurrilous thing. The fiend take you! Our soldiers will eat carrion for three months longer."

Then he explained that Gagneux, the disgusting Gagneux, had a horribly level head and that he had persuaded him—the major—to strike a bargain. He would refrain from informing the colonel, and he would even make a present of the two thousand francs and replace the forged receipts by genuine ones, on condition that the major bound himself to renew the meat contract. It was a settled thing.

"Ah," continued Laguitte, "calculate what profits the brute must make out of the meat to part with such a sum as two thousand francs."

Burle, choking with emotion, grasped his old friend's hands, stammering confused words of thanks. The vileness of the action committed for his sake brought tears into his eyes.

"I never did such a thing before," growled Laguitte, "but I was driven to it. Curse it, to think that I haven't those two thousand francs in my drawer! It is enough to make one hate cards. It is my own fault. I am not worth much; only, mark my words, don't begin again, for, curse it—I shan't."

The captain embraced him, and when he had entered the house the major stood a moment before the closed door to make certain that he had gone upstairs to bed. Then as midnight was striking and the rain was still belaboring the dark town, he slowly turned homeward. The thought of his men almost broke his heart, and, stopping short, he said aloud in a voice full of compassion:

"Poor devils! what a lot of cow beef they'll have to swallow for those two thousand francs!"

CHAPTER III
AGAIN?

The regiment was altogether nonplused: Petticoat Burle had quarreled with Melanie. When a week had elapsed it became a proved and undeniable fact; the captain no longer set foot inside the Cafe de Paris, where the chemist, it was averred, once more reigned in his stead, to the profound sorrow of the retired magistrate. An even more incredible statement was that Captain Burle led the life of a recluse in the Rue des Recollets. He was becoming a reformed character; he spent his evenings at his own fireside, hearing little Charles repeat his lessons. His mother, who had never breathed a word to him of his manipulations with Gagneux, maintained her old severity of demeanor as she sat opposite to him in her armchair, but her looks seemed to imply that she believed him reclaimed.

A fortnight later Major Laguitte came one evening to invite himself to dinner. He felt some awkwardness at the prospect of meeting Burle again, not on his own account but because he dreaded awakening painful memories. However, as the captain was mending his ways he wished to shake hands and break a crust with him. He thought this would please his old friend.

When Laguitte arrived Burle was in his room, so it was the old lady who received the major. The latter, after announcing that he had come to have a plate of soup with them, added, lowering his voice:

"Well, how goes it?"

"It is all right," answered the old lady.

"Nothing queer?"

"Absolutely nothing. Never away—in bed at nine—and looking quite happy."

"Ah, confound it," replied the major, "I knew very well he only wanted a shaking. He has some heart left, the dog!"

When Burle appeared he almost crushed the major's hands in his grasp, and standing before the fire, waiting for the dinner, they conversed peacefully, honestly, together, extolling the charms of home life. The captain vowed he wouldn't exchange his home for a kingdom and declared that when he had removed his braces, put on his slippers and settled himself in his armchair, no king was fit to hold a candle to him. The major assented and examined him. At all events his virtuous conduct had not made him any thinner; he still looked bloated; his eyes were bleared, and his mouth was heavy. He seemed to be half asleep as he repeated mechanically: "Home life! There's nothing like home life, nothing in the world!"

"No doubt," said the major; "still, one mustn't exaggerate—take a little exercise and come to the cafe now and then."

"To the cafe, why?" asked Burle. "Do I lack anything here? No, no, I remain at home."

When Charles had laid his books aside Laguitte was surprised to see a maid come in to lay the cloth.

"So you keep a servant now," he remarked to Mrs. Burle.

"I had to get one," she answered with a sigh. "My legs are not what they used to be, and the household was going to rack and ruin. Fortunately Cabrol let me have his daughter. You know old Cabrol, who sweeps the market? He did not know what to do with Rose—I am teaching her how to work."

Just then the girl left the room.

"How old is she?" asked the major.

"Barely seventeen. She is stupid and dirty, but I only give her ten francs a month, and she eats nothing but soup."

When Rose returned with an armful of plates Laguitte, though he did not care about women, began to scrutinize her and was amazed at seeing so ugly a creature. She was very short, very dark and slightly deformed, with a face like an ape's: a flat nose, a huge mouth and narrow greenish eyes. Her broad back and long arms gave her an appearance of great strength.

"What a snout!" said Laguitte, laughing, when the maid had again left the room to fetch the cruets.

"Never mind," said Burle carelessly, "she is very obliging and does all one asks her. She suits us well enough as a scullion."

The dinner was very pleasant. It consisted of boiled beef and mutton hash. Charles was encouraged to relate some stories of his school, and Mrs. Burle repeatedly asked him the same question: "Don't you want to be a soldier?" A faint smile hovered over the child's wan lips as he answered with the frightened obedience of a trained dog, "Oh yes, Grandmother." Captain Burle, with his elbows on the table, was masticating slowly with an absent-minded expression. The big room was getting warmer; the single lamp placed on the table left the corners in vague gloom. There was a certain amount of heavy comfort, the familiar intimacy of penurious people who do not change their plates at every course but become joyously excited at the unexpected appearance of a bowl of whipped egg cream at the close of the meal.

Rose, whose heavy tread shook the floor as she paced round the table, had not yet opened her mouth. At last she stopped behind the captain's chair and asked in a gruff voice: "Cheese, sir?"

Burle started. "What, eh? Oh yes—cheese. Hold the plate tight."

He cut a piece of Gruyere, the girl watching him the while with her narrow eyes. Laguitte laughed; Rose's unparalleled ugliness amused him immensely. He whispered in the captain's ear, "She is ripping! There never was such a nose and such a mouth! You ought to send her to the colonel's someday as a curiosity. It would amuse him to see her."

More and more struck by this phenomenal ugliness, the major felt a paternal desire to examine the girl more closely.

"Come here," he said, "I want some cheese too."

She brought the plate, and Laguitte, sticking the knife in the Gruyere, stared at her, grinning the while because he discovered that she had one nostril broader than the other. Rose gravely allowed herself to be looked at, waiting till the gentleman had done laughing.

She removed the cloth and disappeared. Burle immediately went to sleep in the chimney corner while the major and Mrs. Burle began to chat. Charles had returned to his exercises. Quietude fell from the loft ceiling; the quietude of a middle-class household gathered in concord around their fireside. At nine o'clock Burle woke up, yawned and announced that he was going off to bed; he apologized but declared that he could not keep his eyes open. Half an hour later, when the major took his leave, Mrs. Burle vainly called for Rose to light him downstairs; the girl must have gone up to her room; she was, indeed, a regular hen, snoring the round of the clock without waking.

"No need to disturb anybody," said Laguitte on the landing; "my legs are not much better than yours, but if I get hold of the banisters I shan't break any bones. Now, my dear lady, I leave you happy; your troubles are ended at last. I watched Burle closely, and I'll take my oath that he's guileless as a child. Dash it—after all, it was high time for Petticoat Burle to reform; he was going downhill fast."

The major went away fully satisfied with the house and its inmates; the walls were of glass and could harbor no equivocal conduct. What particularly delighted him in his friend's return to virtue was that it absolved him from the obligation of verifying the accounts. Nothing was more distasteful to him than the inspection of a number of ledgers, and as long as Burle kept steady, he—Laguitte—could smoke his pipe in peace and sign the books in all confidence. However, he continued to keep one eye open for a little while longer and found the receipts genuine, the entries correct, the columns admirably balanced. A month later he contented himself with glancing at the receipts and running his eye over the totals. Then one morning, without the slightest suspicion of there being anything wrong, simply because he had lit a second pipe and had nothing to do, he carelessly added up a row of figures and fancied that he detected an error of thirteen francs. The balance seemed perfectly correct, and yet he was not mistaken; the total outlay was thirteen francs more than the various sums for which receipts were furnished. It looked queer, but he said nothing to Burle, just making up his mind to examine the next accounts closely. On the following week he detected a fresh error of nineteen francs, and then, suddenly becoming alarmed, he shut himself up with the books and spent a wretched morning poring over them, perspiring, swearing and feeling as if his very skull were bursting with the figures. At every page he discovered thefts of a few francs—the most miserable petty thefts—ten, eight, eleven francs, latterly, three and four; and, indeed, there was one column showing that Burle had pilfered just one franc and a half. For two months, however, he had been steadily robbing the cashbox, and by comparing dates the major found to his disgust that the famous lesson respecting Gagneux had only kept him straight for one week! This last discovery infuriated Laguitte, who struck the books with his clenched fists, yelling through a shower of oaths, "This is more abominable still! At least there was some pluck about those forged receipts of Gagneux. But this time he is as contemptible as a cook charging twopence extra for her cabbages. Powers of hell! To pilfer a franc and a half and clap it in his pocket! Hasn't the brute got any pride then? Couldn't he run away with the safe or play the fool with actresses?"

The pitiful meanness of these pilferings revolted the major, and, moreover, he was enraged at having been duped a second time, deceived by the simple, stupid dodge of falsified additions. He rose at last and paced his office for a whole hour, growling aloud.

"This gives me his measure. Even if I were to thresh him to a jelly every morning he would still drop a couple of coins into his pocket every afternoon. But where can he spend it all? He is never seen abroad; he goes to bed at nine, and everything looks so clean and proper over there. Can the brute have vices that nobody knows of?"

He returned to the desk, added up the subtracted money and found a total of five hundred and forty-five francs. Where was this deficiency to come from? The inspection was close at hand, and if the crotchety colonel should take it into his head to examine a single page, the murder would be out and Burle would be done for.

This idea froze the major, who left off cursing, picturing Mrs. Burle erect and despairing, and at the same time he felt his heart swell with personal grief and shame.

"Well," he muttered, "I must first of all look into the rogue's business; I will act afterward."

As he walked over to Burle's office he caught sight of a skirt vanishing through the doorway. Fancying that he had a clue to the mystery, he slipped up quietly and listened and speedily recognized Melanie's shrill voice. She was complaining of the gentlemen of the divan. She had signed a promissory note which she was unable to meet; the bailiffs were in the house, and all her goods would be sold. The captain, however, barely replied to her. He alleged that he had no money, whereupon she burst into tears and began to coax him. But her blandishments were apparently ineffectual, for Burle's husky voice could be heard repeating, "Impossible! Impossible!" And finally the widow withdrew in a towering passion. The major, amazed at the turn affairs were taking, waited a few moments longer before entering the office, where Burle had remained alone. He found him very calm, and despite his furious inclination to call him names he also remained calm, determined to begin by finding out the exact truth.

The office certainly did not look like a swindler's den. A cane-seated chair, covered with an honest leather cushion, stood before the captain's desk, and in a corner there was the locked safe. Summer was coming on, and the song of a canary sounded through the open window. The apartment was very neat and tidy, redolent of old papers, and altogether its appearance inspired one with confidence.

"Wasn't it Melanie who was leaving here as I came along?" asked Laguitte.

Burle shrugged his shoulders.

"Yes," he mumbled. "She has been dunning me for two hundred francs, but she can't screw ten out of me—not even ten cents."

"Indeed!" said the major, just to try him. "I heard that you had made up with her."

"I? Certainly not. I have done with the likes of her for good."

Laguitte went away, feeling greatly perplexed. Where had the five hundred and forty-five francs gone? Had the idiot taken to drinking or gambling? He decided to pay Burle a surprise visit that very evening at his own house, and maybe by questioning his mother he might learn something. However, during the afternoon his leg became very painful; latterly he had been feeling in ill-health, and he had to use a stick so as not to limp too outrageously. This stick grieved him sorely, and he declared with angry despair that he was now no better than a pensioner. However, toward the evening, making a strong effort, he pulled himself out of his armchair and, leaning heavily on his stick, dragged himself through the darkness to the Rue des Recollets, which he reached about nine o'clock. The street door was still unlocked, and on going up he stood panting on the third landing, when he heard voices on the upper floor. One of these voices was Burle's, so he fancied, and out of curiosity he ascended another flight of stairs. Then at the end of a passage on the left he saw a ray of light coming from a door which stood ajar. As the creaking of his boots resounded, this door was sharply closed, and he found himself in the dark.

"Some cook going to bed!" he muttered angrily. "I'm a fool."

All the same he groped his way as gently as possible to the door and listened. Two people were talking in the room, and he stood aghast, for it was Burle and that fright Rose! Then he listened, and the conversation he heard left him no doubt of the awful truth. For a moment he lifted his stick as if to beat down the door. Then he shuddered and, staggering back, leaned against the wall. His legs were trembling under him, while in the darkness of the staircase he brandished his stick as if it had been a saber.

What was to be done? After his first moment of passion there had come thoughts of the poor old lady below. And these made him hesitate. It was all over with the captain now; when a man sank as low as that he was hardly worth the few shovelfuls of earth that are thrown over carrion to prevent them from polluting the atmosphere. Whatever might be said of Burle, however much one might try to shame him, he would assuredly begin the next day. Ah, heavens, to think of it! The money! The honor of the army! The name of Burle, that respected name, dragged through the mire! By all that was holy this could and should not be!

Presently the major softened. If he had only possessed five hundred and forty-five francs! But he had not got such an amount. On the previous day he had drunk too much cognac, just like a mere sub, and had lost shockingly at cards. It served him right—he ought to have known better! And if he was so lame he richly deserved it too; by rights, in fact, his leg ought to be much worse.

At last he crept downstairs and rang at the bell of Mrs. Burle's flat.

Five minutes elapsed, and then the old lady appeared.

"I beg your pardon for keeping you waiting," she said; "I thought that dormouse Rose was still about. I must go and shake her."

But the major detained her.

"Where is Burle?" he asked.

"Oh, he has been snoring since nine o'clock. Would you like to knock at his door?"

"No, no, I only wanted to have a chat with you."

In the parlor Charles sat at his usual place, having just finished his exercises. He looked terrified, and his poor little white hands were tremulous. In point of fact, his grandmother, before sending him to bed, was wont to read some martial stories aloud so as to develop the latent family heroism in his bosom. That night she had selected the episode of the Vengeur, the man-of-war freighted with dying heroes and sinking into the sea. The child, while listening, had become almost hysterical, and his head was racked as with some ghastly nightmare.

Mrs. Burle asked the major to let her finish the perusal. "Long live the republic!" She solemnly closed the volume. Charles was as white as a sheet.

"You see," said the old lady, "the duty of every French soldier is to die for his country."

"Yes, Grandmother."

Then the lad kissed her on the forehead and, shivering with fear, went to bed in his big room, where the faintest creak of the paneling threw him into a cold sweat.

The major had listened with a grave face. Yes, by heavens! Honor was honor, and he would never permit that wretched Burle to disgrace the old woman and the boy! As the lad was so devoted to the military profession, it was necessary that he should be able to enter Saint-Cyr with his head erect.

When Mrs. Burle took up the lamp to show the major out, she passed the door of the captain's room, and stopped short, surprised to see the key outside, which was a most unusual occurrence.

"Do go in," she said to Laguitte; "it is bad for him to sleep so much."

And before he could interpose she had opened the door and stood transfixed on finding the room empty. Laguitte turned crimson and looked so foolish that she suddenly understood everything, enlightened by the sudden recollection of several little incidents to which she had previously attached no importance.

"You knew it—you knew it!" she stammered. "Why was I not told? Oh, my God, to think of it! Ah, he has been stealing again—I feel it!"

She remained erect, white and rigid. Then she added in a harsh voice, "Look you—I wish he were dead!"

Laguitte caught hold of both her hands, which for a moment he kept tightly clasped in his own. Then he left her hurriedly, for he felt a lump rising in his throat and tears coming to his eyes. Ah, by all the powers, this time his mind was quite made up.

CHAPTER IV
INSPECTION

The regimental inspection was to take place at the end of the month. The major had ten days before him. On the very next morning, however, he crawled, limping, as far as the Cafe de Paris, where he ordered some beer. Melanie grew pale when she saw him enter, and it was with a lively recollection of a certain slap that Phrosine hastened to serve him. The major seemed very calm, however; he called for a second chair to rest his bad leg upon and drank his beer quietly like any other thirsty man. He had sat there for about an hour when he saw two officers crossing the Place du Palais—Morandot, who commanded one of the battalions of the regiment, and Captain Doucet. Thereupon he excitedly waved his cane and shouted: "Come in and have a glass of beer with me!"

The officers dared not refuse, but when the maid had brought the beer Morandot said to the major: "So you patronize this place now?"

"Yes—the beer is good."

Captain Doucet winked and asked archly: "Do you belong to the divan, Major?"

Laguitte chuckled but did not answer. Then the others began to chaff him about Melanie, and he took their remarks good-naturedly, simply shrugging his shoulders. The widow was undoubtedly a fine woman, however much people might talk. Some of those who disparaged her would, in reality, be only too pleased to win her good graces. Then turning to the little counter and assuming an engaging air, he shouted, "Three more glasses, madame."

Melanie was so taken aback that she rose and brought the beer herself. The major detained her at the table and forgot himself so far as to softly pat the hand which she had carelessly placed on the back of a chair. Used as she was to alternate brutality and flattery, she immediately became confident, believing in a sudden whim of gallantry on the part of the "old wreck," as she was wont to style the major when talking with Phrosine. Doucet and Morandot looked at each other in surprise. Was the major actually stepping into Petticoat Burle's shoes? The regiment would be convulsed if that were the case.

Suddenly, however, Laguitte, who kept his eye on the square, gave a start.

"Hallo, there's Burle!" he exclaimed.

"Yes, it is his time," explained Phrosine. "The captain passes every afternoon on his way from the office."

In spite of his lameness the major had risen to his feet, pushing aside the chairs as he called out: "Burle! I say—come along and have a glass."

The captain, quite aghast and unable to understand why Laguitte was at the widow's, advanced mechanically. He was so perplexed that he again hesitated at the door.

"Another glass of beer," ordered the major, and then turning to Burle, he added, "What's the matter with you? Come in. Are you afraid of being eaten alive?"

The captain took a seat, and an awkward pause followed. Melanie, who brought the beer with trembling hands, dreaded some scene which might result in the closing of her establishment. The major's gallantry made her uneasy, and she endeavored to slip away, but he invited her to drink with them, and before she could refuse he had ordered Phrosine to bring a liqueur glass of anisette, doing so with as much coolness as if he had been master of the house. Melanie was thus compelled to sit down between the captain and Laguitte, who exclaimed aggressively: "I WILL have ladies respected. We are French officers! Let us drink Madame's health!"

Burle, with his eyes fixed on his glass, smiled in an embarrassed way. The two officers, shocked at the proceedings, had already tried to get off. Fortunately the cafe was deserted, save that the domino players were having their afternoon game. At every fresh oath which came from the major they glanced around, scandalized by such an unusual accession of customers and ready to threaten Melanie that they would leave her for the Cafe de la Gare if the soldiery was going to invade her place like flies that buzzed about, attracted by the stickiness of the tables which Phrosine scoured only on Saturdays. She was now reclining behind the counter, already reading a novel again.

"How's this—you are not drinking with Madame?" roughly said the major to Burle. "Be civil at least!"

Then as Doucet and Morandot were again preparing to leave, he stopped them.

"Why can't you wait? We'll go together. It is only this brute who never knows how to behave himself."

The two officers looked surprised at the major's sudden bad temper. Melanie attempted to restore peace and with a light laugh placed her hands on the arms of both men. However, Laguitte disengaged himself.

"No," he roared, "leave me alone. Why does he refuse to chink glasses with you? I shall not allow you to be insulted—do you hear? I am quite sick of him."

Burle, paling under the insult, turned slightly and said to Morandot, "What does this mean? He calls me in here to insult me. Is he drunk?"

With a wild oath the major rose on his trembling legs and struck the captain's cheek with his open hand. Melanie dived and thus escaped one half of the smack. An appalling uproar ensued. Phrosine screamed behind the counter as if she herself had received the blow; the domino players also entrenched themselves behind their table in fear lest the soldiers should draw their swords and massacre them. However, Doucet and Morandot pinioned the captain to prevent him from springing at the major's throat and forcibly let him to the door. When they got him outside they succeeded in quieting him a little by repeating that Laguitte was quite in the wrong. They would lay the affair before the colonel, having witnessed it, and the colonel would give his decision. As soon as they had got Burle away they returned to the cafe where they found Laguitte in reality greatly disturbed, with tears in his eyes but affecting stolid indifference and slowly finishing his beer.

"Listen, Major," began Morandot, "that was very wrong on your part. The captain is your inferior in rank, and you know that he won't be allowed to fight you."

"That remains to be seen," answered the major.

"But how has he offended you? He never uttered a word. Two old comrades too; it is absurd."

The major made a vague gesture. "No matter. He annoyed me."

He could never be made to say anything else. Nothing more as to his motive was ever known. All the same, the scandal was a terrible one. The regiment was inclined to believe that Melanie, incensed by the captain's defection, had contrived to entrap the major, telling him some abominable stories and prevailing upon him to insult and strike Burle publicly. Who would have thought it of that old fogy Laguitte, who professed to be a woman hater? they said. So he, too, had been caught at last. Despite the general indignation against Melanie, this adventure made her very conspicuous, and her establishment soon drove a flourishing business.

On the following day the colonel summoned the major and the captain into his presence. He censured them sternly, accusing them of disgracing their uniform by frequenting unseemly haunts. What resolution had they come to, he asked, as he could not authorize them to fight? This same question had occupied the whole regiment for the last twenty-four hours. Apologies were unacceptable on account of the blow, but as Laguitte was almost unable to stand, it was hoped that, should the colonel insist upon it, some reconciliation might be patched up.

"Come," said the colonel, "will you accept me as arbitrator?"

"I beg your pardon, Colonel," interrupted the major; "I have brought you my resignation. Here it is. That settles everything. Please name the day for the duel."

Burle looked at Laguitte in amazement, and the colonel thought it his duty to protest.

"This is a most serious step, Major," he began. "Two years more and you would be entitled to your full pension."

But again did Laguitte cut him short, saying gruffly, "That is my own affair."

"Oh, certainly! Well, I will send in your resignation, and as soon as it is accepted I will fix a day for the duel."

The unexpected turn that events had taken startled the regiment. What possessed that lunatic major to persist in cutting the throat of his old comrade Burle? The officers again discussed Melanie; they even began to dream of her. There must surely be something wonderful about her since she had completely fascinated two such tough old veterans and brought them to a deadly feud. Morandot, having met Laguitte, did not disguise his concern. If he—the major—was not killed, what would he live upon? He had no fortune, and the pension to which his cross of the Legion of Honor entitled him, with the half of a full regimental pension which he would obtain on resigning, would barely find him in bread. While Morandot was thus speaking Laguitte simply stared before him with his round eyes, persevering in the dumb obstinacy born of his narrow mind; and when his companion tried to question him regarding his hatred for Burle, he simply made the same vague gesture as before and once again repeated:

"He annoyed me; so much the worse."

Every morning at mess and at the canteen the first words were: "Has the acceptance of the major's resignation arrived?" The duel was impatiently expected and ardently discussed. The majority believed that Laguitte would be run through the body in three seconds, for it was madness for a man to fight with a paralyzed leg which did not even allow him to stand upright. A few, however, shook their heads. Laguitte had never been a marvel of intellect, that was true; for the last twenty years, indeed, he had been held up as an example of stupidity, but there had been a time when he was known as the best fencer of the regiment, and although he had begun as a drummer he had won his epaulets as the commander of a battalion by the sanguine bravery of a man who is quite unconscious of danger. On the other hand, Burle fenced indifferently and passed for a poltroon. However, they would soon know what to think.

Meanwhile the excitement became more and more intense as the acceptance of Laguitte's resignation was so long in coming. The major was unmistakably the most anxious and upset of everybody. A week had passed by, and the general inspection would commence two days later. Nothing, however, had come as yet. He shuddered at the thought that he had, perhaps, struck his old friend and sent in his resignation all in vain, without delaying the exposure for a single minute. He had in reality reasoned thus: If he himself were killed he would not have the worry of witnessing the scandal, and if he killed Burle, as he expected to do, the affair would undoubtedly be hushed up. Thus he would save the honor of the army, and the little chap would be able to get in at Saint-Cyr. Ah, why wouldn't those wretched scribblers at the War Office hurry up a bit? The major could not keep still but was forever wandering about before the post office, stopping the estafettes and questioning the colonel's orderly to find out if the acceptance had arrived. He lost his sleep and, careless as to people's remarks, he leaned more and more heavily on his stick, hobbling about with no attempt to steady his gait.

On the day before that fixed for the inspection he was, as usual, on his way to the colonel's quarters when he paused, startled, to see Mrs. Burle (who was taking Charles to school) a few paces ahead of him. He had not met her since the scene at the Cafe de Paris, for she had remained in seclusion at home. Unmanned at thus meeting her, he stepped down to leave the whole sidewalk free. Neither he nor the old lady bowed, and the little boy lifted his large inquisitive eyes in mute surprise. Mrs. Burle, cold and erect, brushed past the major without the least sign of emotion or recognition. When she had passed he looked after her with an expression of stupefied compassion.

"Confound it, I am no longer a man," he growled, dashing away a tear.

When he arrived at the colonel's quarters a captain in attendance greeted him with the words: "It's all right at last. The papers have come."

"Ah!" murmured Laguitte, growing very pale.

And again he beheld the old lady walking on, relentlessly rigid and holding the little boy's hand. What! He had longed so eagerly for those papers for eight days past, and now when the scraps had come he felt his brain on fire and his heart lacerated.

The duel took place on the morrow, in the barrack yard behind a low wall. The air was keen, the sun shining brightly. Laguitte had almost to be carried to the ground; one of his seconds supported him on one side, while on the other he leaned heavily, on his stick. Burle looked half asleep; his face was puffy with unhealthy fat, as if he had spent a night of debauchery. Not a word was spoken. They were all anxious to have it over.

Captain Doucet crossed the swords of the two adversaries and then drew back, saying: "Set to, gentlemen."

Burle was the first to attack; he wanted to test Laguitte's strength and ascertain what he had to expect. For the last ten days the encounter had seemed to him a ghastly nightmare which he could not fathom. At times a hideous suspicion assailed him, but he put it aside with terror, for it meant death, and he refused to believe that a friend could play him such a trick, even to set things right. Besides, Laguitte's leg reasssured him; he would prick the major on the shoulder, and then all would be over.

During well-nigh a couple of minutes the swords clashed, and then the captain lunged, but the major, recovering his old suppleness of wrist, parried in a masterly style, and if he had returned the attack Burle would have been pierced through. The captain now fell back; he was livid, for he felt that he was at the mercy of the man who had just spared him. At last he understood that this was an execution.

Laguitte, squarely poised on his infirm legs and seemingly turned to stone, stood waiting. The two men looked at each other fixedly. In Burle's blurred eyes there arose a supplication—a prayer for pardon. He knew why he was going to die, and like a child he promised not to transgress again. But the major's eyes remained implacable; honor had spoken, and he silenced his emotion and his pity.

"Let it end," he muttered between his teeth.

Then it was he who attacked. Like a flash of lightning his sword flamed, flying from right to left, and then with a resistless thrust it pierced the breast of the captain, who fell like a log without even a groan.

Laguitte had released his hold upon his sword and stood gazing at that poor old rascal Burle, who was stretched upon his back with his fat stomach bulging out.

"Oh, my God! My God!" repeated the major furiously and despairingly, and then he began to swear.

They led him away, and, both his legs failing him, he had to be supported on either side, for he could not even use his stick.

Two months later the ex-major was crawling slowly along in the sunlight down a lonely street of Vauchamp, when he again found himself face to face with Mrs. Burle and little Charles. They were both in deep mourning. He tried to avoid them, but he now only walked with difficulty, and they advanced straight upon him without hurrying or slackening their steps. Charles still had the same gentle, girlish, frightened face, and Mrs. Burle retained her stern, rigid demeanor, looking even harsher than ever.

As Laguitte shrank into the corner of a doorway to leave the whole street to them, she abruptly stopped in front of him and stretched out her hand. He hesitated and then took it and pressed it, but he trembled so violently that he made the old lady's arm shake. They exchanged glances in silence.

"Charles," said the boy's grandmother at last, "shake hands with the major." The boy obeyed without understanding. The major, who was very pale, barely ventured to touch the child's frail fingers; then, feeling that he ought to speak, he stammered out: "You still intend to send him to Saint-Cyr?"

"Of course, when he is old enough," answered Mrs. Burle.

But during the following week Charles was carried off by typhoid fever. One evening his grandmother had again read him the story of the Vengeur to make him bold, and in the night he had become delirious. The poor little fellow died of fright.

THE DEATH OF OLIVIER BECAILLE

CHAPTER I
MY PASSING

It was on a Saturday, at six in the morning, that I died after a three days' illness. My wife was searching a trunk for some linen, and when she rose and turned she saw me rigid, with open eyes and silent pulses. She ran to me, fancying that I had fainted, touched my hands and bent over me. Then she suddenly grew alarmed, burst into tears and stammered:

"My God, my God! He is dead!"

I heard everything, but the sounds seemed to come from a great distance. My left eye still detected a faint glimmer, a whitish light in which all objects melted, but my right eye was quite bereft of sight. It was the coma of my whole being, as if a thunderbolt had struck me. My will was annihilated; not a fiber of flesh obeyed my bidding. And yet amid the impotency of my inert limbs my thoughts subsisted, sluggish and lazy, still perfectly clear.

My poor Marguerite was crying; she had dropped on her knees beside the bed, repeating in heart-rending tones:

"He is dead! My God, he is dead!"

Was this strange state of torpor, this immobility of the flesh, really death, although the functions of the intellect were not arrested? Was my soul only lingering for a brief space before it soared away forever? From my childhood upward I had been subject to hysterical attacks, and twice in early youth I had nearly succumbed to nervous fevers. By degrees all those who surrounded me had got accustomed to consider me an invalid and to see me sickly. So much so that I myself had forbidden my wife to call in a doctor when I had taken to my bed on the day of our arrival at the cheap lodging house of the Rue Dauphine in Paris. A little rest would soon set me right again; it was only the fatigue of the journey which had caused my intolerable weariness. And yet I was conscious of having felt singularly uneasy. We had left our province somewhat abruptly; we were very poor and had barely enough money to support ourselves till I drew my first month's salary in the office where I had obtained a situation. And now a sudden seizure was carrying me off!

Was it really death? I had pictured to myself a darker night, a deeper silence. As a little child I had already felt afraid to die. Being weak and compassionately petted by everyone, I had concluded that I had not long to live, that I should soon be buried, and the thought of the cold earth filled me with a dread I could not master—a dread which haunted me day and night. As I grew older the same terror pursued me. Sometimes, after long hours spent in reasoning with myself, I thought that I had conquered my fear. I reflected, "After all, what does it matter? One dies and all is over. It is the common fate; nothing could be better or easier."

I then prided myself on being able to look death boldly in the face, but suddenly a shiver froze my blood, and my dizzy anguish returned, as if a giant hand had swung me over a dark abyss. It was some vision of the earth returning and setting reason at naught. How often at night did I start up in bed, not knowing what cold breath had swept over my slumbers but clasping my despairing hands and moaning, "Must I die?" In those moments an icy horror would stop my pulses while an appalling vision of dissolution rose before me. It was with difficulty that I could get to sleep again. Indeed, sleep alarmed me; it so closely resembled death. If I closed my eyes they might never open again—I might slumber on forever.

I cannot tell if others have endured the same torture; I only know that my own life was made a torment by it. Death ever rose between me and all I loved; I can remember how the thought of it poisoned the happiest moments I spent with Marguerite. During the first months of our married life, when she lay sleeping by my side and I dreamed of a fair future for her and with her, the foreboding of some fatal separation dashed my hopes aside and embittered my delights. Perhaps we should be parted on the morrow—nay, perhaps in an hour's time. Then utter discouragement assailed me; I wondered what the bliss of being united availed me if it were to end in so cruel a disruption.

My morbid imagination reveled in scenes of mourning. I speculated as to who would be the first to depart, Marguerite or I. Either alternative caused me harrowing grief, and tears rose to my eyes at the thought of our shattered lives. At the happiest periods of my existence I often became a prey to grim dejection such as nobody could understand but which was caused by the thought of impending nihility. When I was most successful I was to general wonder most depressed. The fatal question, "What avails it?" rang like a knell in my ears. But the sharpest sting of this torment was that it came with a secret sense of shame, which rendered me unable to confide my thoughts to another. Husband and wife lying side by side in the darkened room may quiver with the same shudder and yet remain mute, for people do not mention death any more than they pronounce certain obscene words. Fear makes it nameless.

I was musing thus while my dear Marguerite knelt sobbing at my feet. It grieved me sorely to be unable to comfort her by telling her that I suffered no pain. If death were merely the annihilation of the flesh it had been foolish of me to harbor so much dread. I experienced a selfish kind of restfulness in which all my cares were forgotten. My memory had become extraordinarily vivid. My whole life passed before me rapidly like a play in which I no longer acted a part; it was a curious and enjoyable sensation—I seemed to hear a far-off voice relating my own history.

I saw in particular a certain spot in the country near Guerande, on the way to Piriac. The road turns sharply, and some scattered pine trees carelessly dot a rocky slope. When I was seven years old I used to pass through those pines with my father as far as a crumbling old house, where Marguerite's parents gave me pancakes. They were salt gatherers and earned a scanty livelihood by working the adjacent salt marshes. Then I remembered the school at Nantes, where I had grown up, leading a monotonous life within its ancient walls and yearning for the broad horizon of Guerande and the salt marshes stretching to the limitless sea widening under the sky.

Next came a blank—my father was dead. I entered the hospital as clerk to the managing board and led a dreary life with one solitary diversion: my Sunday visits to the old house on Piriac road. The saltworks were doing badly; poverty reigned in the land, and Marguerite's parents were nearly penniless. Marguerite, when merely a child, had been fond of me because I trundled her about in a wheelbarrow, but on the morning when I asked her in marriage she shrank from me with a frightened gesture, and I realized that she thought me hideous. Her parents, however, consented at once; they looked upon my offer as a godsend, and the daughter submissively acquiesced. When she became accustomed to the idea of marrying me she did not seem to dislike it so much. On our wedding day at Guerande the rain fell in torrents, and when we got home my bride had to take off her dress, which was soaked through, and sit in her petticoats.

That was all the youth I ever had. We did not remain long in our province. One day I found my wife in tears. She was miserable; life was so dull; she wanted to get away. Six months later I had saved a little money by taking in extra work after office hours, and through the influence of a friend of my father's I obtained a petty appointment in Paris. I started off to settle there with the dear little woman so that she might cry no more. During the night, which we spent in the third-class railway carriage, the seats being very hard, I took her in my arms in order that she might sleep.

That was the past, and now I had just died on the narrow couch of a Paris lodging house, and my wife was crouching on the floor, crying bitterly. The white light before my left eye was growing dim, but I remembered the room perfectly. On the left there was a chest of drawers, on the right a mantelpiece surmounted by a damaged clock without a pendulum, the hands of which marked ten minutes past ten. The window overlooked the Rue Dauphine, a long, dark street. All Paris seemed to pass below, and the noise was so great that the window shook.

We knew nobody in the city; we had hurried our departure, but I was not expected at the office till the following Monday. Since I had taken to my bed I had wondered at my imprisonment in this narrow room into which we had tumbled after a railway journey of fifteen hours, followed by a hurried, confusing transit through the noisy streets. My wife had nursed me with smiling tenderness, but I knew that she was anxious. She would walk to the window, glance out and return to the bedside, looking very pale and startled by the sight of the busy thoroughfare, the aspect of the vast city of which she did not know a single stone and which deafened her with its continuous roar. What would happen to her if I never woke up again—alone, friendless and unknowing as she was?

Marguerite had caught hold of one of my hands which lay passive on the coverlet, and, covering it with kisses, she repeated wildly: "Olivier, answer me. Oh, my God, he is dead, dead!"

So death was not complete annihilation. I could hear and think. I had been uselessly alarmed all those years. I had not dropped into utter vacancy as I had anticipated. I could not picture the disappearance of my being, the suppression of all that I had been, without the possibility of renewed existence. I had been wont to shudder whenever in any book or newspaper I came across a date of a hundred years hence. A date at which I should no longer be alive, a future which I should never see, filled me with unspeakable uneasiness. Was I not the whole world, and would not the universe crumble away when I was no more?

To dream of life had been a cherished vision, but this could not possibly be death. I should assuredly awake presently. Yes, in a few moments I would lean over, take Marguerite in my arms and dry her tears. I would rest a little while longer before going to my office, and then a new life would begin, brighter than the last. However, I did not feel impatient; the commotion had been too strong. It was wrong of Marguerite to give way like that when I had not even the strength to turn my head on the pillow and smile at her. The next time that she moaned out, "He is dead! Dead!" I would embrace her and murmur softly so as not to startle her: "No, my darling, I was only asleep. You see, I am alive, and I love you."

CHAPTER II
FUNERAL PREPARATIONS

Marguerite's cries had attracted attention, for all at once the door was opened and a voice exclaimed: "What is the matter, neighbor? Is he worse?"

I recognized the voice; it was that of an elderly woman, Mrs. Gabin, who occupied a room on the same floor. She had been most obliging since our arrival and had evidently become interested in our concerns. On her own side she had lost no time in telling us her history. A stern landlord had sold her furniture during the previous winter to pay himself his rent, and since then she had resided at the lodginghouse in the Rue Dauphine with her daughter Dede, a child of ten. They both cut and pinked lamp shades, and between them they earned at the utmost only two francs a day.

"Heavens! Is it all over?" cried Mrs. Gabin, looking at me.

I realized that she was drawing nearer. She examined me, touched me and, turning to Marguerite, murmured compassionately: "Poor girl! Poor girl!"

My wife, wearied out, was sobbing like a child. Mrs. Gabin lifted her, placed her in a dilapidated armchair near the fireplace and proceeded to comfort her.

"Indeed, you'll do yourself harm if you go on like this, my dear. It's no reason because your husband is gone that you should kill yourself with weeping. Sure enough, when I lost Gabin I was just like you. I remained three days without swallowing a morsel of food. But that didn't help me—on the contrary, it pulled me down. Come, for the Lord's sake, be sensible!"

By degrees Marguerite grew calmer; she was exhausted, and it was only at intervals that she gave way to a fresh flow of tears. Meanwhile the old woman had taken possession of the room with a sort of rough authority.

"Don't worry yourself," she said as she bustled about. "Neighbors must help each other. Luckily Dede has just gone to take the work home. Ah, I see your trunks are not yet all unpacked, but I suppose there is some linen in the chest of drawers, isn't there?"

I heard her pull a drawer open; she must have taken out a napkin which she spread on the little table at the bedside. She then struck a match, which made me think that she was lighting one of the candles on the mantelpiece and placing it near me as a religious rite. I could follow her movements in the room and divine all her actions.

"Poor gentleman," she muttered. "Luckily I heard you sobbing, poor dear!" Suddenly the vague light which my left eye had detected vanished. Mrs. Gabin had just closed my eyelids, but I had not felt her finger on my face. When I understood this I felt chilled.

The door had opened again, and Dede, the child of ten, now rushed in, calling out in her shrill voice: "Mother, Mother! Ah, I knew you would be here! Look here, there's the money—three francs and four sous. I took back three dozen lamp shades."

"Hush, hush! Hold your tongue," vainly repeated the mother, who, as the little girl chattered on, must have pointed to the bed, for I guessed that the child felt perplexed and was backing toward the door.

"Is the gentleman asleep?" she whispered.

"Yes, yes—go and play," said Mrs. Gabin.

But the child did not go. She was, no doubt, staring at me with widely opened eyes, startled and vaguely comprehending. Suddenly she seemed convulsed with terror and ran out, upsetting a chair.

"He is dead, Mother; he is dead!" she gasped.

Profound silence followed. Marguerite, lying back in the armchair, had left off crying. Mrs. Gabin was still rummaging about the room and talking under her breath.

"Children know everything nowadays. Look at that girl. Heaven knows how carefully she's brought up! When I send her on an errand or take the shades back I calculate the time to a minute so that she can't loiter about, but for all that she learns everything. She saw at a glance what had happened here—and yet I never showed her but one corpse, that of her uncle Francois, and she was then only four years old. Ah well, there are no children left—it can't be helped."

She paused and without any transition passed to another subject.

"I say, dearie, we must think of the formalities—there's the declaration at the municipal offices to be made and the seeing about the funeral. You are not in a fit state to attend to business. What do you say if I look in at Monsieur Simoneau's to find out if he's at home?"

Marguerite did not reply. It seemed to me that I watched her from afar and at times changed into a subtle flame hovering above the room, while a stranger lay heavy and unconscious on my bed. I wished that Marguerite had declined the assistance of Simoneau. I had seen him three or four times during my brief illness, for he occupied a room close to ours and had been civil and neighborly. Mrs. Gabin had told us that he was merely making a short stay in Paris, having come to collect some old debts due to his father, who had settled in the country and recently died. He was a tall, strong, handsome young man, and I hated him, perhaps on account of his healthy appearance. On the previous evening he had come in to make inquiries, and I had much disliked seeing him at Marguerite's side; she had looked so fair and pretty, and he had gazed so intently into her face when she smilingly thanked him for his kindness.

"Ah, here is Monsieur Simoneau," said Mrs. Gabin, introducing him.

He gently pushed the door ajar, and as soon as Marguerite saw him enter she burst into a flood of tears. The presence of a friend, of the only person she knew in Paris besides the old woman, recalled her bereavement. I could not see the young man, but in the darkness that encompassed me I conjured up his appearance. I pictured him distinctly, grave and sad at finding poor Marguerite in such distress. How lovely she must have looked with her golden hair unbound, her pale face and her dear little baby hands burning with fever!

"I am at your disposal, madame," he said softly. "Pray allow me to manage everything."

She only answered him with broken words, but as the young man was leaving, accompanied by Mrs. Gabin, I heard the latter mention money. These things were always expensive, she said, and she feared that the poor little body hadn't a farthing—anyhow, he might ask her. But Simoneau silenced the old woman; he did not want to have the widow worried; he was going to the municipal office and to the undertaker's.

When silence reigned once more I wondered if my nightmare would last much longer. I was certainly alive, for I was conscious of passing incidents, and I began to realize my condition. I must have fallen into one of those cataleptic states that I had read of. As a child I had suffered from syncopes which had lasted several hours, but surely my heart would beat anew, my blood circulate and my muscles relax. Yes, I should wake up and comfort Marguerite, and, reasoning thus, I tried to be patient.

Time passed. Mrs. Gabin had brought in some breakfast, but Marguerite refused to taste any food. Later on the afternoon waned. Through the open window I heard the rising clamor of the Rue Dauphine. By and by a slight ringing of the brass candlestick on the marble-topped table made me think that a fresh candle had been lighted. At last Simoneau returned.

"Well?" whispered the old woman.

"It is all settled," he answered; "the funeral is ordered for tomorrow at eleven. There is nothing for you to do, and you needn't talk of these things before the poor lady."

Nevertheless, Mrs. Gabin remarked: "The doctor of the dead hasn't come yet."

Simoneau took a seat beside Marguerite and after a few words of encouragement remained silent. The funeral was to take place at eleven! Those words rang in my brain like a passing bell. And the doctor coming—the doctor of the dead, as Mrs. Gabin had called him. HE could not possibly fail to find out that I was only in a state of lethargy; he would do whatever might be necessary to rouse me, so I longed for his arrival with feverish anxiety.

The day was drawing to a close. Mrs. Gabin, anxious to waste no time, had brought in her lamp shades and summoned Dede without asking Marguerite's permission. "To tell the truth," she observed, "I do not like to leave children too long alone."

"Come in, I say," she whispered to the little girl; "come in, and don't be frightened. Only don't look toward the bed or you'll catch it."

She thought it decorous to forbid Dede to look at me, but I was convinced that the child was furtively glancing at the corner where I lay, for every now and then I heard her mother rap her knuckles and repeat angrily: "Get on with your work or you shall leave the room, and the gentleman will come during the night and pull you by the feet."

The mother and daughter had sat down at our table. I could plainly hear the click of their scissors as they clipped the lamp shades, which no doubt required very delicate manipulation, for they did not work rapidly. I counted the shades one by one as they were laid aside, while my anxiety grew more and more intense.

The clicking of the scissors was the only noise in the room, so I concluded that Marguerite had been overcome by fatigue and was dozing. Twice Simoneau rose, and the torturing thought flashed through me that he might be taking advantage of her slumbers to touch her hair with his lips. I hardly knew the man and yet felt sure that he loved my wife. At last little Dede began to giggle, and her laugh exasperated me.

"Why are you sniggering, you idiot?" asked her mother. "Do you want to be turned out on the landing? Come, out with it; what makes you laugh so?"

The child stammered: she had not laughed; she had only coughed, but I felt certain she had seen Simoneau bending over Marguerite and had felt amused.

The lamp had been lit when a knock was heard at the door.

"It must be the doctor at last," said the old woman.

It was the doctor; he did not apologize for coming so late, for he had no doubt ascended many flights of stairs during the day. The room being but imperfectly lighted by the lamp, he inquired: "Is the body here?"

"Yes, it is," answered Simoneau.

Marguerite had risen, trembling violently. Mrs. Gabin dismissed Dede, saying it was useless that a child should be present, and then she tried to lead my wife to the window, to spare her the sight of what was about to take place.

The doctor quickly approached the bed. I guessed that he was bored, tired and impatient. Had he touched my wrist? Had he placed his hand on my heart? I could not tell, but I fancied that he had only carelessly bent over me.

"Shall I bring the lamp so that you may see better?" asked Simoneau obligingly.

"No it is not necessary," quietly answered the doctor.

Not necessary! That man held my life in his hands, and he did not think it worth while to proceed to a careful examination! I was not dead! I wanted to cry out that I was not dead!

"At what o'clock did he die?" asked the doctor.

"At six this morning," volunteered Simoneau.

A feeling of frenzy and rebellion rose within me, bound as I was in seemingly iron chains. Oh, for the power of uttering one word, of moving a single limb!

"This close weather is unhealthy," resumed the doctor; "nothing is more trying than these early spring days."

And then he moved away. It was like my life departing. Screams, sobs and insults were choking me, struggling in my convulsed throat, in which even my breath was arrested. The wretch! Turned into a mere machine by professional habits, he only came to a deathbed to accomplish a perfunctory formality; he knew nothing; his science was a lie, since he could not at a glance distinguish life from death—and now he was going—going!

"Good night, sir," said Simoneau.

There came a moment's silence; the doctor was probably bowing to Marguerite, who had turned while Mrs. Gabin was fastening the window. He left the room, and I heard his footsteps descending the stairs.

It was all over; I was condemned. My last hope had vanished with that man. If I did not wake before eleven on the morrow I should be buried alive. The horror of that thought was so great that I lost all consciousness of my surroundings—'twas something like a fainting fit in death. The last sound I heard was the clicking of the scissors handled by Mrs. Gabin and Dede. The funeral vigil had begun; nobody spoke.

Marguerite had refused to retire to rest in the neighbor's room. She remained reclining in her armchair, with her beautiful face pale, her eyes closed and her long lashes wet with tears, while before her in the gloom Simoneau sat silently watching her.

CHAPTER III
THE PROCESSION

I cannot describe my agony during the morning of the following day. I remember it as a hideous dream in which my impressions were so ghastly and so confused that I could not formulate them. The persistent yearning for a sudden awakening increased my torture, and as the hour for the funeral drew nearer my anguish became more poignant still.

It was only at daybreak that I had recovered a fuller consciousness of what was going on around me. The creaking of hinges startled me out of my stupor. Mrs. Gabin had just opened the window. It must have been about seven o'clock, for I heard the cries of hawkers in the street, the shrill voice of a girl offering groundsel and the hoarse voice of a man shouting "Carrots!" The clamorous awakening of Paris pacified me at first. I could not believe that I should be laid under the sod in the midst of so much life; and, besides, a sudden thought helped to calm me. It had just occurred to me that I had witnessed a case similar to my own when I was employed at the hospital of Guerande. A man had been sleeping twenty-eight hours, the doctors hesitating in presence of his apparent lifelessness, when suddenly he had sat up in bed and was almost at once able to rise. I myself had already been asleep for some twenty-five hours; if I awoke at ten I should still be in time.

I endeavored to ascertain who was in the room and what was going on there. Dede must have been playing on the landing, for once when the door opened I heard her shrill childish laughter outside. Simoneau must have retired, for nothing indicated his presence. Mrs. Gabin's slipshod tread was still audible over the floor. At last she spoke.

"Come, my dear," she said. "It is wrong of you not to take it while it is hot. It would cheer you up."

She was addressing Marguerite, and a slow trickling sound as of something filtering indicated that she had been making some coffee.

"I don't mind owning," she continued, "that I needed it. At my age sitting up IS trying. The night seems so dreary when there is a misfortune in the house. DO have a cup of coffee, my dear—just a drop."

She persuaded Marguerite to taste it.

"Isn't it nice and hot?" she continued, "and doesn't it set one up? Ah, you'll be wanting all your strength presently for what you've got to go through today. Now if you were sensible you'd step into my room and just wait there."

"No, I want to stay here," said Marguerite resolutely.

Her voice, which I had not heard since the previous evening, touched me strangely. It was changed, broken as by tears. To feel my dear wife near me was a last consolation. I knew that her eyes were fastened on me and that she was weeping with all the anguish of her heart.

The minutes flew by. An inexplicable noise sounded from beyond the door. It seemed as if some people were bringing a bulky piece of furniture upstairs and knocking against the walls as they did so. Suddenly I understood, as I heard Marguerite begin to sob; it was the coffin.

"You are too early," said Mrs. Gabin crossly. "Put it behind the bed."

What o'clock was it? Nine, perhaps. So the coffin had come. Amid the opaque night around me I could see it plainly, quite new, with roughly planed boards. Heavens! Was this the end then? Was I to be borne off in that box which I realized was lying at my feet?

However, I had one supreme joy. Marguerite, in spite of her weakness, insisted upon discharging all the last offices. Assisted by the old woman, she dressed me with all the tenderness of a wife and a sister. Once more I felt myself in her arms as she clothed me in various garments. She paused at times, overcome by grief; she clasped me convulsively, and her tears rained on my face. Oh, how I longed to return her embrace and cry, "I live!" And yet I was lying there powerless, motionless, inert!

"You are foolish," suddenly said Mrs. Gabin; "it is all wasted."

"Never mind," answered Marguerite, sobbing. "I want him to wear his very best things."

I understood that she was dressing me in the clothes I had worn on my wedding day. I had kept them carefully for great occasions. When she had finished she fell back exhausted in the armchair.

Simoneau now spoke; he had probably just entered the room.

"They are below," he whispered.

"Well, it ain't any too soon," answered Mrs. Gabin, also lowering her .voice. "Tell them to come up and get it over."

"But I dread the despair of the poor little wife."

The old woman seemed to reflect and presently resumed: "Listen to me, Monsieur Simoneau. You must take her off to my room. I wouldn't have her stop here. It is for her own good. When she is out of the way we'll get it done in a jiffy."

These words pierced my heart, and my anguish was intense when I realized that a struggle was actually taking place. Simoneau had walked up to Marguerite, imploring her to leave the room.

"Do, for pity's sake, come with me!" he pleaded. "Spare yourself useless pain."

"No, no!" she cried. "I will remain till the last minute. Remember that I have only him in the world, and when he is gone I shall be all alone!"

From the bedside Mrs. Gabin was prompting the young man.

"Don't parley—take hold of her, carry her off in your arms." Was Simoneau about to lay his hands on Marguerite and bear her away? She screamed. I wildly endeavored to rise, but the springs of my limbs were broken. I remained rigid, unable to lift my eyelids to see what was going on. The struggle continued, and my wife clung to the furniture, repeating, "Oh, don't, don't! Have mercy! Let me go! I will not."

He must have lifted her in his stalwart arms, for I heard her moaning like a child. He bore her away; her sobs were lost in the distance, and I fancied I saw them both—he, tall and strong, pressing her to his breast; she, fainting, powerless and conquered, following him wherever he listed.

"Drat it all! What a to-do!" muttered Mrs. Gabin. "Now for the tug of war, as the coast is clear at last."

In my jealous madness I looked upon this incident as a monstrous outrage. I had not been able to see Marguerite for twenty-four hours, but at least I had still heard her voice. Now even this was denied me; she had been torn away; a man had eloped with her even before I was laid under the sod. He was alone with her on the other side of the wall, comforting her—embracing her, perhaps!

But the door opened once more, and heavy footsteps shook the floor.

"Quick, make haste," repeated Mrs. Gabin. "Get it done before the lady comes back."

She was speaking to some strangers, who merely answered her with uncouth grunts.

"You understand," she went on, "I am not a relation; I'm only a neighbor. I have no interest in the matter. It is out of pure good nature that I have mixed myself up in their affairs. And I ain't overcheerful, I can tell you. Yes, yes, I sat up the whole blessed night—it was pretty cold, too, about four o'clock. That's a fact. Well, I have always been a fool—I'm too softhearted."

The coffin had been dragged into the center of the room. As I had not awakened I was condemned. All clearness departed from my ideas; everything seemed to revolve in a black haze, and I experienced such utter lassitude that it seemed almost a relief to leave off hoping.

"They haven't spared the material," said one of the undertaker's men in a gruff voice. "The box is too long."

"He'll have all the more room," said the other, laughing.

I was not heavy, and they chuckled over it since they had three flights of stairs to descend. As they were seizing me by the shoulders and feet I heard Mrs. Gabin fly into a violent passion.

"You cursed little brat," she screamed, "what do you mean by poking your nose where you're not wanted? Look here, I'll teach you to spy and pry."

Dede had slipped her tousled head through the doorway to see how the gentleman was being put into the box. Two ringing slaps resounded, however, by an explosion of sobs. And as soon as the mother returned she began to gossip about her daughter for the benefit of the two men who were settling me in the coffin.

"She is only ten, you know. She is not a bad girl, but she is frightfully inquisitive. I do not beat her often; only I WILL be obeyed."

"Oh," said one of the men, "all kids are alike. Whenever there is a corpse lying about they always want to see it."

I was commodiously stretched out, and I might have thought myself still in bed, had it not been that my left arm felt a trifle cramped from being squeezed against a board. The men had been right. I was pretty comfortable inside on account of my diminutive stature.

"Stop!" suddenly exclaimed Mrs. Gabin. "I promised his wife to put a pillow under his head."

The men, who were in a hurry, stuffed in the pillow roughly. One of them, who had mislaid his hammer, began to swear. He had left the tool below and went to fetch it, dropping the lid, and when two sharp blows of the hammer drove in the first nail, a shock ran through my being—I had ceased to live. The nails then entered in rapid succession with a rhythmical cadence. It was as if some packers had been closing a case of dried fruit with easy dexterity. After that such sounds as reached me were deadened and strangely prolonged, as if the deal coffin had been changed into a huge musical box. The last words spoken in the room of the Rue Dauphine—at least the last ones that I heard distinctly—were uttered by Mrs. Gabin.

"Mind the staircase," she said; "the banister of the second flight isn't safe, so be careful."

While I was being carried down I experienced a sensation similar to that of pitching as when one is on board a ship in a rough sea. However, from that moment my impressions became more and more vague. I remember that the only distinct thought that still possessed me was an imbecile, impulsive curiosity as to the road by which I should be taken to the cemetery. I was not acquainted with a single street of Paris, and I was ignorant of the position of the large burial grounds (though of course I had occasionally heard their names), and yet every effort of my mind was directed toward ascertaining whether we were turning to the right or to the left. Meanwhile the jolting of the hearse over the paving stones, the rumbling of passing vehicles, the steps of the foot passengers, all created a confused clamor, intensified by the acoustical properties of the coffin.

At first I followed our course pretty closely; then came a halt. I was again lifted and carried about, and I concluded that we were in church, but when the funeral procession once more moved onward I lost all consciousness of the road we took. A ringing of bells informed me that we were passing another church, and then the softer and easier progress of the wheels indicated that we were skirting a garden or park. I was like a victim being taken to the gallows, awaiting in stupor a deathblow that never came.

At last they stopped and pulled me out of the hearse. The business proceeded rapidly. The noises had ceased; I knew that I was in a deserted space amid avenues of trees and with the broad sky over my head. No doubt a few persons followed the bier, some of the inhabitants of the lodging-house, perhaps—Simoneau and others, for instance—for faint whisperings reached my ear. Then I heard a psalm chanted and some Latin words mumbled by a priest, and afterward I suddenly felt myself sinking, while the ropes rubbing against the edges of the coffin elicited lugubrious sounds, as if a bow were being drawn across the strings of a cracked violoncello. It was the end. On the left side of my head I felt a violent shock like that produced by the bursting of a bomb, with another under my feet and a third more violent still on my chest. So forcible, indeed, was this last one that I thought the lid was cleft atwain. I fainted from it.

CHAPTER IV
THE NAIL

It is impossible for me to say how long my swoon lasted. Eternity is not of longer duration than one second spent in nihility. I was no more. It was slowly and confusedly that I regained some degree of consciousness. I was still asleep, but I began to dream; a nightmare started into shape amid the blackness of my horizon, a nightmare compounded of a strange fancy which in other days had haunted my morbid imagination whenever with my propensity for dwelling upon hideous thoughts I had conjured up catastrophes.

Thus I dreamed that my wife was expecting me somewhere—at Guerande, I believe—and that I was going to join her by rail. As we passed through a tunnel a deafening roll thundered over our head, and a sudden subsidence blocked up both issues of the tunnel, leaving our train intact in the center. We were walled up by blocks of rock in the heart of a mountain. Then a long and fearful agony commenced. No assistance could possibly reach us; even with powerful engines and incessant labor it would take a month to clear the tunnel. We were prisoners there with no outlet, and so our death was only a question of time.

My fancy had often dwelt on that hideous drama and had constantly varied the details and touches. My actors were men, women and children; their number increased to hundreds, and they were ever furnishing me with new incidents. There were some provisions in the train, but these were soon exhausted, and the hungry passengers, if they did not actually devour human flesh, at least fought furiously over the last piece of bread. Sometimes an aged man was driven back with blows and slowly perished; a mother struggled like a she-wolf to keep three or four mouthfuls for her child. In my own compartment a bride and bridegroom were dying, clasped in each other's arms in mute despair.

The line was free along the whole length of the train, and people came and went, prowling round the carriages like beasts of prey in search of carrion. All classes were mingled together. A millionaire, a high functionary, it was said, wept on a workman's shoulder. The lamps had been extinguished from the first, and the engine fire was nearly out. To pass from one carriage to another it was necessary to grope about, and thus, too, one slowly reached the engine, recognizable by its enormous barrel, its cold, motionless flanks, its useless strength, its grim silence, in the overwhelming night. Nothing could be more appalling than this train entombed alive with its passengers perishing one by one.

I gloated over the ghastliness of each detail; howls resounded through the vault; somebody whom one could not see, whose vicinity was not even suspected, would suddenly drop upon another's shoulder. But what affected me most of all was the cold and the want of air. I have never felt so chilled; a mantle of snow seemed to enwrap me; heavy moisture rained upon my skull; I was gasping; the rocky vault seemed to crush my chest; the whole mountain was seemingly weighing upon me.

Suddenly a cry of deliverance sounded. For some time past we fancied that we could hear a dull sound, and we tried to hope that men were at work and that help was coming, but it came not thus. One of the passengers, however, had discovered an air shaft in the tunnel, and, crowding round, we all saw this shaft, above which we could discern a blue patch about the size of a wafer. That blue patch filled us with rapture, for it was the sky. We stretched ourselves and stood on tiptoes to breathe more freely. Then we distinguished some black specks moving about, specks that must surely be workmen about to deliver us. A furious clamor arose. The cry "Saved! Saved!" burst from every mouth, while trembling arms were uplifted toward the tiny azure patch above.

That roar of voices aroused me. Where was I? In the tunnel, of course. I was lying at full length; hard walls were pressing against my ribs. Then I attempted to rise and struck my head roughly. Was it the rock closing in on all sides? The blue speck had vanished—aye, the sky had disappeared and I was still suffocating, shivering, with chattering teeth.

All at once I remembered. Intense horror raised my hair on end. I felt the hideous truth freeze me from head to foot like ice. I had shaken off the long coma which for many hours had stricken me with corpselike rigidity. Yes, I could move; my hands could feel the boards of my coffin; my lips parted; words came to me, and instinctively I called out Marguerite's name. It was a scream I raised. In that deal box my voice took so hoarse and weird a sound that it terrified me. Oh, my God, was this thing true? I was able to walk, speak, cry out that I was living, and yet my voice could not be heard; I was entombed under the earth.

I made a desperate effort to remain calm and reflect. Was there no means of getting out? Then my dream began afresh in my troubled brain. The fanciful air shaft with the blue bit of sky overhead was mingled with the real grave in which I was lying. I stared at the darkness with widely opened eyes; perhaps I might discover a hole, a slit, a glimmer of light, but only sparks of fire flitted through that night, with rays that broadened and then faded away. I was in a somber abyss again. With returning lucidity I struggled against these fatal visions. Indeed, I should need all my reason if I meant to try to save myself.

The most immediate peril lay in an increasing sense of suffocation. If

I had been able to live so long without air it was owing to suspended animation, which had changed all the normal conditions of my existence, but now that my heart beat and my lungs breathed I should die, asphyxiated, if I did not promptly liberate myself. I also suffered from cold and dreaded lest I should succumb to the mortal numbness of those who fall asleep in the snow, never to wake again. Still, while unceasingly realizing the necessity of remaining calm, I felt maddening blasts sweep through my brain, and to quiet my senses I exhorted myself to patience, trying to remember the circumstances of my burial. Probably the ground had been bought for five years, and this would be against my chances of self-deliverance, for I remembered having noticed at Nantes that in the trenches of the common graves one end of the last lowered coffins protruded into the next open cavity, in which case I should only have had to break through one plank. But if I were in a separate hole, filled up above me with earth, the obstacles would prove too great. Had I not been told that the dead were buried six feet deep in Paris? How was I to get through the enormous mass of soil above me? Even if I succeeded in slitting the lid of my bier open the mold would drift in like fine sand and fill my mouth and eyes. That would be death again, a ghastly death, like drowning in mud.

However, I began to feel the planks carefully. The coffin was roomy, and I found that I was able to move my arms with tolerable ease. On both sides the roughly planed boards were stout and resistive. I slipped my arm onto my chest to raise it over my head. There I discovered in the top plank a knot in the wood which yielded slightly at my pressure. Working laboriously, I finally succeeded in driving out this knot, and on passing my finger through the hole I found that the earth was wet and clayey. But that availed me little. I even regretted having removed the knot, vaguely dreading the irruption of the mold. A second experiment occupied me for a while. I tapped all over the coffin to ascertain if perhaps there were any vacuum outside. But the sound was everywhere the same. At last, as I was slightly kicking the foot of the coffin, I fancied that it gave out a clearer echoing noise, but that might merely be produced by the sonority of the wood.

At any rate, I began to press against the boards with my arms and my closed fists. In the same way, too, I used my knees, my back and my feet without eliciting even a creak from the wood. I strained with all my strength, indeed, with so desperate an effort of my whole frame, that my bruised bones seemed breaking. But nothing moved, and I became insane.

Until that moment I had held delirium at bay. I had mastered the intoxicating rage which was mounting to my head like the fumes of alcohol; I had silenced my screams, for I feared that if I again cried out aloud I should be undone. But now I yelled; I shouted; unearthly howls which I could not repress came from my relaxed throat. I called for help in a voice that I did not recognize, growing wilder with each fresh appeal and crying out that I would not die. I also tore at the wood with my nails; I writhed with the contortions of a caged wolf. I do not know how long this fit of madness lasted, but I can still feel the relentless hardness of the box that imprisoned me; I can still hear the storm of shrieks and sobs with which I filled it; a remaining glimmer of reason made me try to stop, but I could not do so.

Great exhaustion followed. I lay waiting for death in a state of somnolent pain. The coffin was like stone, which no effort could break, and the conviction that I was powerless left me unnerved, without courage to make any fresh attempts. Another suffering—hunger—was presently added to cold and want of air. The torture soon became intolerable. With my finger I tried to pull small pinches of earth through the hole of the dislodged knot, and I swallowed them eagerly, only increasing my torment. Tempted by my flesh, I bit my arms and sucked my skin with a fiendish desire to drive my teeth in, but I was afraid of drawing blood.

Then I ardently longed for death. All my life long I had trembled at the thought of dissolution, but I had come to yearn for it, to crave for an everlasting night that could never be dark enough. How childish it had been of me to dread the long, dreamless sleep, the eternity of silence and gloom! Death was kind, for in suppressing life it put an end to suffering. Oh, to sleep like the stones, to be no more!

With groping hands I still continued feeling the wood, and suddenly I pricked my left thumb. That slight pain roused me from my growing numbness. I felt again and found a nail—a nail which the undertaker's men had driven in crookedly and which had not caught in the lower wood. It was long and very sharp; the head was secured to the lid, but it moved. Henceforth I had but one idea—to possess myself of that nail—and I slipped my right hand across my body and began to shake it. I made but little progress, however; it was a difficult job, for my hands soon tired, and I had to use them alternately. The left one, too, was of little use on account of the nail's awkward position.

While I was obstinately persevering a plan dawned on my mind. That nail meant salvation, and I must have it. But should I get it in time? Hunger was torturing me; my brain was swimming; my limbs were losing their strength; my mind was becoming confused. I had sucked the drops that trickled from my punctured finger, and suddenly I bit my arm and drank my own blood! Thereupon, spurred on by pain, revived by the tepid, acrid liquor that moistened my lips, I tore desperately at the nail and at last I wrenched it off!

I then believed in success. My plan was a simple one; I pushed the point of the nail into the lid, dragging it along as far as I could in a straight line and working it so as to make a slit in the wood. My fingers stiffened, but I doggedly persevered, and when I fancied that I had sufficiently cut into the board I turned on my stomach and, lifting myself on my knees and elbows thrust the whole strength of my back against the lid. But although it creaked it did not yield; the notched line was not deep enough. I had to resume my old position—which I only managed to do with infinite trouble—and work afresh. At last after another supreme effort the lid was cleft from end to end.

I was not saved as yet, but my heart beat with renewed hope. I had ceased pushing and remained motionless, lest a sudden fall of earth should bury me. I intended to use the lid as a screen and, thus protected, to open a sort of shaft in the clayey soil. Unfortunately I was assailed by unexpected difficulties. Some heavy clods of earth weighed upon the boards and made them unmanageable; I foresaw that I should never reach the surface in that way, for the mass of soil was already bending my spine and crushing my face.

Once more I stopped, affrighted; then suddenly, while I was stretching my legs, trying to find something firm against which I might rest my feet, I felt the end board of the coffin yielding. I at once gave a desperate kick with my heels in the faint hope that there might be a freshly dug grave in that direction.

It was so. My feet abruptly forced their way into space. An open grave was there; I had only a slight partition of earth to displace, and soon I rolled into the cavity. I was saved!

I remained for a time lying on my back in the open grave, with my eyes raised to heaven. It was dark; the stars were shining in a sky of velvety blueness. Now and then the rising breeze wafted a springlike freshness, a perfume of foliage, upon me. I was saved! I could breathe;

I felt warm, and I wept and I stammered, with my arms prayerfully extended toward the starry sky. O God, how sweet seemed life!

CHAPTER V
MY RESURRECTION

My first impulse was to find the custodian of the cemetery and ask him to have me conducted home, but various thoughts that came to me restrained me from following that course. My return would create general alarm; why should I hurry now that I was master of the situation? I felt my limbs; I had only an insignificant wound on my left arm, where I had bitten myself, and a slight feverishness lent me unhoped-for strength. I should no doubt be able to walk unaided.

Still I lingered; all sorts of dim visions confused my mind. I had felt beside me in the open grave some sextons' tools which had been left there, and I conceived a sudden desire to repair the damage I had done, to close up the hole through which I had crept, so as to conceal all traces of my resurrection. I do not believe that I had any positive motive in doing so. I only deemed it useless to proclaim my adventure aloud, feeling ashamed to find myself alive when the whole world thought me dead. In half an hour every trace of my escape was obliterated, and then I climbed out of the hole.

The night was splendid, and deep silence reigned in the cemetery; the black trees threw motionless shadows over the white tombs. When I endeavored to ascertain my bearings I noticed that one half of the sky was ruddy, as if lit by a huge conflagration; Paris lay in that direction, and I moved toward it, following a long avenue amid the darkness of the branches.

However, after I had gone some fifty yards I was compelled to stop, feeling faint and weary. I then sat down on a stone bench and for the first time looked at myself. I was fully attired with the exception that I had no hat. I blessed my beloved Marguerite for the pious thought which had prompted her to dress me in my best clothes—those which I had worn at our wedding. That remembrance of my wife brought me to my feet again. I longed to see her without delay.

At the farther end of the avenue I had taken a wall arrested my progress. However, I climbed to the top of a monument, reached the summit of the wall and then dropped over the other side. Although roughly shaken by the fall, I managed to walk for a few minutes along a broad deserted street skirting the cemetery. I had no notion as to where I might be, but with the reiteration of monomania I kept saying to myself that I was going toward Paris and that I should find the Rue Dauphine somehow or other. Several people passed me but, seized with sudden distrust, I would not stop them and ask my way. I have since realized that I was then in a burning fever and already nearly delirious. Finally, just as I reached a large thoroughfare, I became giddy and fell heavily upon the pavement.

Here there is a blank in my life. For three whole weeks I remained unconscious. When I awoke at last I found myself in a strange room. A man who was nursing me told me quietly that he had picked me up one morning on the Boulevard Montparnasse and had brought me to his house. He was an old doctor who had given up practicing.

When I attempted to thank him he sharply answered that my case had seemed a curious one and that he had wished to study it. Moreover, during the first days of my convalescence he would not allow me to ask a single question, and later on he never put one to me. For eight days longer I remained in bed, feeling very weak and not even trying to remember, for memory was a weariness and a pain. I felt half ashamed and half afraid. As soon as I could leave the house I would go and find out whatever I wanted to know. Possibly in the delirium of fever a name had escaped me; however, the doctor never alluded to anything I may have said. His charity was not only generous; it was discreet.

The summer had come at last, and one warm June morning I was permitted to take a short walk. The sun was shining with that joyous brightness which imparts renewed youth to the streets of old Paris. I went along slowly, questioning the passers-by at every crossing I came to and asking the way to Rue Dauphine. When I reached the street I had some difficulty in recognizing the lodging house where we had alighted on our arrival in the capital. A childish terror made me hesitate. If I appeared suddenly before Marguerite the shock might kill her. It might be wiser to begin by revealing myself to our neighbor Mrs. Gabin; still I shrank from taking a third party into confidence. I seemed unable to arrive at a resolution, and yet in my innermost heart I felt a great void, like that left by some sacrifice long since consummated.

The building looked quite yellow in the sunshine. I had just recognized it by a shabby eating house on the ground floor, where we had ordered our meals, having them sent up to us. Then I raised my eyes to the last window of the third floor on the left-hand side, and as I looked at it a young woman with tumbled hair, wearing a loose dressing gown, appeared and leaned her elbows on the sill. A young man followed and printed a kiss upon her neck. It was not Marguerite. Still I felt no surprise. It seemed to me that I had dreamed all this with other things, too, which I was to learn presently.

For a moment I remained in the street, uncertain whether I had better go upstairs and question the lovers, who were still laughing in the sunshine. However, I decided to enter the little restaurant below. When I started on my walk the old doctor had placed a five-franc piece in my hand. No doubt I was changed beyond recognition, for my beard had grown during the brain fever, and my face was wrinkled and haggard. As I took a seat at a small table I saw Mrs. Gabin come in carrying a cup; she wished to buy a penny-worth of coffee. Standing in front of the counter, she began to gossip with the landlady of the establishment.

"Well," asked the latter, "so the poor little woman of the third floor has made up her mind at last, eh?"

"How could she help herself?" answered Mrs. Gabin. "It was the very best thing for her to do. Monsieur Simoneau showed her so much kindness. You see, he had finished his business in Paris to his satisfaction, for he has inherited a pot of money. Well, he offered to take her away with him to his own part of the country and place her with an aunt of his, who wants a housekeeper and companion."

The landlady laughed archly. I buried my face in a newspaper which I picked off the table. My lips were white and my hands shook.

"It will end in a marriage, of course," resumed Mrs. Gabin. "The little widow mourned for her husband very properly, and the young man was extremely well behaved. Well, they left last night—and, after all, they were free to please themselves."

Just then the side door of the restaurant, communicating with the passage of the house, opened, and Dede appeared.

"Mother, ain't you coming?" she cried. "I'm waiting, you know; do be quick."

"Presently," said the mother testily. "Don't bother."

The girl stood listening to the two women with the precocious shrewdness of a child born and reared amid the streets of Paris.

"When all is said and done," explained Mrs. Gabin, "the dear departed did not come up to Monsieur Simoneau. I didn't fancy him overmuch; he was a puny sort of a man, a poor, fretful fellow, and he hadn't a penny to bless himself with. No, candidly, he wasn't the kind of husband for a young and healthy wife, whereas Monsieur Simoneau is rich, you know, and as strong as a Turk."

"Oh yes!" interrupted Dede. "I saw him once when he was washing—his door was open. His arms are so hairy!"

"Get along with you," screamed the old woman, shoving the girl out of the restaurant. "You are always poking your nose where it has no business to be."

Then she concluded with these words: "Look here, to my mind the other one did quite right to take himself off. It was fine luck for the little woman!"

When I found myself in the street again I walked along slowly with trembling limbs. And yet I was not suffering much; I think I smiled once at my shadow in the sun. It was quite true. I WAS very puny. It had been a queer notion of mine to marry Marguerite. I recalled her weariness at Guerande, her impatience, her dull, monotonous life. The dear creature had been very good to me, but I had never been a real lover; she had mourned for me as a sister for her brother, not otherwise. Why should I again disturb her life? A dead man is not jealous.

When I lifted my eyelids I saw the garden of the Luxembourg before me. I entered it and took a seat in the sun, dreaming with a sense of infinite restfulness. The thought of Marguerite stirred me softly. I pictured her in the provinces, beloved, petted and very happy. She had grown handsomer, and she was the mother of three boys and two girls. It was all right. I had behaved like an honest man in dying, and I would not commit the cruel folly of coming to life again.

Since then I have traveled a good deal. I have been a little everywhere. I am an ordinary man who has toiled and eaten like anybody else. Death no longer frightens me, but it does not seem to care for me now that I have no motive in living, and I sometimes fear that I have been forgotten upon earth.

THE SPREE AT COQUEVILLE

Coqueville is a little village planted in a cleft in the rocks, two leagues from Grandport. A fine sandy beach stretches in front of the huts lodged halfway up in the side of the cliff like shells left there by the tide. As one climbs to the heights of Grandport, on the left the yellow sheet of sand can be very clearly seen to the west like a river of gold dust streaming from the gaping cleft in the rock; and with good eyes one can even distinguish the houses, whose tones of rust spot the rock and whose chimneys send up their bluish trails to the very crest of the great slope, streaking the sky. It is a deserted hole. Coqueville has never been able to attain to the figure of two hundred inhabitants. The gorge which opens into the sea, and on the threshold of which the village is planted, burrows into the earth by turns so abrupt and by descents so steep that it is almost impossible to pass there with wagons. It cuts off all communication and isolates the country so that one seems to be a hundred leagues from the neighboring hamlets.

Moreover, the inhabitants have communication with Grandport only by water. Nearly all of them fishermen, living by the ocean, they carry their fish there every day in their barks. A great commission house, the firm of Dufeu, buys their fish on contract. The father Dufeu has been dead some years, but the widow Dufeu has continued the business; she has simply engaged a clerk, M. Mouchel, a big blond devil, charged with beating up the coast and dealing with the fishermen. This M. Mouchel is the sole link between Coqueville and the civilized world.

Coqueville merits a historian. It seems certain that the village, in the night of time, was founded by the Mahes; a family which happened to establish itself there and which grew vigorous at the foot of the cliff. These Mahes continued to prosper at first, marrying continually among themselves, for during centuries one finds none but Mahes there. Then under Louis XIII appeared one Floche. No one knew too much of where he came from. He married a Mahe, and from that time a phenomenon was brought forth; the Floches in their turn prospered and multiplied exceedingly, so that they ended little by little in absorbing the Mahes, whose numbers diminished until their fortune passed entirely into the hands of the newcomers. Without doubt, the Floches brought new blood, more vigorous physical organs, a temperament which adapted itself better to that hard condition of high wind and of high sea. At any rate, they are to-day masters of Coqueville.

It can easily be understood that this displacement of numbers and of riches was not accomplished without terrible disturbances. The Mahes and the Hoches detest each other. Between them is a hatred of centuries. The Mahes in spite of their decline retain the pride of ancient conquerors. After all they are the founders, the ancestors. They speak with contempt of the first Floche, a beggar, a vagabond picked up by them from feelings of pity, and to have given away one of their daughters to whom was their eternal regret. This Floche, to hear them speak, had engendered nothing but a descent of libertines and thieves, who pass their nights in raising children and their days in coveting legacies. And there is not an insult they do not heap upon the powerful tribe of Floche, seized with that bitter rage of nobles, decimated, ruined, who see the spawn of the bourgeoisie master of their rents and of their chateau. The Floches, on their side, naturally have the insolence of those who triumph. They are in full possession, a thing to make them insolent. Full of contempt for the ancient race of the Mahes, they threaten to drive them from the village if they do not bow their heads. To them they are starvelings, who instead of draping themselves in their rags would do much better to mend them.

So Coqueville finds itself a prey to two fierce factions something like one hundred and thirty inhabitants bent upon devouring the other fifty for the simple reason that they are the stronger.

The struggle between two great empires has no other history.

Among the quarrels which have lately upset Coqueville, they cite the famous enmity of the brothers, Fouasse and Tupain, and the ringing battles of the Rouget ménage. You must know that every inhabitant in former days received a surname, which has become to-day the regular name of the family; for it was difficult to distinguish one's self among the cross-breedings of the Mahes and the Floches. Rouget assuredly had an ancestor of fiery blood. As for Fouasse and Tupain, they were called thus without knowing why, many surnames having lost all rational meaning in course of time. Well, old Francoise, a wanton of eighty years who lived forever, had had Fouasse by a Mahe, then becoming a widow; she remarried with a Floche and brought forth Tupain. Hence the hatred of the two brothers, made especially lively by the question of inheritance. At the Rouget's they beat each other to a jelly because Rouget accused his wife, Marie, of being unfaithful to him for a Floche, the tall Brisemotte, a strong, dark man, on whom he had already twice thrown himself with a knife, yelling that he would rip open his belly. Rouget, a small, nervous man, was a great spitfire.

But that which interested Coqueville most deeply was neither the tantrums of Rouget nor the differences between Tupain and Fouasse. A great rumor circulated: Delphin, a Mahe, a rascal of twenty years, dared to love the beautiful Margot, the daughter of La Queue, the richest of the Floches and chief man of the country. This La Queue was, in truth, a considerable personage. They called him La Queue because his father, in the days of Louis Philippe, had been the last to tie up his hair, with the obstinacy of old age that clings to the fashions of its youth. Well, then, La Queue owned one of the two large fishing smacks of Coqueville, the "Zephyr," by far the best, still quite new and seaworthy. The other big boat, the "Beeline," a rotten old barge, belonged to Rouget, whose sailors were Delphin and Fouasse, while La Queue took with him Tupain and Brisemotte. These last had grown weary of laughing contemptuously at the "Beeline"; a sabot, they said, which would disappear some fine day under the billows like a handful of mud. So when La Queue learned that that ragamuffin of a Delphin, the froth of the "Beeline," allowed himself to go prowling around his daughter, he delivered two sound whacks at Margot, a trifle merely to warn her that she should never be the wife of a Mahe. As a result, Margot, furious, declared that she would pass that pair of slaps on to Delphin if he ever ventured to rub against her skirts. It was vexing to be boxed on the ears for a boy whom she had never looked in the face!

Margot, at sixteen years strong as a man and handsome as a lady, had the reputation of being a scornful person, very hard on lovers. And from that, added to the trifle of the two slaps, of the presumptuousness of Delphin, and of the wrath of Margot, one ought easily to comprehend the endless gossip of Coqueville.

Notwithstanding, certain persons said that Margot, at bottom, was not so very furious at sight of Delphin circling around her. This Delphin was a little blonde, with skin bronzed by the sea-glare, and with a mane of curly hair that fell over his eyes and in his neck. And very powerful despite his slight figure; quite capable of thrashing any one three times his size. They said that at times he ran away and passed the night in Grandport. That gave him the reputation of a werewolf with the girls, who accused him, among themselves, of "making a life of it" a vague expression in which they included all sorts of unknown pleasures. Margot, when she spoke of Delphin, betrayed too much feeling. He, smiling with an artful air, looked at her with eyes half shut and glittering, without troubling himself the least in the world over her scorn or her transports of passion. He passed before her door, he glided along by the bushes watching for her hours at a time, full of the patience and the I cunning of a cat lying in wait for a tomtit; and when suddenly she discovered him behind her skirts, so close to her at times that she guessed it by the warmth of his breath, he did not fly, he took on an air gentle and melancholy which left her abashed, stifled, not regaining her wrath until he was some distance away. Surely, if her father saw her he would smite her again. But she boasted in vain that Delphin would some day get that pair of slaps she had promised him; she never seized the moment to apply them when he was there; which made people say that she ought not to talk so much, since in the end she kept the slaps herself.

No one, however, supposed she could ever be Delphin's wife. In her case they saw the weakness of a coquette. As for a marriage between the most beggardly of the Mahes, a fellow who had not six shirts to set up housekeeping with, and the daughter of the mayor, the richest heiress of the Floches, it would seem simply monstrous.

Evil tongues insinuated that she could perfectly go with him all the same, but that she would certainly not marry him. A rich girl takes her pleasure as it suits her; only, if she has a head, she does not commit a folly. Finally all Coqueville interested itself in the matter, curious to know how things would turn out. Would Delphin get his two slaps? Or else Margot, would she let herself be kissed on both cheeks in some hole in the cliff? They must see! There were some for the slaps and there were some for the kisses. Coqueville was in revolution.

In the village two people only, the priest and the police chief belonged neither to the Mahes nor to the Floches. The police chief, a tall, dried-up fellow, whose name no one knew, but who was called the Emperor, no doubt because he had served under Charles X, as a matter of fact exercised no burdensome supervision over the commune which was all bare rocks and waste lands. A sub-prefect who patronized him had created for him the sinecure where he devoured in peace his very small living.

As for the Abbe Radiguet, he was one of those simple-minded priests whom the bishop, in his desire to be rid of him, buries in some out of the way hole. He lived the life of an honest man, once more turned peasant, hoeing his little garden redeemed from the rock, smoking his pipe and watching his salads grow. His sole fault was a gluttony which he knew not how to refine, reduced to adoring mackerel and to drinking, at times, more cider than he could contain. In other respects, the father of his parishioners, who came at long intervals to hear a mass to please him.

But the priest and the police chief were obliged to take sides after having succeeded for a long time in remaining neutral. Now, the Emperor held for the Mahes, while the Abbe Radiguet supported the Floches. Hence complications. As the Emperor, from morning to night, lived like a bourgeois [citizen], and as he wearied of counting the boats which put out from Grand-port, he took it upon himself to act as village police. Having become the partisan of the Mahes, through native instinct for the preservation of society, he sided with Fouasse against Tupain; he tried to catch the wife of Rouget in flagrante delicto with Brisemotte, and above all he closed his eyes when he saw Delphin slipping into Margot's courtyard. The worst of it was that these tactics brought about heated quarrels between the Emperor and his natural superior, the mayor La Queue. Respectful of discipline, the former heard the reproaches of the latter, then recommenced to act as his head dictated; which disorganized the public authority of Coqueville. One could not pass before the shed ornamented with the name of the town hall without being deafened by the noise of some dispute. On the other hand, the Abbe Radiguet rallied to the triumphant Floches, who loaded him with superb mackerel, secretly encouraged the resistance of Rouget's wife and threatened Margot with the flames of hell if she should ever allow Delphin to touch her with his finger. It was, to sum up, complete anarchy; the army in revolt against the civil power, religion making itself complaisant toward the pleasures of the bourgeoisie; a whole people, a hundred and eighty inhabitants, devouring each other in a hole, in face of the vast sea, and of the infinite sky.

Alone, in the midst of topsy-turvy Coqueville, Delphin preserved the laughter of a love-sick boy, who scorned the rest, provided Margot was for him. He followed her zigzags as one follows hares. Very wise, despite his simple look, he wanted the priest to marry them, so that his bliss might last forever.

One evening, in a byway where he was watching for her, Margot at last raised her hand. But she stopped, all red; for without waiting for the slap, he had seized the hand that threatened him and kissed it furiously. As she trembled, he said to her in a low voice: "I love you. Won't you have me?"

"Never!" she cried, in rebellion.

He shrugged his shoulders, then with an air, calm and tender, "Pray do not say that we shall be very comfortable together, we two. You will see how nice it is."

That Sunday the weather was appalling, one of those sudden calamities of September that unchain such fearful tempests on the rocky coast of Grandport. At nightfall Coqueville sighted a ship in distress driven by the wind. But the shadows deepened, they could not dream of rendering help. Since the evening before, the "Zephyr" and the "Beeline" had been moored in the little natural harbor situated at the left of the beach, between two walls of granite. Neither La Queue nor Rouget had dared to go out, the worst of it was that M. Mouchel, representing the Widow Dufeu, had taken the trouble to come in person that Saturday to promise them a reward if they would make a serious effort; fish was scarce, they were complaining at the markets. So, Sunday evening, going to bed under squalls of rain, Coqueville growled in a bad humor. It was the everlasting story: orders kept coming in while the sea guarded its fish. And all the village talked of the ship which they had seen passing in the hurricane, and which must assuredly by that time be sleeping at the bottom of the water. The next day, Monday, the sky was dark as ever. The sea, still high, raged without being able to calm itself, although the wind was blowing less strong. It fell completely, but the waves kept up their furious motion. In spite of everything, the two boats went out in the afternoon. Toward four o'clock, the "Zephyr" came in again, having caught nothing. While the sailors, Tupain and Brisemotte, anchored in the little harbor, La Queue, exasperated, on the shore, shook his fist at the ocean. And M. Mouchel was waiting! Margot was there, with the half of Coqueville, watching the last surging of the tempest, sharing her father's rancor against the sea and the sky.

"But where is the 'Beeline'?" demanded some one.

"Out there beyond the point," said La Queue. "If that carcass comes back whole to-day, it will be by a chance."

He was full of contempt. Then he informed them that it was good for the Mahes to risk their skins in that way; when one is not worth a sou, one may perish. As for him, he preferred to break his word to M. Mouchel.

In the meantime, Margot was examining the point of rocks behind which the "Beeline" was hidden.

"Father," she asked at last, "have they caught something?"

"They?" he cried. "Nothing at all."

He calmed himself and added more gently, seeing the Emperor, who was sneering at him:

"I do not know whether they have caught anything, but as they never do catch anything "

"Perhaps, to-day, all the same, they have taken something," said the Emperor ill-naturedly. "Such things have been seen." La Queue was about to reply angrily. But the Abbe Radiguet, who came up, calmed him. From the porch of the church the abbe had happened to observe the "Beeline"; and the bark seemed to be giving chase to some big fish. This news greatly interested Coqueville. In the groups reunited on the shore there were Mahes and Floches, the former praying that the boat might come in with a miraculous catch, the others making vows that it might come in empty.

Margot, holding herself very straight, did not take her eyes from the sea. "There they are!" said she simply.

And in fact a black dot showed itself beyond the point. All looked at it. One would have said a cork dancing on the water. The Emperor did not see even the black dot. One must be of Coqueville to recognize at that distance the "Beeline" and those who manned her.

"See!" said Margot, who had the best eyes of the coast, "it is Fouasse and Rouget who are rowing The little one is standing up in the bow."

She called Delphin "the little one" so as not to mention his name. And from then on they followed the course of the bark, trying to account for her strange movements. As the priest said, she appeared to be giving chase to some great fish that might be fleeing before her. That seemed extraordinary. The Emperor pretended that their net was without doubt being carried away. But La Queue cried that they were do-nothings, and that they were just amusing themselves. Quite certain they were not fishing for seals! All the Floches made merry over that joke; while the Mahes, vexed, declared that Rouget was a fine fellow all the same, and that he was risking his skin while others at the least puff of wind preferred terra firma. The Abbe Radiguet was forced to interpose again for there were slaps in the air.

"What ails them?" said Margot abruptly. "They are off again!" They ceased menacing one another, and every eye searched the horizon, The "Beeline" was once more hidden behind the point. This time La Queue himself became uneasy. He could not account for such maneuvers. The fear that Rouget was really in a fair way to catch some fish threw him off his mental balance. No one left the beach, although there was nothing strange to be seen. They stayed there nearly two hours, they watched incessantly for the bark, which appeared from time to time, then disappeared. It finished by not showing itself at all any more. La Queue, enraged, breathing in his heart the abominable wish, declared that she must have sunk; and, as just at that moment Rouget's wife appeared with Brisemotte, he looked at them both, sneering, while he patted Tupain on the shoulder to console him already for the death of his brother, Fouasse. But he stopped laughing when he caught sight of his daughter Margot, silent and looming, her eyes on the distance; it was quite possibly for Delphin.

"What are you up to over there?" he scolded. "Be off home with you! Mind, Margot!"

She did not stir. Then all at once: "Ah! There they are!"

He gave a cry of surprise. Margot, with her good eyes, swore that she no longer saw a soul in the bark; neither Rouget, nor Fouasse, nor any one! The "Beeline," as if abandoned, ran before the wind, tacking about every minute, rocking herself with a lazy air.

A west wind had fortunately risen and was driving her toward the land, but with strange caprices which tossed her to right and to left. Then all Coqueville ran down to the shore. One half shouted to the other half, there remained not a girl in the houses to look after the soup. It was a catastrophe; something inexplicable, the strangeness of which completely turned their heads. Marie, the wife of Rouget, after a moment's reflection, thought it her duty to burst into tears. Tupain succeeded in merely carrying an air of affliction. All the Mahes were in great distress, while the Floches tried to appear conventional. Margot collapsed as if she had her legs broken.

"What are you up to again!" cried La Queue, who stumbled upon her.

"I am tired," she answered simply.

And she turned her face toward the sea, her cheeks between her hands, shading her eyes with the ends of her fingers, gazing fixedly at the bark rocking itself idly on the waves with the air of a good fellow who has drunk too much.

In the meanwhile suppositions were rife. Perhaps the three men had fallen into the water? Only, all three at a time, that seemed absurd.

La Queue would have liked well to persuade them that the "Beeline" had gone to pieces like a rotten egg; but the boat still held the sea; they shrugged their shoulders. Then, as if the three men had actually perished, he remembered that he was Mayor and spoke of formalities.

"Leave off!" cried the Emperor, "Does one die in such a silly way?" "If they had fallen overboard, little Delphin would have been here by this!"

All Coqueville had to agree, Delphin swam like a herring. But where then could the three men be? They shouted: "I tell you, yes!" "I tell you, no!" "Too stupid!" "Stupid yourself!" And matters came to the point of exchanging blows. The Abbe Radiguet was obliged to make an appeal for reconciliation, while the Emperor hustled the crowd about to establish order. Meanwhile, the bark, without haste, continued to dance before the world. It waltzed, seeming to mock at the people; the sea carried her in, making her salute the land in long rhythmic reverences. Surely it was a bark in a crazy fit. Margot, her cheeks between her hands, kept always gazing. A yawl had just put out of the harbor to go to meet the "Beeline." It was Brisemotte, who had exhibited that impatience, as if he had been delayed in giving certainty to Rouget's wife. From that moment all Coqueville interested itself in the yawl. The voices rose higher: "Well, does he see anything?"

The "Beeline" advanced with her mysterious and mocking air. At last they saw him draw himself up and look into the bark that he had succeeded in taking in tow. All held their breath. But, abruptly, he burst out laughing. That was a surprise; what had he to be amused at? "What is it? What have you got there?" they shouted to him furiously.

He, without replying, laughed still louder. He made gestures as if to say that they would see. Then having fastened the "Beeline" to the yawl, he towed her back. And an unlooked-for spectacle stunned Coqueville. In the bottom of the bark, the three men Rouget, Delphin, Fouasse were beatifically stretched out on their backs, snoring, with fists clenched, dead drunk. In their midst was found a little cask stove in, some full cask they had come across at sea and which they had appreciated. Without doubt, it was very good, for they had drunk it all save a liter's worth which had leaked into the bark and which was mixed with the sea water.

"Ah! The pig!" cried the wife of Rouget, brutally, ceasing to whimper.

"Well, it's characteristic their catch!" said La Queue, who affected great disgust.

"Forsooth!" replied the Emperor, "they catch what they can! They have at least caught a cask, while others have not caught anything at all."

The Mayor shut up, greatly vexed. Coqueville brayed. They understood now. When barks are intoxicated, they dance as men do; and that one, in truth, had her belly full of liquor. Ah, the slut! What a minx! She festooned over the ocean with the air of a sot who could no longer recognize his home. And Coqueville laughed, and fumed, the Mahes found it funny, while the Floches found it disgusting. They surrounded the "Beeline," they craned their necks, they strained their eyes to see sleeping there the three jolly dogs who were exposing the secret springs of their jubilation, oblivious of the crowd hanging over them. The abuse and the laughter troubled them but little. Rouget did not hear his wife accuse him of drinking up all they had; Fouasse did not feel the stealthy kicks with which his brother Tupain rammed his sides. As for Delphin, he was pretty, after he had drunk, with his blond hair, his rosy face drowned in bliss. Mar-got had gotten up, and silently, for the present, she contemplated the little fellow with a hard expression.

"Must put them to bed!" cried a voice.

But just then Delphin opened his eyes. He rolled looks of rapture over the people. They questioned him on all sides with an eagerness that dazed him somewhat, the more easily since he was still as drunk as a thrush.

"Well! What?" he stuttered; "it was a little cask. There is no fish. Therefore, we have caught a little cask."

He did not get beyond that. To every sentence he added simply: "It was very good!"

"But what was it in the cask?" they asked him hotly.

"Ah! I don't know it was very good."

By this time Coqueville was burning to know. Every one lowered their noses to the boat, sniffing vigorously. With one opinion, it smelt of liquor; only no one could guess what liquor. The Emperor, who flattered himself that he had drunk of everything that a man can drink, said that he would see. He solemnly took in the palm of his hand a little of the liquor that was swimming in the bottom of the bark. The crowd became all at once silent. They waited. But the Emperor, after sucking up a mouthful, shook his head as if still badly informed. He sucked twice, more and more embarrassed, with an air of uneasiness and surprise. And he was bound to confess:

"I do not know. It's strange If there was no salt water in it, I would know, no doubt My word of honor, it is very strange!"

They looked at him. They stood struck with awe before that which the

Emperor himself did not venture to pronounce. Coqueville contemplated with respect the little empty cask.

"It was very good!" once more said Delphin, who seemed to be making game of the people. Then, indicating the sea with a comprehensive sweep, he added: "If you want some, there is more there I saw them little casks little casks little casks "

And he rocked himself with the refrain which he kept singing, gazing tenderly at Margot. He had just caught sight of her. Furious, she made a motion as if to slap him; but he did not even close his eyes; he awaited the slap with an air of tenderness.

The Abbe Radiguet, puzzled by that unknown tipple, he, too, dipped his finger in the bark and sucked it. Like the Emperor, he shook his head: no, he was not familiar with that, it was very extraordinary. They agreed on but one point: the cask must have been wreckage from the ship in distress, signaled Sunday evening. The English ships often carried to Grandport such cargoes of liquor and fine wines.

Little by little the day faded and the people were withdrawn into shadow. But La Queue remained absorbed, tormented by an idea which he no longer expressed. He stopped, he listened a last time to Delphin, whom they were carrying along, and who was repeating in his sing-song voice: "Little casks little casks little casks if you want some, there are more!"

That night the weather changed completely. When Coqueville awoke the following day an unclouded sun was shining; the sea spread out without a wrinkle, like a great piece of green satin. And it was warm, one of those pale glows of autumn.

First of the village, La Queue had risen, still clouded from the dreams of the night. He kept looking for a long time toward the sea, to the right, to the left. At last, with a sour look, he said that he must in any event satisfy M. Mouchel. And he went away at once with Tupain and Brisemotte, threatening Margot to touch up her sides if she did not walk straight. As the "Zephyr" left the harbor, and as he saw the "Beeline" swinging heavily at her anchor, he cheered up a little saying: "To-day, I guess, not a bit of it! Blow out the candle, Jeanetton! Those gentlemen have gone to bed!"

And as soon as the "Zephyr" had reached the open sea, La Queue cast his nets. After that he went to visit his "traps." The traps are a kind of elongated eel-pot in which they catch more, especially lobsters and red garnet. But in spite of the calm sea, he did well to visit his traps one by one. All were empty; at the bottom of the last one, as if in mockery, he found a little mackerel, which he threw back angrily into the sea. It was fate; there were weeks like that when the fish flouted Coqueville, and always at a time when M. Mouchel had expressed a particular desire for them. When La Queue drew in his nets, an hour later, he found nothing but a bunch of seaweed. Straightway he swore, his fists clenched, raging so much the more for the vast serenity of the ocean, lazy and sleeping like a sheet of burnished silver under the blue sky. The "Zephyr," without a waver, glided along in gentle ease. La Queue decided to go in again, after having cast his nets once more. In the afternoon he came to see them, and he menaced God and the saints, cursing in abominable words. In the meanwhile, Rouget, Fouasse, and Delphin kept on sleeping. They did not succeed in standing up until the dinner hour. They recollected nothing, they were conscious only of having been treated to something extraordinary, something which they did not understand. In the afternoon, as they were all three down at the harbor, the Emperor tried to question them concerning the liquor, now that they had recovered their senses. It was like, perhaps, eau-de-vie with liquorice-juice in it; or rather one might say rum, sugared and burned. They said "Yes"; they said "No." From their replies, the Emperor suspected that it was ratafia; but he would not have sworn to it. That day Rouget and his men had too many pains in their sides to go a-fishing. Moreover, they knew that La Queue had gone out without success that morning, and they talked of waiting until the next day before visiting their traps. All three of them, seated on blocks of stone, watched the tide come in, their backs rounded, their mouths clammy, half-asleep.

But suddenly Delphin woke up; he jumped on to the stone, his eyes on the distance, crying: "Look, Boss, off there!"

"What?" asked Rouget, who stretched his limbs.

"A cask."

Rouget and Fouasse were at once on their feet, their eyes gleaming, sweeping the horizon.

"Where is it, lad? Where is the cask?" repeated the boss, greatly moved.

"Off there to the left that black spot."

The others saw nothing. Then Rouget swore an oath. "Nom de Dieu!"

He had just spotted the cask, big as a lentil on the white water in a slanting ray of the setting sun. And he ran to the "Beeline," followed by Delphin and Fouasse, who darted forward tapping their backs with their heels and making the pebbles roll.

The "Beeline" was just putting out from the harbor when the news that they saw a cask out at sea was circulated in Coqueville. The children, the women, began to run. They shouted: "A cask! A cask!"

"Do you see it? The current is driving it toward Grandport."

"Ah, yes! On the left a cask! Come, quick!"

And Coqueville came; tumbled down from its rock; the children arrived head over heels, while the women picked up their skirts with both hands to descend quickly. Soon the entire village was on the beach as on the night before.

Margot showed herself for an instant, then she ran back at full speed to the house, where she wished to forestall her father, who was discussing an official process with the Emperor. At last La Queue appeared. He was livid; he said to the police chief: "Hold your peace! It's Rouget who has sent you here to beguile me. Well, then, he shall not get it. You'll see!"

When he saw the "Beeline," three hundred meters out, making with all her oars toward the black dot, rocking in the distance, his fury redoubled. And he shoved Tupain and Brisemotte into the "Zephyr," and he pulled out in turn, repeating: "No, they shall not have it; I'll die sooner!"

Then Coqueville had a fine spectacle; a mad race between the "Zephyr" and the "Beeline." When the latter saw the first leave the harbor, she understood the danger, and shot off with all her speed. She may have been four hundred meters ahead; but the chances remained even, for the "Zephyr" was otherwise light and swift; so excitement was at its height on the beach. The Mahes and the Floches had instinctively formed into two groups, following eagerly the vicissitudes of the struggle, each upholding its own boat. At first the "Beeline" kept her advantage, but as soon as the "Zephyr" spread herself, they saw that she was gaining little by little. The "Beeline" made a supreme effort and succeeded for a few minutes in holding her distance. Then the "Zephyr" once more gained upon the "Beeline," came up with her at extraordinary speed. From that moment on, it was evident that the two barks would meet in the neighborhood of the cask. Victory hung on a circumstance, on the slightest mishap.

"The 'Beeline'!" cried the Mahes.

But they soon ceased shouting. When the "Beeline" was almost touching the cask, the "Zephyr," by a bold maneuver, managed to pass in front of her and throw the cask to the left, where La Queue harpooned it with a thrust of the boat-hook.

"The 'Zephyr'! The 'Zephyr!" screamed the Floches.

And the Emperor, having spoken of foul play, big words were exchanged. Margot clapped her hands. The Abbe Radiguet came down with his breviary, made a profound remark which abruptly calmed the people, and then threw them into consternation.

"They will, perhaps, drink it all, these, too," he murmured with a melancholy air.

At sea, between the "Beeline" and the "Zephyr," a violent quarrel broke out. Rouget called La Queue a thief, while the latter called Rouget a good-for-nothing. The men even took up their oars to beat each other down, and the adventure lacked little of turning into a naval combat. More than this, they engaged to meet on land, showing their fists and threatening to disembowel each other as soon as they found each other again.

"The rascal!" grumbled Rouget. "You know, that cask is bigger than the one of yesterday. It's yellow, this one it ought to be great." Then in accents of despair: "Let's go and see the traps; there may very possibly be lobsters in them."

And the "Beeline" went on heavily to the left, steering toward the point.

In the "Zephyr," La Queue had to get in a passion in order to hold Tupain and Brisemotte from the cask. The boat-hook, in smashing a hoop, had made a leaking for the red liquid, which the two men tasted from the ends of their fingers and which they found exquisite. One might easily drink a glass without its producing much effect. But La Queue would not have it. He caulked the cask and declared that the first who sucked it should have a talk with him. On land, they would see.

"Then," asked Tupain, sullenly, "are we going to draw out the traps?"

"Yes, right away; there is no hurry!" replied La Queue.

He also gazed lovingly at the barrel. He felt his limbs melt with longing to go in at once and taste it. The fish bored him.

"Bah!" said he at the end of a silence. "Let's go back, for it's late. We will return to-morrow." And he was relaxing his fishing when he noticed another cask at his right, this one very small, and which stood on end, turning on itself like a top. That was the last straw for the nets and the traps. No one even spoke of them any longer. The "Zephyr" gave chase to the little barrel, which was caught very easily.

During this time a similar adventure overtook the "Beeline." After

Rouget had already visited five traps completely empty, Delphin, always on the watch, cried out that he saw something. But it did not have the appearance of a cask, it was too long.

"It's a beam," said Fouasse.

Rouget let fall his sixth trap without drawing it out of the water. "Let's go and see, all the same," said he.

As they advanced, they thought they recognized at first a beam, a chest, the trunk of a tree. Then they gave a cry of joy.

It was a real cask, but a very queer cask, such as they had never seen before. One would have said a tube, bulging in the middle and closed at the two ends by a layer of plaster.

"Ah, that's comical!" cried Rouget, in rapture. "This one I want the Emperor to taste. Come, children, let's go in."

They all agreed not to touch it, and the "Beeline" returned to Coqueville at the same moment as the "Zephyr," in its turn, anchored in the little harbor. Not one inquisitive had left the beach. Cries of joy greeted that unexpected catch of three casks. The gamins hurled their caps into the air, while the women had at once gone on the run to look for glasses. It was decided to taste the liquid on the spot. The wreckage belonged to the village. Not one protest arose. Only they formed into two groups, the Mahes surrounded Rouget, the Floches would not let go of La Queue.

"Emperor, the first glass for you!" cried Rouget. "Tell us what it is."

The liquor was of a beautiful golden yellow. The police chief raised his glass, looked at it, smelt it, then decided to drink.

"That comes from Holland," said he, after a long silence.

He did not give any other information. All the Mahes drank with deference. It was rather thick, and they stood surprised, for it tasted of flowers. The women found it very good. As for the men, they would have preferred less sugar. Nevertheless, at the bottom it ended by being strong at the third or fourth glass. The more they drank, the better they liked it. The men became jolly, the women grew funny.

But the Emperor, in spite of his recent quarrels with the Mayor, had gone to hang about the group of Floches.

The biggest cask gave out a dark-red liquor, while they drew from the smallest a liquid white as water from the rock; and it was this latter that was the stiffest, a regular pepper, something that skinned the tongue.

Not one of the Floches recognized it, neither the red nor the white.

There were, however, some wags there. It annoyed them to be regaling themselves without knowing over what.

"I say, Emperor, taste that for me!" said La Queue, thus taking the first step.

The Emperor, who had been waiting for the invitation, posed once more as connoisseur.

"As for the red," he said, "there is orange in that! And for the white," he declared, "that that is excellent!"

They had to content themselves with these replies, for he shook his head with a knowing air, with the happy look of a man who has given satisfaction to the world.

The Abbe Radiguet, alone, did not seem convinced. As for him, he had the names on the tip of his tongue; and to thoroughly reassure himself, he drank small glasses, one after the other, repeating: "Wait, wait, I know what it is. In a moment I will tell you."

In the mean while, little by little, merriment grew in the group of the Mahes and the group of the Floches. The latter, particularly, laughed very loud because they had mixed the liquors, a thing that excited them the more. For the rest, the one and the other of the groups kept apart. They did not offer each other of their casks, they simply cast sympathetic glances, seized with the unavowed desire to taste their neighbor's liquor, which might possibly be better. The inimical brothers, Tupain and Fouasse, were in close proximity all the evening without showing their fists. It was remarked, also, that Rouget and his wife drank from the same glass. As for Margot, she distributed the liquor among the Floches, and as she filled the glasses too full, and the liquor ran over her fingers, she kept sucking them continually, so well that, though obeying her father who forbade her to drink, she became as fuddled as a girl in vintage time. It was not unbecoming to her; on the contrary, she got rosy all over, her eyes were like candles.

The sun set, the evening was like the softness of springtime. Coqueville had finished the casks and did not dream of going home to dine. They found themselves too comfortable on the beach. When it was pitch night, Margot, sitting apart, felt some one blowing on her neck. It was Delphin, very gay, walking on all fours, prowling behind her like a wolf. She repressed a cry so as not to awaken her father, who would have sent Delphin a kick in the back.

"Go away, imbecile!" she murmured, half angry, half laughing; "you will get yourself caught!"

The following day Coqueville, in rising, found the sun already high above the horizon. The air was softer still, a drowsy sea under a clear sky, one of those times of laziness when it is so good to do nothing. It was a Wednesday. Until breakfast time, Coqueville rested from the fête of the previous evening. Then they went down to the beach to see.

That Wednesday the fish, the Widow Dufeu, M. Mouchel, all were forgotten. La Queue and Rouget did not even speak of visiting their jam-bins. Toward three o'clock they sighted some casks. Four of them were dancing before the village. The "Zephyr" and the "Beeline" went in chase; but as there was enough for all, they disputed no longer. Each boat had its share. At six o'clock, after having swept all over the little gulf, Rouget and La Queue came in, each with three casks. And the fête began again. The women had brought down tables for convenience. They had brought benches as well; they set up two cafes in the open air, such as they had at Grandport. The Mahes were on the left; the Floches on the right, still separated by a bar of sand. Nevertheless, that evening the Emperor, who went from one group to the other, carried his glasses full, so at to give every one a taste of the six casks. At about nine o'clock they were much gayer than the night before.

The next day Coqueville could never remember how it had gone to bed.

Thursday the "Zephyr" and the "Beeline" caught but four casks, two each, but they were enormous. Friday the fishing was superb, undreamed of; there were seven casks, three for Rouget and four for La Queue. Coqueville was entering upon a golden age. They never did anything any more. The fishermen, working off the alcohol of the night before, slept till noon. Then they strolled down to the beach and interrogated the sea. Their sole anxiety was to know what liquor the sea was going to bring them. They waited there for hours, their eyes strained; they raised shouts of joy when wreckage appeared.

The women and the children, from the tops of the rocks, pointed with sweeping gestures even to the least bunch of seaweed rolled in by the waves. And, at all hours, the "Zephyr" and the "Beeline" stood ready to leave. They put out, they beat the gulf, they fished for casks, as they had fished for tuna; disdaining now the tame mackerel that capered about in the sun, and the lazy sole rocked on the foam of the water. Coqueville watched the fishing, dying of laughter on the sands. Then in the evening they drank the catch.

That which enraptured Coqueville was that the casks did not cease. When there were no more, there were still more! The ship that had been lost must truly have had a pretty cargo aboard; and Coqueville became egoist and merry, joked over the wrecked ship, a regular wine-cellar, enough to intoxicate all the fish of the ocean. Added to that, never did they catch two casks alike; they were of all shapes, of all sizes, of all colors. Then, in every cask there was a different liquor. So the Emperor was plunged into profound reveries; he who had drunk everything, he could identify nothing any more. La Queue declared that never had he seen such a cargo. The Abbe Radiguet guessed it was an order from some savage king, wishing to set up his wine-cellar. Coqueville, rocked in mysterious intoxication, no longer tried to understand.

The ladies preferred the "creams"; they had cream of mocha, of cacao, of mint, of vanilla. Marie Rouget drank one night so much anisette that she was sick.

Margot and the other young ladies tapped the curaçao, the bénédictine, the trappistine, the chartreuse. As to the cassis, it was reserved for the little children. Naturally the men rejoiced more when they caught cognacs, rums, gins, everything that burned the mouth. Then surprises produced themselves. A cask of raki of Chio, flavored with mastic, stupefied Coqueville, which thought that it had fallen on a cask of essence of turpentine. All the same they drank it, for they must lose nothing; but they talked about it for a long time. Arrack from Batavia, Swedish eau-de-vie with cumin, tuica calugaresca from Rumania, slivowitz from Serbia, all equally overturned every idea that Coqueville had of what one should endure. At heart they had a weakness for kuemmel and kirschwasser, for liqueurs as pale as water and stiff enough to kill a man.

Heavens! Was it possible so many good things had been invented! At Coqueville they had known nothing but eau-de-vie; and, moreover, not every one at that. So their imaginations finished in exultation; they arrived at a state of veritable worship, in face of that inexhaustible variety, for that which intoxicates. Oh! To get drunk every night on something new, on something one does not even know the name of! It seemed like a fairy-tale, a rain, a fountain that would spout extraordinary liquids, all the distilled alcohols, perfumed with all the flowers and all the fruits of creation.

So then, Friday evening, there were seven casks on the beach! Coqueville did not leave the beach. They lived there, thanks to the mildness of the season. Never in September had they enjoyed so fine a week. The fête had lasted since Monday, and there was no reason why it should not last forever if Providence should continue to send them casks; for the Abbe Radiguet saw therein the hand of Providence. All business was suspended; what use drudging when pleasure came to them in their sleep? They were all bourgeois, bourgeois who were drinking expensive liquors without having to pay anything at the cafe. With hands in pocket, Coqueville basked in the sunshine waiting for the evening's spree. Moreover, it did not sober up; it enjoyed side by side the gaieties of kuemmel, of kirsch-wasser, of ratafia; in seven days they knew the wraths of gin, the tendernesses of curaçao, the laughter of cognac. And Coqueville remained as innocent as a newborn child, knowing nothing about anything, drinking with conviction that which the good Lord sent them.

It was on Friday that the Mahes and the Floches fraternized. They were very jolly that evening. Already, the evening before, distances had drawn nearer, the most intoxicated had trodden down the bar of sand which separated the two groups. There remained but one step to take. On the side of the Floches the four casks were emptying, while the Mahes were equally finishing their three little barrels; just three liqueurs which made the French flag; one blue, one white, and one red. The blue filled the Floches with jealousy, because a blue liqueur seemed to them something really supernatural. La Queue, grown good-natured since he had been drunk, advanced, a glass in his hand, feeling that he ought to take the first step as magistrate.

"See here, Rouget," he stuttered, "will you drink with me?"

"Willingly," replied Rouget, who was staggering under a feeling of tenderness.

And they fell upon each other's necks. Then they all wept, so great was their emotion. The Mahes and the Floches embraced, they who had been devouring one another for three centuries. The Abbe Radiguet, greatly touched, again spoke of the finger of God. They drank to each other in the three liqueurs, the blue, the white, and the red.

"Vive la France!" cried the Emperor.

The blue was worthless, the white of not much account, but the red was really a success. Then they tapped the casks of the Floches. Then they danced. As there was no band, some good-natured boys clapped their hands, whistling, which excited the girls. The fête became superb. The seven casks were placed in a row; each could choose that which he liked best. Those who had had enough stretched themselves out on the sands, where they slept for a while; and when they awoke they began again. Little by little the others spread the fun until they took up the whole beach. Right up to midnight they skipped in the open air. The sea had a soft sound, the stars shone in a deep sky, a sky of vast peace. It was the serenity of the infant ages enveloping the joy of a tribe of savages, intoxicated by their first cask of eau-de-vie.

Nevertheless, Coqueville went home to bed again. When there was nothing more left to drink, the Floches and the Mahes helped one another, carried one another, and ended by finding their beds again one way or another. On Saturday the fête lasted until nearly two o'clock in the morning. They had caught six casks, two of them enormous. Fouasse and Tupain almost fought. Tupain, who was wicked when drunk, talked of finishing his brother. But that quarrel disgusted every one, the Floches as well as the Mahes. Was it reasonable to keep on quarreling when the whole village was embracing? They forced the two brothers to drink together. They were sulky. The Emperor promised to watch them. Neither did the Rouget household get on well. When Marie had taken anisette she was prodigal in her attentions to Brisemotte, which Rouget could not behold with a calm eye, especially since having become sensitive, he also wished to be loved. The Abbe Radiguet, full of forbearance, did well in preaching forgiveness; they feared an accident. "Bah!" said La Queue; "all will arrange itself. If the fishing is good tomorrow, you will see your health!"

However, La Queue himself was not yet perfect. He still kept his eye on Delphin and leveled kicks at him whenever he saw him approach Margot. The Emperor was indignant, for there was no common sense in preventing two young people from laughing. But La Queue always swore to kill his daughter sooner than give her to "the little one." Moreover, Margot would not be willing.

"Isn't it so? You are too proud," he cried. "Never would you marry a ragamuffin!"

"Never, papa!" answered Margot.

Saturday, Margot drank a great deal of sugary liqueur. No one had any idea of such sugar. As she was no longer on her guard, she soon found herself sitting close to the cask. She laughed, happy, in paradise; she saw stars, and it seemed to her that there was music within her, playing dance tunes. Then it was that Delphin slipped into the shadow of the casks. He took her hand; he asked: "Say, Margot, will you?"

She kept on smiling. Then she replied: "It is papa who will not."

"Oh! That's nothing," said the little one; "you know the old ones never will provided you are willing, you." And he grew bold, he planted a kiss on her neck. She bridled; shivers ran along her shoulders. "Stop! You tickle me."

But she talked no more of giving him a slap. In the first place, she was not able to, for her hands were too weak. Then it seemed nice to her, those little kisses on the neck. It was like the liqueur that enervated her so deliciously. She ended by turning her head and extending her chin, just like a cat.

"There!" she stammered, "there under the ear that tickles me. Oh! That is nice!"

They had both forgotten La Queue. Fortunately the Emperor was on guard. He pointed them out to the Abbe.

"Look there, priest, it would be better to marry them."

"Morals would gain thereby," declared the priest sententiously.

And he charged himself with the matter for the morrow. 'Twas he himself that would speak to La Queue. Meanwhile La Queue had drunk so much that the Emperor and the priest were forced to carry him home. On the way they tried to reason with him on the subject of his daughter; but they could draw from him nothing but growls. Behind them, in the untroubled night, Delphin led Margot home.

The next day by four o'clock the "Zephyr" and the "Beeline" had already caught seven casks. At six o'clock the "Zephyr" caught two more. That made nine.

Then Coqueville feted Sunday. It was the seventh day that it had been drunk. And the fête was complete a fête such as no one had ever seen, and which no one will ever see again. Speak of it in Lower Normandy, and they will tell you with laughter, "Ah! Yes, the fête at Coqueville!"

In the mean while, since the Tuesday, M. Mouchel had been surprised at not seeing either Rouget or La Queue arrive at Grandport. What the devil could those fellows be doing? The sea was fine, the fishing ought to be splendid. Very possibly they wished to bring a whole load of soles and lobsters in all at once. And he was patient until the Wednesday.

Wednesday, M. Mouchel was angry. You must know that the Widow Dufeu was not a commodious person. She was a woman who in a flash came to high words. Although he was a handsome fellow, blond and powerful, he trembled before her, especially since he had dreams of marrying her, always with little attentions, free to subdue her with a slap if he ever became her master. Well, that Wednesday morning the Widow Dufeu stormed, complaining that the bundles were no longer forwarded, that the sea failed; and she accused him of running after the girls of the coast instead of busying himself with the whiting and the mackerel which ought to be yielding in abundance. M. Mouchel, vexed, fell back on Coqueville's singular breach of honor. For a moment surprise calmed the Widow Dufeu. What was Coqueville dreaming about? Never had it so conducted itself before. But she declared immediately that she had nothing to do with Coqueville; that it was M. Mouchel's business to look into matters, that she should take a partner if he allowed himself to be played with again by the fishermen. In a word, much disquieted, he sent Rouget and La Queue to the devil. Perhaps, after all, they would come tomorrow.

The next day, Thursday, neither the one nor the other appeared. Toward evening, M. Mouchel, desperate, climbed the rock to the left of Grandport, from which one could see in the distance Coqueville, with its yellow spot of beach. He gazed at it a long time. The village had a tranquil look in the sun, light smoke was rising from the chimneys; no doubt the women were preparing the soup. M. Mouchel was satisfied that Coqueville was still in its place, that a rock from the cliff had not crushed it, and he understood less and less. As he was about to descend again, he thought he could make out two black points on the gulf; the "Beeline" and the "Zephyr." After that he went back to calm the Widow Dufeu. Coqueville was fishing. The night passed. Friday was here. Still nothing of Coqueville. M. Mouchel climbed to his rock more than ten times. He was beginning to lose his head; the Widow Dufeu behaved abominably to him, without his finding anything to reply. Coqueville was always there, in the sun, warming itself like a lazy lizard. Only, M. Mouchel saw no more smoke. The village seemed dead. Had they all died in their holes? On the beach, there was quite a movement, but that might be seaweed rocked by the tide. Saturday, still no one. The Widow Dufeu scolded no more; her eyes were fixed, her lips white. M. Mouchel passed two hours on the rock. A curiosity grew in him, a purely personal need of accounting to himself for the strange immobility of the village. The old walls sleeping beatifically in the sun ended by worrying him. His resolution was taken; he would set out that Monday very early in the morning and try to get down there near nine o'clock.

It was not a promenade to go to Coqueville. M. Mouchel preferred to follow the route by land, in that way he would come upon the village without their expecting him. A wagon carried him as far as Robineux, where he left it under a shed, for it would not have been prudent to risk it in the middle of the gorge. And he set off bravely, having to make nearly seven kilometers over the most abominable of roads. The route was otherwise of a wild beauty; it descended by continual turns between two enormous ledges of rock, so narrow in places that three men could not walk abreast. Farther on it skirted the precipices; the gorge opened abruptly; and one caught glimpses of the sea, of immense blue horizons. But M. Mouchel was not in a state of mind to admire the landscape. He swore as the pebbles rolled under his feet. It was the fault of Coqueville, he promised to shake up those do-nothings well. But, in the meantime, he was approaching. All at once, in the turning at the last rock, he saw the twenty houses of the village hanging to the flank of the cliff.

Nine o'clock struck. One would have believed it June, so blue and warm was the sky; a superb season, limpid air, gilded by the dust of the sun, refreshed by the good smell of the sea. M. Mouchel entered the only street of the village, where he came very often; and as he passed before Rouget's house, he went in. The house was empty. Then he cast his eye toward Fouasse's Tupain's Brisemotte's. Not a soul; all the doors open, and no one in the rooms. What did it mean? A light chill began to creep over his flesh. Then he thought of the authorities. Certainly, the Emperor would reassure him. But the Emperor's house was empty like the others. Even to the police chief, there was failure! That village, silent and deserted, terrified him now. He ran to the Mayor's. There another surprise awaited him: the house was found in an abominable mess; they had not made the beds in three days; dirty dishes littered the place; chairs seemed to indicate a fight. His mind upset, dreaming of cataclysms, M. Mouchel determined to go on to the end, and he entered the church. No more priest than mayor. All the authorities, even religion itself had vanished. Coqueville abandoned, slept without a breath, without a dog, without a cat. Not even a fowl; the hens had taken themselves off. Nothing, a void, silence, a leaden sleep under the great blue sky.

Good God! It was no wonder that Coqueville brought no more fish! Coqueville had moved away. Coqueville was dead. He must notify the police. The mysterious catastrophe exalted M. Mouchel, when, with the idea of descending to the beach, he uttered a cry. In the midst of the sands, the whole population lay stretched. He thought of a general massacre. But the sonorous snores came to undeceive him. During the night of Sunday, Coqueville had feasted so late that it had found itself in absolute inability to go home to bed. So it had slept on the sand, just where it had fallen, around the nine casks, completely empty.

Yes, all Coqueville was snoring there; I hear the children, the women, the old people, and the men. Not one was on his feet. There were some on their stomachs, there were some on their backs; others held themselves like dogs on all fours. As one makes his bed so must one lie on it. And the fellows found themselves, happen what may, scattered in their drunkenness like a handful of leaves driven by the wind. The men had rolled over, heads lower than heels. It was a scene full of good-fellowship; a dormitory in the open air; honest family folk taking their ease; for where there is care, there is no pleasure.

It was just at the new moon. Coqueville, thinking it had blown out its candle, had abandoned itself to the darkness. Then the day dawned; and now the sun was flaming, a sun which fell perpendicularly on the sleepers, powerless to make them open their eyelids. They slept rudely, all their faces beaming with the fine innocence of drunkards. The hens at early morning must have strayed down to peck at the casks, for they were drunk; they, too, sleeping on the sands. There were also five cats and five dogs, their paws in the air, drunk from licking the glasses glistening with sugar.

For a moment M. Mouchel walked about among the sleepers, taking care not to step on any of them. He understood, for at Grandport they, too, had received casks from the wreck of the English ship. All his wrath left him. What a touching and moral spectacle! Coqueville reconciled, the Mahes and the Floches sleeping together! With the last glass the deadliest enemies had embraced. Tupain and Fouasse lay there snoring, hand in hand, like brothers, incapable of coming to dispute a legacy. As to the Rouget household, it offered a still more amiable picture, Marie slept between Rouget and Brisemotte, as much as to say that henceforth they were to live thus, happy, all the three.

But one group especially exhibited a scene of family tenderness. It was

Delphin and Margot; one on the neck of the other, they slept cheek to cheek, their lips still opened for a kiss. At their feet the Emperor, sleeping crosswise, guarded them. Above them La Queue snored like a father satisfied at having settled his daughter, while the Abbe Radiguet, fallen there like the others, with arms outspread, seemed to bless them. In her sleep Margot still extended her rosy muzzle like an amorous cat who loves to have one scratch her under the chin.

The fête ended with a marriage. And M. Mouchel himself later married the Widow Dufeu, whom he beat to a jelly. Speak of that in Lower Normandy, they will tell you with a laugh, "Ah! Yes, the fête at Coqueville!"

The Flood

I

My name is Louis Roubien. I am seventy years old. I was born in the village of Saint-Jory, several miles up the Garonne from Toulouse.

For fourteen years I battled with the earth for my daily bread. At last, prosperity smiled on we, and last month I was still the richest farmer in the parish.

Our house seemed blessed, happiness reigned there. The sun was our brother, and I cannot recall a bad crop. We were almost a dozen on the farm. There was myself, still hale and hearty, leading the children to work; then my young brother, Pierre, an old bachelor and retired sergeant; then my sister, Agathe, who came to us after the death of her husband. She was a commanding woman, enormous and gay, whose laugh could be heard at the other end of the village. Then came all the brood: my son, Jacques; his wife, Rosie, and their three daughters, Aimee, Veronique, and Marie. The first named was married to Cyprica Bouisson, a big jolly fellow, by whom she had two children, one two years old and the other ten months. Veronique was just betrothed, and was soon to marry Gaspard Rabuteau. The third, Marie, was a real young lady, so white, so fair, that she looked as if born in the city.

That made ten, counting everybody. I was a grandfather and a great-grandfather. When we were at table I had my sister, Agathe, at my right, and my brother, Pierre, at my left. The children formed a circle, seated according to age, with the heads diminishing down to the baby of ten months, who already ate his soup like a man. And let me tell you that the spoons in the plates made a clatter. The brood had hearty appetites. And what gayety between the mouthfuls. I was filled with pride and joy when the little ones held out their hands toward me, crying, "Grandpa, give us some bread. A big piece, grandpa."

Oh, the good days. Our farm sang from every corner. In the evening, Pierre invented games and related stories of his regiment. On Sunday Agathe made cakes for the girls. Marie knew some canticles, which she sang like a chorister. She looked like a saint, with her blond hair falling on her neck and her hands folded on her apron.

I had built another story on the house when Aimee had married Cyprien; and I said laughingly that I would have to build another after the wedding of Veronique and Gaspard. We never cared to leave each other. We would sooner have built a city behind the farm, in our enclosure. When families are united, it is so good to live and die where one has grown up.

The month of May had been magnificent that year. It was long since the crops gave such good promise. That day precisely, I had made a tour of inspection with my son, Jacques. We started at about three o'clock. Our meadows on the banks of the Garonne were of a tender green. The grass was three feet high, and an osier thicket, planted the year before, had sprouts a yard high. From there we went to visit our wheat and our vines, fields bought one by one as fortune came to us. The wheat was growing strong; the vines, in full flower, promised a superb vintage. And Jacques laughed his good laugh as he slapped me on the shoulder.

"Well, father, we shall never want for bread nor for wine. You must be a friend of the Divine Power to have silver showered upon your land in this way."

We often joked among ourselves of our past poverty. Jacques was right. I must have gained the friendship of some saint or of God himself, for all the luck in the country was for us. When it hailed the hail ceased on the border of our fields. If the vines of our neighbors fell sick, ours seemed to have a wall of protection around them. And in the end I grew to consider it only just. Never doing harm to any one, I thought that happiness was my due.

As we approached the house, Rose gesticulated, calling out, "Hurry up."

One of our cows had just had a calf, and everybody was excited. The birth of that little beast seemed one more blessing. We had been obliged recently to enlarge the stables, where we had nearly one hundred head of animals—cows and sheep, without counting the horses.

"Well, a good day's work." I cried. "We will drink to-night a bottle of ripened wine."

Meanwhile, Rose took us aside and told us that Gaspard, Veronique's betrothed, had come to arrange the day for the wedding. She had invited him to remain for dinner.

Gaspard, the oldest son of a farmer of Moranges, was a big boy of twenty years, known throughout the country for his prodigious strength. During a festival at Toulouse he had vanquished Martial, the "Lion of the Midi." With that, a nice boy, with a heart of gold. He was even timid, and he blushed when Veronique looked him squarely in the face.

I told Rose to call him. He was at the bottom of the yard, helping our servants to spread out the freshly-washed linen. When he entered the dining room, where we were, Jacques turned toward me, saying, "You speak, father."

"Well," I said, "you have come, my boy, to have us set the great day?"

"Yes, that is it, Father Roubien," he answered, very red.

"You mustn't blush, my boy," I continued. "It will be, if you wish, on Saint-Felicite day, the 10th of July. This is the 23rd of June, so you will have only twenty days to wait. My poor dead wife was called Felicite, and that will bring you happiness. Well? Is it understood?"

"Yes, that will do—Sainte-Felicite day. Father Roubien."

And he gave each of us a grip that made us wince. Then he embraced Rose, calling her mother. This big boy with the terrific fists loved Veronique to the point of losing his appetite.

"Now," I continued, "you must remain for dinner. Well, everybody to the table. I have a thundering appetite, I have."

That evening we were eleven at table. Gaspard was placed next to Veronique, and he sat looking at her, forgetting his plate, so moved at the thought of her belonging to him that, at times, the tears sprang to his eyes. Cyprien and Aimee, married only three years, smiled. Jacques and Rose, who had had twenty-five years of married life, were more serious, but, surreptitiously, they exchanged tender glances. As for me, I seemed to relive in those two sweethearts, whose happiness seemed to bring a corner of Paradise to our table. What good soup we had that evening. Aunt Agathe, always ready with a witticism, risked several jokes. Then that honest Pierre wanted to relate his love affair with a young lady of Lyons. Fortunately, we were at the dessert, and every one was talking at once. I had brought two bottles of mellowed wine from the cellar. We drank to the good fortune of Gaspard and Veronique. Then we had singing. Gaspard knew some love songs in dialect. We also asked Marie for a canticle. She stood up and sang in a flute-like voice that tickled one's ears.

I went to the window, and Gaspard joined me there.

"Is there no news up your way?" I asked him.

"No," he answered. "There is considerable talk about the heavy rains of the last few days. Some seem to think that they will cause trouble."

In effect, it had rained for sixty hours without stopping. The Garonne was very much swollen since the preceding day, but we had confidence in it, and, as long as it did not overflow its banks, we could not look on it as a bad neighbor.

"Bah." I exclaimed, shrugging my shoulders. "Nothing will happen. It is the same every year. The river puts up her back as if she were furious, and she calms down in a night. You will see, my boy, that it will amount to nothing this time. See how beautiful the weather is."

And I pointed to the sky. It was seven o'clock; the sun was setting. The sky was blue, an immense blue sheet of profound purity, in which the rays of the setting sun were like a golden dust. Never had I seen the village drowsing in so sweet a peace. Upon the tiled roofs a rosy tint was fading. I heard a neighbor's laugh, then the voices of children at the turn in the road in front of our place. Farther away and softened by the distance, rose the sounds of flocks entering their sheds. The great voice of the Garonne roared continually; but it was to me as the voice of the silence, so accustomed to it was I.

Little by little the sky paled; the village became more drowsy. It was the evening of a beautiful day; and I thought that all our good fortune—the big harvests, the happy house, the betrothal of Veronique—came to us from above in the purity of the dying light. A benediction spread over us with the farewell of the evening.

Meanwhile I had returned to the center of the room. The girls were chattering. We listened to them, smiling. Suddenly, across the serenity of the country, a terrible cry sounded, a cry of distress and death, "The Garonne. The Garonne."

II

We rushed out into the yard. Saint-Jory is situated at the bottom of a slope at about five hundred yards from the Garonne. Screens of tall poplars that divide the meadows, hide the river completely.

We could see nothing. And still the cry rang out, "The Garonne. The Garonne."

Suddenly, on the wide road before us, appeared two men and three women, one of them holding a child in her arms. It was they who were crying out, distracted, running with long strides. They turned at times, look-ing behind with terrified faces, as if a band of wolves was pursuing them.

"What's the matter with them?" demanded Cyprien. "Do you see any-thing, grandfather?"

"No," I answered. "The leaves are not even moving."

I was still talking when an exclamation burst from us. Behind the fugi-tives there appeared, between the trunks of the poplars, amongst the large tufts of grass, what looked like a pack of gray beasts speckled with yellow. They sprang up from all directions, waves crowding waves, a helter-skelter of masses of foaming water, shaking the sod with the rumbling gallop of their hordes.

It was our turn to send forth the despairing cry, "The Garonne. The Garonne."

The two men and the three women were still running on the road. They heard the terrible gallop gaining on them. Now the waves arrived in a sin-gle line, rolling, tumbling with the thunder of a charging battalion. With their first shock they had broken three poplars; the tall foliage sank and dis-appeared. A wooden cabin was swallowed up, a wall was demolished; heavy carts were carried away like straws. But the water seemed, above all, to pur-sue the fugitives. At the bend in the road, where there was a steep slope, it fell suddenly in an immense sheet and cut off retreat. They continued to run, nevertheless, splashing through the water, no longer shouting, mad with terror. The water swirled about their knees. An enormous wave felled the woman who was carrying the child. Then all were engulfed.

"Quick. Quick." I cried. "We must get into the house. It is solid—we have nothing to fear."

We took refuge upstairs. The house was built on a hillock above the road. The water invaded the yard, softly, with a little rippling noise. We were not much frightened.

"Bah." said Jacques, to reassure every one, "this will not amount to any-thing. You remember, father, in '55, the water came up into the yard. It was a foot deep. Then it receded."

"It is disastrous for the crops, just the same," murmured Cyprien.

"No, it will not be anything," I said, seeing the large questioning eyes of our girls.

Aimee had put her two children into the bed. She sat beside them, with Veronique and Marie. Aunt Agathe spoke of heating some wine she had brought up, to give us courage.

Jacques and Rose were looking out of a window. I was at the other, with my brother Pierre, Cyprien and Gaspard.

"Come up." I cried to our two servants, who were wading in the yard. "Don't stay there and get all wet."

"But the animals?" they asked. "They are afraid. They are killing each other in the barn."

"No, no; come up. After a while we'll see to them."

The rescue of the animals would be impossible, if the disaster was to attain greater proportions. I thought it unnecessary to frighten the family. So I forced myself to appear hopeful. Leaning on the windowsill, I indicated the progress of the flood. The river, after its attack on the village, was in possession even to the narrowest streets. It was no longer a galloping charge, but a slow and invincible strangulation. The hollow in the bottom of which Saint-Jory is built was changed into a lake. In our yard the water was soon three feet deep. But I asserted that it remained stationary—I even went so far as to pretend that it was going down.

"Well, you will be obliged to sleep here to-night, my boy," I said, turning to Gaspard. "That is, unless the roads are free in a couple of hours—which is quite possible."

He looked at me without answering, his face quite pale; and I saw him look at Veronique with an expression of anguish.

It was half-past eight o'clock. It was still daylight—a pale, sad light beneath the blanched sky. The servants had had the forethought to bring up two lamps with them. I had them lighted, thinking that they would brighten up the somber room. Aunt Agathe, who had rolled a table to the middle of the room, wished to organize a card party. The worthy woman, whose eyes sought mine momentarily, thought above all of diverting the children. Her good humor kept up a superb bravery; and she laughed to combat the terror that she felt growing around her. She forcibly placed Aimee, Veronique, and Marie at the table. She put the cards into their hands, took a hand herself with an air of intense interest, shuffling, cutting, dealing with such a flow of talk that she almost drowned the noise of the water. But our girls could not be diverted; they were pale, with feverish hands, and ears on the alert. Every few moments there was a pause in the play. One of them would turn to me, asking in a low voice, "Grandpa, is it still rising?"

"No, no. Go on with the game. There is no danger."

Never had my heart been gripped by such agony. All the men placed themselves at the windows to hide the terrifying sight. We tried to smile, turned toward the peaceful lamps that threw discs of light upon the table. I recalled our winter evenings, when we gathered around the table. It was the same quiet interior, filled with the warmth of affection. And while peace was there I heard behind me the roaring of the escaped river, that was constantly rising.

"Louis," said my brother Pierre, "the water is within three feet of the window. We ought to tell them."

I hushed him up by pressing his arm. But it was no longer possible to hide the peril. In our barns the animals were killing each other. There were bleatings and bellowings from the crazed herds; and the horses gave the harsh cries that can be heard at great distances when they are in danger of death.

"My God. My God." cried Aimee, who stood up, pressing her hands to her temples.

They all ran to the windows. There they remained, mute, their hair rising with fear. A dim light floated above the yellow sheet of water. The pale sky looked like a white cloth thrown over the earth. In the distance trailed some smoke. Everything was misty. It was the terrified end of a day melting into a night of death. And not a human sound, nothing but the roaring of that sea stretching to infinity; nothing but the bellowings and the neighings of the animals.

"My God. My God." repeated the women, in low voices, as if they feared to speak aloud.

A terrible cracking silenced the exclamations. The maddened animals had burst open the doors of the stables. They passed in the yellow flood, rolled about, carried away by the current. The sheep were tossed about like dead leaves, whirling in bands in the eddies. The cows and the horses struggled, tried to walk, and lost their footing. Our big gray horse fought long for life. He stretched his neck, he reared, snorting like a forge. But the enraged waters took him by the crupper, and we saw him, beaten, abandon himself.

Then we gave way for the first time. We felt the need of tears. Our hands stretched out to those dear animals that were being borne away, we lamented, giving vent to the tears and the sobs that we had suppressed. Ah. What ruin. The harvests destroyed, the cattle drowned, our fortunes changed in a few hours. God was not just. We had done nothing against

Him, and He was taking everything from us. I shook my fist at the horizon. I spoke of our walk that afternoon, of our meadows, our wheat and vines that we had found so full of promise. It was all a lie, then. The sun lied when he sank, so sweet and calm, in the midst of the evening's serenity.

The water was still rising. Pierre, who was watching it, cried, "Louis, we must look out. The water is up to the window."

That warning snatched us from our spell of despair. I was once more myself. Shrugging my shoulders, I said, "Money is nothing. As long as we are all saved, there need be no regrets. We shall have to work again—that is all."

"Yes, yes; you are right, father," said Jacques, feverishly. "And we run no danger—the walls are good and strong. We must get up on the roof."

That was the only refuge left us. The water, which had mounted the stairs step by step, was already coming through the door. We rushed to the attic in a group, holding close to each other. Cyprien had disappeared. I called him, and I saw him return from the next room, his face working with emotion. Then, as I remarked the absence of the servants, for whom I was waiting, he gave me a strange look, then said, in a suppressed voice, "Dead. The corner of the shed under their room caved in."

The poor girls must have gone to fetch their savings from their trunks. I told him to say nothing about it. A cold shiver had passed over me. It was Death entering the house.

When we went up, in our turn, we did not even think of putting out the lights. The cards remained spread upon the table. There was already a foot of water in the room.

III

Fortunately, the roof was vast and sloped gently. We reached it through a lid-like window, above which was a sort of platform. It was there that we took refuge. The women seated themselves. The men went over the tiles to reconnoiter. From my post against the dormer window through which we had climbed, I examined the four points of the horizon.

"Help cannot fail to arrive," I said, bravely. "The people of Saintin have boats; they will come this way. Look over there. Isn't that a lantern on the water?"

But no one answered me. Pierre had lighted his pipe, and he was smoking so furiously that, at each puff, he spit out pieces of the stem. Jacques and Cyprien looked into the distance, with drawn faces; while Gaspard, clenching his fists, continued to walk about, seeking an issue. At our feet the women, silent and shivering, hid their faces to shut out the sight. Yet Rose raised her head, glanced about her and demanded:

"And the servants? Where are they? Why, aren't they here?"

I avoided answering. She then questioned me, her eyes on mine.

"Where are the servants?"

I turned away, unable to lie. I felt that chill that had already brushed me pass over our women and our dear girls. They had understood. Marie burst into tears. Aimee wrapped her two children in her skirt, as if to protect them. Veronique, her face in her hands, did not move. Aunt Agathe, very pale, made the sign of the cross, and mumbled Paters and Aves.

Meanwhile the spectacle about us became of sovereign grandeur. The night retained the clearness of a summer night. There was no moon, but the sky was sprinkled with stars, and was of so pure a blue that it seemed to fill space with a blue light. And the immense sheet of water expanded beneath the softness of the sky. We could no longer see any land.

"The water is rising; the water is rising." repeated my brother Pierre, still crunching the stem of his pipe between his teeth.

The water was within a yard of the roof. It was losing its tranquility; currents were being formed. In less than an hour the water became threatening, dashing against the house, bearing drifting barrels, pieces of wood, clumps of weeds. In the distance there were attacks upon walls, and we could hear the resounding shocks. Poplar trees fell, houses crumbled, like a cartload of stones emptied by the roadside.

Jacques, unnerved by the sobs of the women, cried, "We can't stay here. We must try something. Father, I beg of you, try to do something."

I stammered after him, "Yes, yes; let us try to do something."

And we knew of nothing. Gaspard offered to take Veronique on his back and swim with her to a place of safety. Pierre suggested a raft. Cyprien finally said:

"If we could only reach the church."

Above the waters the church remained standing, with its little square steeple. We were separated from it by seven houses. Our farmhouse, the first of the village, adjoined a higher building, which, in turn, leaned against the next. Perhaps, by way of the roofs, we would be able to reach the parsonage. A number of people must have taken refuge there already, for the neighboring roofs were vacant, and we could hear voices that surely came from the steeple. But what dangers must be run to reach them.

"It is impossible," said Pierre. "The house of the Raimbeaus is too high; we would need ladders."

"I am going to try it," said Cyprien. "I will return if the way is impracticable. Otherwise, we will all go and we will have to carry the girls."

I let him go. He was right. We had to try the impossible. He had succeeded, by the aid of an iron hook fixed in a chimney, in climbing to the next house, when his wife, Aimee, raising her head, noticed that he was no longer with us. She screamed:

"Where is he? I don't want him to leave me. We are together, we shall die together."

When she saw him on the top of the house she ran over the tiles, still holding her children. And she called out:

"Cyprien, wait for me. I am going with you. I am going to die with you."

She persisted. He leaned over, pleading with her, promising to come back, telling her that he was going for the rescue of all of us. But, with a wild air, she shook her head, repeating "I am going with you. I am going with you."

He had to take the children. Then he helped her up. We could follow them along the crest of the house. They walked slowly. She had taken the children again, and at every step he turned and supported her.

"Get her to a safe place, and return." I shouted.

I saw him wave his hand, but the roaring of the water prevented my hearing his answer. Soon we could not see them. They had descended to the roof of the next house. At the end of five minutes they appeared upon the third roof, which must have been very steep, for they went on hands and knees along the summit. A sudden terror seized me. I put my hands to my mouth and shouted, "Come back. Come back."

Then all of us shouted together. Our voices stopped them for a moment, but they continued on their way. They reached the angle formed by the street upon which faced the Raimbeau house, a high structure, with a roof at least ten feet above those of the neighboring houses. For a moment they hesitated. Then Cyprien climbed up a chimney pipe, with the agility of a cat. Aimee, who must have consented to wait for him, stood on the tiles. We saw her plainly, black and enlarged against the pale sky, straining her children to her bosom. And it was then that the horrifying trouble began.

The Raimbeau house, originally intended for a factory, was very flimsily built. Besides, the facade was exposed to the current in the street. I thought I could see it tremble from the attacks of the water; and, with a contraction of the throat, I watched Cyprien cross the roof. Suddenly a rumbling was heard. The moon rose, a round moon, whose yellow face lighted up the immense lake. Not a detail of the catastrophe was lost to us. The Raimbeau house collapsed. We gave a cry of terror as we saw Cyprien disappear. As the house crumbled we could distinguish nothing but a tempest, a swirling of waves beneath the debris of the roof. Then calm was restored, the surface became smooth; and out of the black hole of the engulfed house projected the skeleton of its framework. There was a mass of entangled beams, and, amongst them, I seemed to see a body moving, something living making superhuman efforts.

"He lives." I cried. "Oh, God be praised. He lives."

We laughed nervously; we clapped our hands, as if saved ourselves.

"He is going to raise himself up," said Pierre.

"Yes, yes," said Gaspard, "he is trying to seize the beam on his left."

But our laugh ceased. We had just realized the terrible situation in which Cyprien was placed. During the fall of the house his feet had been caught between two beams, and he hung head downward within a few inches of the water. On the roof of the next house Aimee was still standing, holding her two children. A convulsive tremor shook her. She did not take her eyes from her husband, a few yards below her. And, mad with horror, she emitted without cessation a lamentable sound like the howling of a dog.

"We can't let him die like that," said Jacques, distracted. "We must get down there."

"Perhaps we could slide down the beams and save him," remarked Pierre.

And they started toward the neighboring roof, when the second house collapsed, leaving a gap in the route. Then a chill seized us. We mechanically grasped each other's hands, wringing them cruelly as we watched the harrowing sight.

Cyprien had tried at first to stiffen his body. With extraordinary strength, he had lifted himself above the water, holding his body in an oblique position. Rut the strain was too great. Nevertheless, he struggled, tried to reach some of the beams, felt around him for something to hold to. Then, resigning himself, he fell back again, hanging limp.

Death was slow in coming. The water barely covered his hair, and it rose very gradually. He must have felt its coolness on his brain. A wave wet his brow; others closed his eyes. Slowly we saw his head disappear.

The women, at our feet, had buried their faces in their clasped hands. We, ourselves, fell to our knees, our arms outstretched, weeping, stammering supplications.

On the other roof Aimee, still standing, her children clasped to her bosom, howled mournfully into the night.

IV

I know not how long we remained in a stupor after that tragedy. When I came to, the water had risen. It was now on a level with the tiles. The roof was a narrow island, emerging from the immense sheet. To the right and the left the houses must have crumbled.

"We are moving," murmured Rose, who clung to the tiles.

And we all experienced the effect of rolling, as if the roof had become detached and turned into a raft. The swift currents seemed to be drifting us away. Then, when we looked at the church clock, immovable opposite us, the dizziness ceased; we found ourselves in the same place in the midst of the waves.

Then the water began an attack. Until then the stream had followed the street; but the debris that encumbered it deflected the course. And when a drifting object, a beam, came within reach of the current, it seized it and directed it against the house like a battering-ram. Soon ten, a dozen, beams were attacking us on all sides. The water roared. Our feet were spattered with foam. We heard the dull moaning of the house full of water. There were moments when the attacks became frenzied, when the beams battered fiercely; and then we thought that the end was near, that the walls would open and deliver us to the river.

Gaspard had risked himself upon the edge of the roof. He had seized a rafter and drawn it to him.

"We must defend ourselves," he cried.

Jacques, on his side, had stopped a long pole in its passage. Pierre helped him. I cursed my age that left me without strength, as feeble as a child. But the defense was organized—a drill between three men and a river. Gaspard, holding his beam in readiness, awaited the driftwood that the current sent against us, and he stopped it a short distance from the walls. At times the shock was so rude that he fell. Beside him Jacques and Pierre manipulated the long pole. During nearly an hour that unending fight continued. And the water retained its tranquil obstinacy, invincible.

Then Jacques and Pierre succumbed, prostrated; while Gaspard, in a last violent thrust, had his beam wrested from him by the current. The combat was useless.

Marie and Veronique had thrown themselves into each other's arms. They repeated incessantly one phrase—a phrase of terror that I still hear ringing in my ears:

"I don't want to die. I don't want to die."

Rose put her arms about them. She tried to console them, to reassure them. And she herself, trembling, raised her face and cried out, in spite of herself, "I don't want to die."

Aunt Agathe alone said nothing. She no longer prayed, no longer made the sign of the cross. Bewildered, her eyes roamed about, and she tried to smile when her glance met mine.

The water was beating against the tiles now. There was no hope of help. We still heard the voices in the direction of the church; two lanterns had passed in the distance; and the silence spread over the immense yellow sheet. The people of Saintin, who owned boats, must have been surprised before us.

Gaspard continued to wander over the Roof. Suddenly he called us. "Look." he said. "Help me—hold me tight."

He had a pole and he was watching an enormous black object that was gently drifting toward the house. It was the roof of a shed, made of strong boards, and that was floating like a raft. When it was within reach he stopped it with the pole, and, as he felt himself being carried off, he called to us. We held him around the waist.

Then, as the mass entered the current, it returned against our roof so violently that we were afraid of seeing it smashed into splinters.

Gaspard jumped upon it boldly. He went over it carefully, to assure himself of its solidity. He laughed, saying joyously, "Grandfather, we are saved. Don't cry any more, you women. A real boat. Look, my feet are dry. And it will easily carry all of us."

Still, he thought it well to make it more solid. He caught some floating beams and bound them to it with a rope that Pierre had brought up for an emergency. Gaspard even fell into the water, but at our screams he laughed. He knew the water well; he could swim three miles in the Garonne at a stretch. Getting up again, he shook himself, crying:

"Come, get on it. Don't lose any time."

The women were on their knees. Gaspard had to carry Veronique and Marie to the middle of the raft, where he made them sit down.

Rose and Aunt Agathe slid down the tiles and placed themselves beside the young girls. At this moment I looked toward the church. Aimee was still in the same place. She was leaning now against a chimney, holding her children up at arm's length, for the water was to her waist.

"Don't grieve, grandfather," said Gaspard. "We will take her off on the way."

Pierre and Jacques were already on the raft, so I jumped on. Gaspard was the last one aboard. He gave us poles that he had prepared and that were to serve us as oars. He had a very long one that he used with great skill. We let him do all the commanding. At an order from him, we braced our poles against the tiles to put out into the stream. But it seemed as if the raft was attached to the roof. In spite of all our efforts, we could not budge it. At each new effort the current swung us violently against the house. And it was a dangerous maneuver, for the shock threatened to break up the planks composing the raft.

So once again we were made to feel our helplessness. We had thought ourselves saved, and we were still at the mercy of the river. I even regretted that the women were not on the roof; for, every minute, I expected to see them precipitated into the boiling torrent. But when I suggested regaining our refuge they all cried, "No, no. Let us try again. Better die here."

Gaspard no longer laughed. We renewed our efforts, bending to our poles with redoubled energy. Pierre then had the idea to climb up on the roof and draw us, by means of a rope, towards the left. He was thus able to draw us out of the current. Then, when he again jumped upon the raft, a few thrusts of our poles sent us out into the open. But Gaspard recalled the promise he had made me to stop for our poor Aimee, whose plaintive moans had never ceased. For that purpose it was necessary to cross the street, where the terrible current existed. He consulted me by a glance. I was completely upset. Never had such a combat raged within me. We would have to expose eight lives. And yet I had not the strength to resist the mournful appeal.

"Yes, yes," I said to Gaspard. "We can not possibly go away without her."

He lowered his head without a word, and began using his pole against all the walls left standing. We passed the neighboring house, but as soon as we emerged into the street a cry escaped us. The current, which had again seized us, carried us back against our house. We were whirled round like a leaf, so rapidly that our cry was cut short by the smashing of the raft against the tiles. There was a rending sound, the planks were loosened and wrenched apart, and we were all thrown into the water. I do not know what happened then. I remember that when I sank I saw Aunt Agathe floating, sustained by her skirts, until she went down backward, head first, without a struggle.

A sharp pain brought me to. Pierre was dragging me by the hair along the tiles. I lay still, stupidly watching. Pierre had plunged in again. And, in my confused state, I was surprised to see Gaspard at the spot where my brother had disappeared. The young man had Veronique in his arms. When he had placed her near me he again jumped in, bringing up Marie, her face so waxy white that I thought her dead. Then he plunged again. But this time he searched in vain. Pierre had joined him. They talked and gave each other indications that I could not hear. As they drew themselves up on the roof, I cried, "And Aunt Agathe? And Jacques? And Rose?"

They shook their heads. Large tears coursed down their cheeks. They explained to me that Jacques had struck his head against a beam and that Rose had been carried down with her husband's body, to which she clung. Aunt Agathe had not reappeared.

Raising myself, I looked toward the roof, where Aimee stood. The water was rising constantly. Aimee was now silent. I could see her upstretched arms holding her children out of the water. Then they all sank, the water closed over them beneath the drowsy light of the moon.

V

There were only five of us on the roof now. The water left us but a narrow band along the ridge. One of the chimneys had just been carried away. We had to raise Marie and Veronique, who were still unconscious, and support them almost in a standing position to prevent the waves washing over their legs. At last, their senses returned, and our anguish increased upon seeing them wet, shivering and crying miserably that they did not wish to die.

The end had come. The destroyed village was marked by a few vestiges of walls. Alone, the church reared its steeple intact, from whence came the voices—a murmur of human beings in a refuge. There were no longer any sounds of falling houses, like a cart of stones suddenly discharged. It was as if we were abandoned, shipwrecked, a thousand miles from land.

One moment we thought we heard the dip of oars. Ah. What hopeful music. How we all strained our eyes into space. We held our breath. But we could see nothing. The yellow sheet stretched away, spotted with black shadows. But none of those shadows—tops of trees, remnants of walls— moved. Driftwood, weeds, empty barrels caused us false joy. We waved our handkerchiefs until, realizing our error, we again succumbed to our anxiety.

"Ah, I see it." cried Gaspard, suddenly. "Look over there. A large boat."

And he pointed out a distant speck. I could see nothing, neither could Pierre. But Gaspard insisted it was a boat. The sound of oars became distinct. At last, we saw it. It was proceeding slowly and seemed to be circling about us without approaching. I remember that we were like mad. We raised our arms in our fury; we shouted with all our might. And we insulted the boat, called it cowardly. But, dark and silent, it glided away slowly. Was it really a boat? I do not know to this day. When it disappeared it carried our last hope.

We were expecting every second to be engulfed with the house. It was undermined and was probably supported by one solid wall, which, in giving way, would pull everything with it. But what terrified me most was to feel the roof sway under our feet. The house would perhaps hold out overnight, but the tiles were sinking in, beaten and pierced by beams. We had taken refuge on the left side on some solid rafters. Then these rafters seemed to weaken. Certainly they would sink if all five of us remained in so small a space.

For some minutes my brother Pierre had been twisting his soldierly mustache, frowning and muttering to himself. The growing danger that surrounded him and against which his courage availed nothing, was wearing out his endurance. He spat two or three times into the water, with an expression of contemptuous anger. Then, as we sank lower, he made up his mind; he started down the roof.

"Pierre. Pierre." I cried, fearing to comprehend.

He turned and said quietly:

"Adieu, Louis. You see, it is too long for me. And it will leave more room for you."

And, first throwing in his pipe, he plunged, adding, "Good night. I have had enough."

He did not come up. He was not a strong swimmer, and he probably abandoned himself, heart-broken at the death of our dear ones and at our ruin.

Two o'clock sounded from the steeple of the church. The night would soon end—that horrible night already so filled with agony and tears. Little by little, beneath our feet, the small dry space grew smaller. The current had changed again. The drift, passed to the right of the village, floating slowly, as if the water, nearing its highest level, was reposing, tired and lazy.

Gaspard suddenly took off his shoes and his shirt. I watched him for a moment as he wrung his hands. When I questioned him he said, "Listen, grandfather; it is killing me to wait. I cannot stay here. Let me do as I wish. I will save her."

He was speaking of Veronique. I opposed him. He would never have the strength to carry the young girl to the church. But he was obstinate.

"Yes, I can. My arms are strong. I feel myself able. You will see. I love her—I will save her."

I was silent. I drew Marie to my breast. Then he thought I was reproaching the selfishness of his love. He stammered, "I will return and get Marie. I swear it. I will find a boat and organize a rescue party. Have confidence in me, grandfather."

Rapidly, he explained to Veronique that she must not struggle, that she must submit without a movement, and that she must not be afraid. The young girl answered "yes" to everything, with a distracted look. Then, after making the sign of the cross, he slid down the roof, holding Veronique by a rope that he had looped under her arms. She gave a scream, beat the water with arms and legs, and, suffocated, she fainted.

"I like this better." Gaspard called to me. "Now, I can answer for her."

It can be imagined with what agony I followed them with my eyes. On the white surface, I could see Gaspard's slightest movement. He held the young girl by means of the rope that he coiled around his neck; and he carried her thus, half thrown over his right shoulder. The crushing weight bore him under at times. But he advanced, swimming with superhuman strength. I was no longer in doubt. He had traversed a third of the distance when he struck against something submerged. The shock was terrible. Both disappeared. Then I saw him reappear alone. The rope must have snapped. He plunged twice. At last, he came up with Veronique, whom he again took on his back. But without the rope to hold her, she weighed him down more than ever. Still, he advanced. A tremor shook me as I saw them approaching the church. Suddenly, I saw some beams bearing down upon them. A second shock separated them and the waters closed over them.

From this moment, I was stupefied. I had but the instinct of the animal looking out for its own safety. When the water advanced, I retreated. In that stupor, I heard someone laughing, without explaining to myself who it was. The dawn appeared, a great white daybreak. It was very fresh and very calm, as on the bank of a pond, the surface of which awakens before sunrise. But the laughter sounded continually.

Turning, I saw Marie, standing in her wet clothes. It was she who was laughing.

Ah. The poor, dear child. How sweet and pretty she was at that early hour. I saw her stoop, take up some water in the hollow of her hand, and wash her face. Then she coiled her beautiful blonde hair. Doubtless, she imagined she was in her little room, dressing while the church bell rang merrily. And she continued to laugh her childish laugh, her eyes bright and her face happy.

I, too, began to laugh, infected with her madness. Terror had destroyed her mind; and it was a mercy, so charmed did she appear with the beauty of the morning.

I let her hasten, not understanding, shaking my head tenderly. When she considered herself ready to go, she sang one of her canticles in her clear crystalline voice. But, interrupting herself, she cried, as if responding to someone who had called her:

"I am coming, I am coming."

She took up the canticle again, went down the roof, and entered the water. It covered her softly, without a ripple. I had not ceased smiling. I looked with happiness upon the spot where she had just disappeared.

Then, I remembered nothing more. I was alone on the roof. The water had risen. A chimney was standing, and I must have clung to it with all my strength, like an animal that dreads death. Then, nothing, nothing, a black pit, oblivion.

VI

Why am I still here? They tell me that people from Saintin came toward six o'clock, with boats, and that they found me lying on a chimney, unconscious. The water was cruel not to have carried me away to be with those who were dear to me.

All the others are gone. The babes in swaddling clothes, the girls to be married, the young married couples, the old married couples. And I, I live like a useless weed, coarse and dried, rooted in the rock. If I had the courage, I would say like Pierre, "I have had enough. Good night." And I would throw myself into the Garonne.

I have no child, my house is destroyed, my fields are devastated. Oh. The evenings when we were all at table, and the gaiety surrounded me and kept me young. Oh. The great days of harvest and vintage when we all worked, and when we returned to the house proud of our wealth. Oh. The handsome children and the fruitful vines, the beautiful girls and the golden grain, the joy of my old age, the living recompense of my entire life. Since all that is gone, why should I live?

There is no consolation. I do not want help. I will give my fields to the village people who still have their children. They will find the courage to clear the land of the flotsam and cultivate it anew. When one has no children, a corner is large enough to die in.

I had one desire, one only desire. I wished to recover the bodies of my family, to bury them beneath a slab, where I should soon rejoin them. It was said that, at Toulouse, a large number of bodies carried down the stream, had been taken from the water. I decided to make the trip.

What a terrible disaster. Nearly two thousand houses in ruins; seven hundred deaths; all the bridges carried away; a whole district razed, buried in the mud; atrocious tragedies; twenty thousand half-clad wretches starving to death; the city in a pestilential condition; mourning everywhere; the streets filled with funeral processions; financial aid powerless to heal the wounds. But I walked through it all without seeing anything. I had my ruins; I had my dead, to crush me.

I was told that many of the bodies had been buried in trenches in a corner of the cemetery. Only, they had had the forethought to photograph the unidentified. And it was among these lamentable photographs that I found Gaspard and Veronique. They had been clasped passionately in each other's arms, exchanging in death their bridal kiss. It had been necessary to break their arms in order to separate them. But, first, they had been photographed together; and they sleep together beneath the sod.

I have nothing but them, the image of those two handsome children; bloated by the water, disfigured, retaining upon their livid faces the heroism of their love. I look at them, and I weep.

THE FOUR DAYS OF JEAN GOURDON

I
SPRING

On that particular day, at about five o'clock in the morning, the sun entered with delightful abruptness into the little room I occupied at the house of my uncle Lazare, parish priest of the hamlet of Dourgues. A broad yellow ray fell upon ray closed eyelids, and I awoke in light.

My room, which was whitewashed, and had deal furniture, was full of attractive gaiety. I went to the window and gazed at the Durance, which traced its broad course amidst the dark green verdure of the valley. Fresh puffs of wind caressed my face, and the murmur of the trees and river seemed to call me to them.

I gently opened my door. To get out I had to pass through my uncle's room. I proceeded on tip-toe, fearing the creaking of my thick boots might awaken the worthy man, who was still slumbering with a smiling countenance. And I trembled at the sound of the church bell tolling the Angelus. For some days past my uncle Lazare had been following me about everywhere, looking sad and annoyed. He would perhaps have prevented me going over there to the edge of the river, and hiding myself among the willows on the bank, so as to watch for Babet passing, that tall dark girl who had come with the spring.

But my uncle was sleeping soundly. I felt something like remorse in deceiving him and running away in this manner. I stayed for an instant and gazed on his calm countenance, with its gentle expression enhanced by rest, and I recalled to mind with feeling the day when he had come to fetch me in the chilly and deserted home which my mother's funeral was leaving. Since that day, what tenderness, what devotedness, what good advice he had bestowed on me, He had given me his knowledge and his kindness, all his intelligence and all his heart.

I was tempted for a moment to cry out to him, "Get up, uncle Lazare, let us go for a walk together along that path you are so fond of beside the Durance. You will enjoy the fresh air and morning sun. You will see what an appetite you will have on your return,"

And Babet, who was going down to the river in her light morning gown, and whom I should not be able to see. My uncle would be there, and I would have to lower my eyes. It must be so nice under the willows, lying flat on one's stomach, in the fine grass, I felt a languid feeling creeping over me, and, slowly, taking short steps, holding my breath, I reached the door. I went downstairs, and began running like a madcap in the delightful, warm May morning air.

The sky was quite white on the horizon, with exquisitely delicate blue and pink tints. The pale sun seemed like a great silver lamp, casting a shower of bright rays into the Durance. And the broad, sluggish river, expanding lazily over the red sand, extended from one end of the valley to the other, like a stream of liquid metal. To the west, a line of low rugged hills threw slight violet streaks on the pale sky.

I had been living in this out-of-the-way corner for ten years. How often had I kept my uncle Lazare waiting to give me my Latin lesson; the worthy man wanted to make me learned. But I was on the other side of the Durance, ferreting out magpies, discovering a hill which I had not yet climbed. Then, on my return, there were remonstrances: the Latin was forgotten, my poor uncle scolded me for having torn my trousers, and he shuddered when he noticed sometimes that the skin underneath was cut. The valley was mine, really mine; I had conquered it with my legs, and I was the real landlord by right of friendship. And that bit of river, those two leagues of the Durance, how I loved them, how well we understood one another when together, I knew all the whims of my dear stream, its anger, its charming ways, its different features at each hour of the day.

When I reached the water's edge on that particular morning, I felt something like giddiness at seeing it so gentle and so white. It had never looked so gay. I slipped rapidly beneath the willows, to an open space where a broad patch of sunlight fell on the dark grass. There I laid me down on my stomach, listening, watching the pathway by which Babet would come, through the branches.

"Oh, How sound uncle Lazare must be sleeping," I thought.

And I extended myself at full length on the moss. The sun struck gentle heat into my back, whilst my breast, buried in the grass, was quite cool.

Have you never examined the turf, at close quarters, with your eyes on the blades of grass? Whilst I was waiting for Babet, I pried indiscreetly into a tuft which was really a whole world. In my bunch of grass there were streets, cross roads, public squares, entire cities. At the bottom of it, I distinguished a great dark patch where the shoots of the previous spring were decaying sadly, then slender stalks were growing up, stretching out, bending into a multitude of elegant forms, and producing frail colonnades, churches, virgin forests. I saw two lean insects wandering in the midst of this immensity; the poor children were certainly lost, for they went from colonnade to colonnade, from street to street, in an affrighted, anxious way.

It was just at this moment that, on raising my eyes, I saw Babet's white skirts standing out against the dark ground at the top of the pathway. I recognized her printed calico gown, which was grey, with small blue flowers. I sunk down deeper in the grass, I heard my heart thumping against the earth and almost raising me with slight jerks. My breast was burning now; I no longer felt the freshness of the dew.

The young girl came nimbly down the pathway, her skirts skimming the ground with a swinging motion that charmed me, I saw her at full length, quite erect, in her proud and happy gracefulness. She had no idea I was there behind the willows; she walked with a light step, she ran without giving a thought to the wind, which slightly raised her gown. I could distinguish her feet, trotting along quickly, quickly, and a piece of her white stockings, which was perhaps as large as one's hand, and which made me blush in a manner that was alike sweet and painful.

Oh, then, I saw nothing else, neither the Durance, nor the willows, nor the whiteness of the sky. What cared I for the valley; it was no longer my sweetheart; I was quite indifferent to its joy and its sadness. What cared I for my friends, the stories, and the trees on the hills, the river could run away all at once if it liked; I would not have regretted it.

And the spring, I did not care a bit about the spring, Had it borne away the sun that warmed my back, its leaves, its rays, all its May morning, I should have remained there, in ecstasy, gazing at Babet, running along the pathway, and swinging her skirts deliciously. For Babet had taken the valley's place in my heart, Babet was the spring; I had never spoken to her. Both of us blushed when we met one another in my uncle Lazare's church. I could have vowed she detested me.

She talked on that particular day for a few minutes with the women who were washing. The sound of her pearly laughter reached as far as me, mingled with the loud voice of the Durance. Then she stooped down to take a little water in the hollow of her hand; but the bank was high, and

Babet, who was on the point of slipping, saved herself by clutching the grass. I gave a frightful shudder, which made my blood run cold. I rose hastily, and, without feeling ashamed, without reddening, ran to the young girl. She cast a startled look at me; then she began to smile. I bent down, at the risk of falling. I succeeded in filling my right hand with water by keeping my fingers close together. And I presented this new sort of cup to Babet' asking her to drink.

The women who were washing laughed. Babet, confused, did not dare accept; she hesitated, and half turned her head away. At last she made up her mind, and delicately pressed her lips to the tips of my fingers; but she had waited too long, all the water had run away. Then she burst out laughing, she became a child again, and I saw very well that she was making fun of me.

I was very silly. I bent forward again. This time I took the water in both hands and hastened to put them to Babet's lips. She drank, and I felt the warm kiss from her mouth run up my arms to my breast, which it filled with heat.

"Oh, How my uncle must sleep," I murmured to myself.

Just as I said that, I perceived a dark shadow beside me, and, having turned round, I saw my uncle Lazare, in person, a few paces away, watching Babet and me as if offended. His cassock appeared quite white in the sun; in his look I saw reproaches which made me feel inclined to cry.

Babet was very much afraid. She turned quite red, and hurried off stammering, "Thanks, Monsieur Jean, I thank you very much."

As for me, wiping my wet hands, I stood motionless and confused before my uncle Lazare.

The worthy man, with folded arms, and bringing back a corner of his cassock, watched Babet, who was running up the pathway without turning her head. Then, when she had disappeared behind the hedges, he lowered his eyes to me, and I saw his pleasant countenance smile sadly.

"Jean," he said to me, "come into the broad walk. Breakfast is not ready. We have half an hour to spare."

He set out with his rather heavy tread, avoiding the tufts of grass wet with dew. A part of the bottom of his cassock that was dragging along the ground, made a dull crackling sound. He held his breviary under his arm; but he had forgotten his morning lecture, and he advanced dreamily, with bowed head, and without uttering a word.

His silence tormented me. He was generally so talkative. My anxiety increased at each step. He had certainly seen me giving Babet water to drink. What a sight, O Lord, The young girl, laughing and blushing, kissed the tips of my fingers, whilst I, standing on tip-toe, stretching out my arms, was leaning forward as if to kiss her. My action now seemed to me frightfully audacious. And all my timidity returned. I inquired of myself how I could have dared to have my fingers kissed so sweetly.

And my uncle Lazare, who said nothing, who continued walking with short steps in front of me, without giving a single glance at the old trees he loved, He was assuredly preparing a sermon. He was only taking me into the broad walk to scold me at his ease. It would occupy at least an hour; breakfast would get cold, and I would be unable to return to the water's edge and dream of the warm burns that Babet's lips had left on my hands.

We were in the broad walk. This walk, which was wide and short, ran beside the river; it was shaded by enormous oak trees, with trunks lacerated by seams, stretching out their great, tall branches. The fine grass spread like a carpet beneath the trees, and the sun, riddling the foliage, embroidered this carpet with a rosaceous pattern in gold. In the distance, all around, extended raw green meadows.

My uncle went to the bottom of the walk, without altering his step and without turning round. Once there, he stopped, and I kept beside him, understanding that the terrible moment had arrived.

The river made a sharp curve; a low parapet at the end of the walk formed a sort of terrace. This vault of shade opened on a valley of light. The country expanded wide before us, for several leagues. The sun was rising in the heavens, where the silvery rays of morning had become transformed into a stream of gold; blinding floods of light ran from the horizon, along the hills, and spread out into the plain with the glare of fire.

After a moment's silence, my uncle Lazare turned towards me.

"Good heavens, the sermon," I thought, and I bowed my head. My uncle pointed out the valley to me, with an expansive gesture; then, drawing himself up, he said, slowly, "Look, Jean, there is the spring. The earth is full of joy, my boy, and I have brought you here, opposite this plain of light, to show you the first smiles of the young season. Observe what brilliancy and sweetness, Warm perfumes rise from the country and pass across our faces like puffs of life."

He was silent and seemed dreaming. I had raised my head, astonished, breathing at ease. My uncle was not preaching.

"It is a beautiful morning," he continued, "a morning of youth. Your eighteen summers find full enjoyment amidst this verdure which is at most eighteen days old. All is great brightness and perfume, is it not? The broad valley seems to you a delightful place: the river is there to give you its freshness, the trees to lend you their shade, the whole country to speak to you of tenderness, the heavens themselves to kiss those horizons that you are searching with hope and desire. The spring belongs to fellows of your age. It teaches the boys how to give young girls to drink."

I hung my head again. My uncle Lazare had certainly seen me.

"An old fellow like me," he continued, "unfortunately knows what trust to place in the charms of spring. I, my poor Jean, I love the Durance because it waters these meadows and gives life to all the valley; I love this young foliage because it proclaims to me the coming of the fruits of summer and autumn; I love this sky because it is good to us, because its warmth hastens the fecundity of the earth. I should have had to tell you this one day or other; I prefer telling it you now, at this early hour. It is spring itself that is giving you the lesson. The earth is a vast workshop wherein there is never a slack season. Observe this flower at our feet; to you it is perfume; to me it is labor, it accomplishes its task by producing its share of life, a little black seed which will work in its turn, next spring. And, now, search the vast horizon. All this joy is but the act of generation. If the country be smiling, it is because it is beginning the everlasting task again. Do you hear it now, breathing hard, full of activity and haste? he leaves sigh, the flowers are in a hurry, the corn grows without pausing; all the plants, all the herbs are quarrelling as to which shall spring up the quickest; and the running water, the river comes to assist in the common labor, and the young sun which rises in the heavens is entrusted with the duty of enlivening the everlasting task of the laborers."

At this point my uncle made me look him straight in the face. He concluded in these terms, "Jean, you hear what your friend the spring says to you. He is youth, but he is preparing ripe age; his bright smile is but the gaiety of labor. Summer will be powerful, autumn bountiful, for the spring is singing at this moment, while courageously performing its work."

I looked very stupid. I understood my uncle Lazare. He was positively preaching me a sermon, in which he told me I was an idle fellow and that the time had come to work.

My uncle appeared as much embarrassed as myself. After having hesitated for some instants he said, slightly stammering, "Jean, you were wrong not to have come and told me all, as you love Babet and Babet loves you."

"Babet loves me," I exclaimed.

My uncle made me an ill-humored gesture.

"Eh, allow me to speak. I don't want another avowal. She owned it to me herself."

"She owned that to you, she owned that to you,"

And I suddenly threw my arms round my uncle Lazare's neck.

"Oh, how nice that is," I added. "I had never spoken to her, truly. She told you that at the confessional, didn't she? I would never have dared ask her if she loved me, and I would never have known anything. Oh, how I thank you,"

My uncle Lazare was quite red. He felt that he had just committed a blunder. He had imagined that this was not my first meeting with the young girl, and here he gave me a certainty, when as yet I only dared dream of a hope. He held his tongue now; it was I who spoke with volubility.

"I understand all," I continued. "You are right, I must work to win Babet. But you will see how courageous I shall be. Ah, how good you are, my uncle Lazare, and how well you speak, I understand what the spring says: I, also, will have a powerful summer and an autumn of abundance. One is well placed here, one sees all the valley; I am young like it, I feel youth within me demanding to accomplish its task."

My uncle calmed me.

"Very good, Jean," he said to me. "I had long hoped to make a priest of you, and I imparted to you my knowledge with that sole aim. But what I saw this morning at the waterside compels me to definitely give up my fondest hope. It is Heaven that disposes of us. You will love the Almighty in another way. You cannot now remain in this village, and I only wish you to return when ripened by age and work. I have chosen the trade of printer for you; your education will serve you. One of my friends, who is a printer at Grenoble, is expecting you next Monday."

I felt anxious.

"And I shall come back and marry Babet?" I inquired. My uncle smiled imperceptibly; and, without answering in a direct manner, said, "The remainder is the will of Heaven."

"You are heaven, and I have faith in your kindness. Oh, uncle, see that Babet does not forget me. I will work for her."

Then my uncle Lazare again pointed out to me the valley which the warm golden light was overspreading more and more.

"There is hope," he said to me. "Do not be as old as I am, Jean. Forget my sermon, be as ignorant as this land. It does not trouble about the autumn; it is all engrossed with the joy of its smile; it labors, courageously and without a care. It hopes."

And we returned to the parsonage, strolling along slowly in the grass, which was scorched by the sun, and chatting with concern of our approaching separation.

Breakfast was cold, as I had foreseen; but that did not trouble me much. I had tears in my eyes each time I looked at my uncle Lazare. And, at the thought of Babet, my heart beat fit to choke me.

I do not remember what I did during the remainder of the day. I think I went and lay down under the willows at the riverside. My uncle was right, the earth was at work. On placing my ear to the grass I seemed to hear continual sounds. Then I dreamed of what my life would be. Buried in the grass until nightfall, I arranged an existence full of labor divided between Babet and my uncle Lazare. The energetic youthfulness of the soil had penetrated my breast, which I pressed with force against the common mother, and at times I imagined myself to be one of the strong willows that lived around me. In the evening I could not dine. My uncle, no doubt, understood the thoughts that were choking me, for he feigned not to notice my want of appetite. As soon as I was able to rise from table, I hastened to return and breathe the open air outside.

A fresh breeze rose from the river, the dull splashing of which I heard in the distance. A soft light fell from the sky. The valley expanded, peaceful and transparent, like a dark shoreless ocean. There were vague sounds in the air, a sort of impassioned tremor, like a great flapping of wings passing above my head. Penetrating perfumes rose with the cool air from the grass.

I had gone out to see Babet; I knew she came to the parsonage every night and I went and placed myself in ambush behind a hedge. I had got rid of my timidity of the morning; I considered it quite natural to be waiting for her there, because she loved me and I had to tell her of my departure.

"When I perceived her skirts in the limpid night, I advanced noiselessly. Then I murmured in a low voice, "Babet, Babet, I am here.""

She did not recognize me, at first, and started with fright. When she discovered who it was, she seemed still more frightened, which very much surprised me.

"It's you, Monsieur Jean," she said to me. "What are you doing there? What do you want?"

I was beside her and took her hand.

"You love me fondly, do you not?"

"I who told you that?"

"My uncle Lazare."

She stood there in confusion. Her hand began to tremble in mine. As she was on the point of running away, I took her other hand. We were face to face, in a sort of hollow in the hedge, and I felt Babet's panting breath running all warm over my face. The freshness of the air, the rustling silence of the night, hung around us.

"I don't know," stammered the young girl, "I never said that, his reverence the curée misunderstood. For mercy's sake, let me be, I am in a hurry."

"No, no," I continued, "I want you to know that I am going away to-morrow and to promise to love me always."

"You are leaving tomorrow,"

Oh, that sweet cry, and how tenderly Babet uttered it, I seem still to hear her apprehensive voice full of affliction and love.

"You see," I exclaimed in my turn, "that my uncle Lazare said the truth. Besides, he never tells fibs. You love me, you love me, Babet, Your lips, this morning confided the secret very softly to my fingers."

And I made her sit down at the foot of the hedge. My memory has retained my first chat of love in its absolute innocence. Babet listened to me like a little sister. She was no longer afraid; she told me the story of her love. And there were solemn sermons, ingenious avowals, projects without end. She vowed she would marry no one but me, I vowed to deserve her hand by labor and tenderness. There was a cricket behind the hedge, who accompanied our chat with his chant of hope, and all the valley, whispering in the dark, took pleasure in hearing us talk so softly. On separating, we forgot to kiss each other.

When I returned to my little room, it appeared to me that I had left it for at least a year. That day which was so short, seemed an eternity of happiness. It was the warmest and most sweetly-scented spring-day of my life, and the remembrance of it is now like the distant, faltering voice of my youth.

II
SUMMER

When I awoke at about three o'clock in the morning on that particular day, I was lying on the hard ground tired out, and with my face bathed in perspiration. The hot heavy atmosphere of a July night weighed me down.

My companions were sleeping around me, wrapped in their hooded cloaks; they speckled the grey ground with black, and the obscure plain panted; I fancied I heard the heavy breathing of a slumbering multitude. Indistinct sounds, the neighing of horses, the clash of arms rang out amidst the rustling silence.

The army had halted at about midnight, and we had received orders to lie down and sleep. We had been marching for three days, scorched by the sun and blinded by dust. The enemy were at length in front of us, over there on those hills on the horizon. At daybreak a decisive battle would be fought.

I had been a victim to despondency. For three days I had been as if trampled on, without energy and without thought for the future. It was the excessive fatigue, indeed, that had just awakened me. Now, lying on my back, with my eyes wide open, I was thinking whilst gazing into the night, I thought of this battle, this butchery, which the sun was about to light up. For more than six years, at the first shot in each fight, I had been saying good-bye to those I loved the most fondly, Babet and uncle Lazare. And now, barely a month before my discharge, I had to say good-bye again, and this time perhaps for ever.

Then my thoughts softened. With closed eyelids I saw Babet and my uncle Lazare. How long it was since I had kissed them, I remembered the day of our separation; my uncle weeping because he was poor, and allowing me to leave like that, and Babet, in the evening, had vowed she would wait for me, and that she would never love another. I had had to quit all, my master at Grenoble, my friends at Dourgues. A few letters had come from time to time to tell me they always loved me, and that happiness was awaiting me in my well-beloved valley. And I, I was going to fight; I was going to get killed.

I began dreaming of my return. I saw my poor old uncle on the threshold of the parsonage extending his trembling arms; and behind him was Babet, quite red, smiling through her tears. I fell into their arms and kissed them, seeking for expressions.

Suddenly the beating of drums recalled me to stern reality. Daybreak had come, the grey plain expanded in the morning mist. The ground became full of life, indistinct forms appeared on all sides; a sound that became louder and louder filled the air; it was the call of bugles, the galloping of horses, the rumble of artillery, the shouting out of orders. War came threatening, amidst my dream of tenderness. I rose with difficulty; it seemed to me that my bones were broken, and that my head was about to split. I hastily got my men together; for I must tell you that I had won the rank of sergeant. We soon received orders to bear to the left and occupy a hillock above the plain.

As we were about to move, the sergeant-major came running along and shouting, "A letter for Sergeant Gourdon,"

And he handed me a dirty crumpled letter, which had been lying perhaps for a week in the leather bags of the post-office. I had only just time to recognize the writing of my uncle Lazare.

"Forward, march," shouted the major.

I had to march. For a few seconds I held the poor letter in my hand, devouring it with my eyes; it burnt my fingers; I would have given everything in the world to have sat down and wept at ease whilst reading it. I had to content myself with slipping it under my tunic against my heart.

I have never experienced such agony. By way of consolation I said to myself what my uncle had so often repeated to me: I was in the summer of my life, at the moment of the fierce struggle, and it was essential that I should perform my duty bravely, if I would have a peaceful and bountiful autumn. But these reasons exasperated me the more: this letter, which had come to speak to me of happiness, burnt my heart, which had revolted against the folly of war. And I could not even read it, I was perhaps going to die without knowing what it contained, without perusing my uncle Lazare's affectionate remarks for the last time.

We had reached the top of the hill. We were to await orders there to advance. The battle-field had been marvelously chosen to slaughter one another at ease. The immense plain expanded for several leagues, and was quite bare, without a house or tree. Hedges and bushes made slight spots on the whiteness of the ground. I have never since seen such a country, an ocean of dust, a chalky soil, bursting open here and there, and displaying its tawny bowels. And never either have I since witnessed a sky of such intense purity, a July day so lovely and so warm; at eight o'clock the sultry heat was already scorching our faces. Oh, the splendid morning, and what a sterile plain to kill and die in,

Firing had broken out with irregular crackling sounds, a long time since, supported by the solemn growl of the cannon. The enemy, Austrians dressed in white, had quitted the heights, and the plain was studded with long files of men, who looked to me about as big as insects. One might have thought it was an ant-hill in insurrection. Clouds of smoke hung over the battle-field. At times, when these clouds broke asunder, I perceived soldiers in flight, smitten with terrified panic. Thus there were currents of fright which bore men away, and outbursts of shame and courage which brought them back under fire.

I could neither hear the cries of the wounded, nor see the blood flow. I could only distinguish the dead which the battalions left behind them, and which resembled black patches. I began to watch the movements of the troops with curiosity, irritated at the smoke which hid a good half of the show, experiencing a sort of egotistic pleasure at the knowledge that I was in security, whilst others were dying.

At about nine o'clock we were ordered to advance. We went down the hill at the double and proceeded towards the centre which was giving way. The beat of our footsteps appeared to me funeral-like. The bravest among us were panting, pale and with haggard features.

I have made up my mind to tell the truth. At the first whistle of the bullets, the battalion suddenly came to a halt, tempted to fly.

"Forward, forward," shouted the chiefs.

But we were riveted to the ground, bowing our heads when a bullet whistled by our ears. This movement is instinctive; if shame had not restrained me, I would have thrown myself flat on my stomach in the dust.

"Before us was a huge veil of smoke which we dared not penetrate. Red flashes passed through this smoke. And, shuddering, we still stood still. But the bullets reached us; soldiers fell with yells. The chiefs shouted louder, "Forward, forward,"

The rear ranks, which they pushed on, compelled us to march. Then, closing our eyes, we made a fresh dash and entered the smoke.

We were seized with furious rage. When the cry of "Halt," resounded, we experienced difficulty in coming to a standstill. As soon as one is motionless, fear returns and one feels a wish to run away. Firing commenced. We shot in front of us, without aiming, finding some relief in discharging bullets into the smoke. I remember I pulled my trigger mechanically, with lips firmly set together and eyes wide open; I was no longer afraid, for, to tell the truth, I no longer knew if I existed. The only idea I had in my head, was that I would continue firing until all was over. My companion on the left received a bullet full in the face and fell on me; I brutally pushed him away, wiping my cheek which he had drenched with blood. And I resumed firing.

I still remember having seen our colonel, M. de Montrevert, firm and erect upon his horse, gazing quietly towards the enemy. That man appeared to me immense. He had no rifle to amuse himself with, and his breast was expanded to its full breadth above us. From time to time, he looked down, and exclaimed in a dry voice, "Close the ranks, close the ranks,"

We closed our ranks like sheep, treading on the dead, stupefied, and continuing firing. Until then, the enemy had only sent us bullets; a dull explosion was heard and a shell carried off five of our men. A battery which must have been opposite us and which we could not see, had just opened fire. The shells struck into the middle of us, almost at one spot, making a sanguinary gap which we closed unceasingly with the obstinacy of ferocious brutes.

"Close the ranks, close the ranks," the colonel coldly repeated.

We were giving the cannon human flesh. Each time a soldier was struck down, I was taking a step nearer death, I was approaching the spot where the shells were falling heavily, crushing the men whose turn had come to die. The corpses were forming heaps in that place, and soon the shells would strike into nothing more than a mound of mangled flesh; shreds of limbs flew about at each fresh discharge. We could no longer close the ranks.

The soldiers yelled, the chiefs themselves were moved.

"With the bayonet, with the bayonet,"

And amidst a shower of bullets the battalion rushed in fury towards the shells. The veil of smoke was torn asunder; we perceived the enemy's battery flaming red, which was firing at us from the mouths of all its pieces, on the summit of a hillock. But the dash forward had commenced, the shells stopped the dead only.

I ran beside Colonel Montrevert, whose horse had just been killed, and who was fighting like a simple soldier. Suddenly I was struck down; it seemed to me as if my breast opened and my shoulder was taken away. A frightful wind passed over my face.

And I fell. The colonel fell beside me. I felt myself dying. I thought of those I loved, and fainted whilst searching with a withering hand for my uncle Lazare's letter.

When I came to myself again I was lying on my side in the dust. I was annihilated by profound stupor. I gazed before me with my eyes wide open without seeing anything; it seemed to me that I had lost my limbs, and that my brain was empty. I did not suffer, for life seemed to have departed from my flesh.

The rays of a hot implacable sun fell upon my face like molten lead. I did not feel it. Life returned to me little by little; my limbs became lighter, my shoulder alone remained crushed beneath an enormous weight. Then, with the instinct of a wounded animal, I wanted to sit up. I uttered a cry of pain, and fell back upon the ground.

But I lived now, I saw, I understood. The plain spread out naked and deserted, all white in the broad sunlight. It exhibited its desolation beneath the intense serenity of heaven; heaps of corpses were sleeping in the warmth, and the trees that had been brought down, seemed to be other dead who were dying. There was not a breath of air. A frightful silence came from those piles of inanimate bodies; then, at times, there were dismal groans which broke this silence, and conveyed a long tremor to it. Slender clouds of grey smoke hanging over the low hills on the horizon, was all that broke the bright blue of the sky. The butchery was continuing on the heights.

I imagined we were conquerors, and I experienced selfish pleasure in thinking I could die in peace on this deserted plain. Around me the earth was black. On raising my head I saw the enemy's battery on which we had charged, a few feet away from me. The struggle must have been horrible: the mound was covered with hacked and disfigured bodies; blood had flowed so abundantly that the dust seemed like a large red carpet. The cannon stretched out their dark muzzles above the corpses. I shuddered when I observed the silence of those guns.

Then gently, with a multitude of precautions, I succeeded in turning on my stomach. I rested my head on a large stone all splashed with gore, and drew my uncle Lazare's letter from my breast. I placed it before my eyes; but my tears prevented my reading it.

And whilst the sun was roasting me in the back, the acrid smell of blood was choking me. I could form an idea of the woeful plain around me, and was as if stiffened with the rigidness of the dead. My poor heart was weeping in the warm and loathsome silence of murder.

Uncle Lazare wrote to me, "My Dear Boy, I hear war has been declared; but I still hope you will get your discharge before the campaign opens. Every morning I beseech the Almighty to spare you new dangers; He will grant my prayer; He will, one of these days, let you close my eyes.

"Ah, my poor Jean, I am becoming old, I have great need of your arm. Since your departure I no more feel your youthfulness beside me, which gave me back my twenty summers. Do you remember our strolls in the morning along the oak-tree walk? Now I no longer dare to go beneath those trees; I am alone, I am afraid. The Durance weeps. Come quickly and console me, assuage my anxiety."

The tears were choking me, I could not continue. At that moment a heartrending cry was uttered a few steps away from me; I saw a soldier suddenly rise, with the muscles of his face contracted; he extended his arms in agony, and fell to the ground, where he writhed in frightful convulsions; then he ceased moving.

"I have placed my hope in the Almighty," continued my uncle, "He will bring you back safe and sound to Dourgues, and we will resume our peaceful existence. Let me dream out loud and tell you my plans for the future.

"You will go no more to Grenoble, you will remain with me; I will make my child a son of the soil, a peasant who shall live gaily whilst tilling the fields.

"And I will retire to your farm. In a short time my trembling hands will no longer be able to hold the Host. I only ask Heaven for two years of such an existence. That will be my reward for the few good deeds I may have done. Then you will sometimes lead me along the paths of our dear valley, where every rock, every hedge will remind me of your youth which I so greatly loved."

I had to stop again. I felt such a sharp pain in my shoulder, that I almost fainted a second time. A terrible anxiety had just taken possession of me; it, seemed as if the sound of the fusillade was approaching, and I thought with terror that our army was perhaps retreating, and that in its flight it would descend to the plain and pass over my body. But I still saw nothing but the slight cloud, of smoke hanging over the low hills.

My uncle Lazare added, "And we shall be three to love one another. Ah, my well-beloved Jean, how right you were to give her to drink that morning beside the Durance. I was afraid of Babet, I was ill-humored, and now I am jealous, for I can see very well that I shall never be able to love you as much as she does, 'Tell him,' she repeated to me yesterday, blushing, 'that if he gets killed, I shall go and throw myself into the river at the spot where he gave me to drink.'

"For the love of God, be careful of your life. There are things that I cannot understand, but I feel that happiness awaits you here. I already call Babet my daughter; I can see her on your arm, in the church, when I shall bless your union. I wish that to be my last mass.

"Babet is a fine, tall girl now. She will, assist you in your work."

The sound of the fusillade had gone farther away. I was weeping sweet tears. There were dismal moans among soldiers who were in their last agonies between the cannon wheels. I perceived one who was endeavoring to get rid of a comrade, wounded as he was, whose body was crushing his chest; and, as this wounded man struggled and complained, the soldier pushed him brutally away, and made him roll down the slope of the mound, whilst the wretched creature yelled with pain. At that cry a murmur came from the heap of corpses. The sun, which was sinking, shed rays of a light fallow color. The blue of the sky was softer.

I finished reading my uncle Lazare's letter.

"I simply wished," he continued, "to give you news of ourselves, and to beg you to come as soon as possible and make us happy. And here I am weeping and gossiping like an old child. Hope, my poor Jean, I pray, and God is good.

"Answer me quickly, and give me, if possible, the date of your return. Babet and I are counting the weeks. We trust to see you soon; be hopeful."

The date of my return, I kissed the letter, sobbing, and fancied for a moment that I was kissing Babet and my uncle. No doubt I should never see them again. I would die like a dog in the dust, beneath the leaden sun. And it was on that desolated plain, amidst the death-rattle of the dying, that those whom I loved dearly were saying good-bye. A buzzing silence filled my ears; I gazed at the pale earth spotted with blood, which extended, deserted, to the grey lines of the horizon. I repeated: "I must die." Then, I closed my eyes, and thought of Babet and my uncle Lazare.

I know not how long I remained in a sort of painful drowsiness. My heart suffered as much as my flesh. Warm tears ran slowly down my cheeks. Amidst the nightmare that accompanied the fever, I heard a moan similar to the continuous plaintive cry of a child in suffering. At times, I awoke and stared at the sky in astonishment.

At last I understood that it was M. de Montrevert, lying a few paces off, who was moaning in this manner. I had thought him dead. He was stretched out with his face to the ground and his arms extended. This man had been good to me; I said to myself that I could not allow him to die thus, with his face to the ground, and I began crawling slowly towards him.

Two corpses separated us. For a moment I thought of passing over the stomachs of these dead men to shorten the distance; for, my shoulder made me suffer frightfully at every movement. But I did not dare. I proceeded on my knees, assisting myself with one hand. When I reached the colonel, I gave a sigh of relief; it seemed to me that I was less alone; we would die together, and this death shared by both of us no longer terrified me.

I wanted him to see the sun, and I turned him over as gently as possible. When the rays fell upon his face, he breathed hard; he opened his eyes. Leaning over his body, I tried to smile at him. He closed his eyelids again; I understood by his trembling lips that he was conscious of his sufferings.

"It's you, Gourdon," he said to me at last, in a feeble voice; "is the battle won?"

"I think so, colonel," I answered him.

There was a moment of silence. Then, opening his eyes and looking at me, he inquired "Where are you wounded?"

"In the shoulder and you, colonel?"

"My elbow must be smashed. I remember; it was the same bullet that arranged us both like this, my boy."

He made an effort to sit up.

"But come," he said with sudden gaiety, "we are not going to sleep here?"

You cannot believe how much this courageous display of joviality contributed towards giving me strength and hope. I felt quite different since we were two to struggle against death.

"Wait," I exclaimed, "I will bandage up your arm with my handkerchief, and we will try and support one another as far as the nearest ambulance."

"That's it, my boy. Don't make it too tight. Now, let us take each other by the good hand and try to get up."

We rose staggering. We had lost a great deal of blood; our heads were swimming and our legs failed us. Any one would have mistaken us for drunkards, stumbling, supporting, pushing one another, and making zig-zags to avoid the dead. The sun was setting with a rosy blush, and our gigantic shadows danced in a strange way over the field of battle. It was the end of a fine day.

The colonel joked; his lips were crisped by shudders, his laughter resembled sobs. I could see that we were going to fall down in some corner never to rise again. At times we were seized with giddiness, and were obliged to stop and close our eyes. The ambulances formed small grey patches on the dark ground at the extremity of the plain.

We knocked up against a large stone, and were thrown down one on the other. The colonel swore like a pagan. We tried to walk on all-fours, catching hold of the briars. In this way we did a hundred yards on our knees. But our knees were bleeding.

"I have had enough of it," said the colonel, lying down; "they may come and fetch me if they will. Let us sleep."

I still had the strength to sit half up, and shout with all the breath that remained within me. Men were passing along in the distance picking up the wounded; they ran to us and placed us side by side on a stretcher.

"Comrade," the colonel said to me during the journey, "Death will not have us. I owe you my life; I will pay my debt, whenever you have need of me. Give me your hand."

I placed my hand in his, and it was thus that we reached the ambulances. They had lighted torches; the surgeons were cutting and sawing, amidst frightful yells; a sickly smell came from the blood-stained linen, whilst the torches cast dark rosy flakes into the basins.

The colonel bore the amputation of his arm with courage; I only saw his lips turn pale and a film come over his eyes. When it was my turn, a surgeon examined my shoulder.

"A shell did that for you," he said; "an inch lower and your shoulder would have been carried away. The flesh, only, has suffered."

And when I asked the assistant, who was dressing my wound, whether it was serious, he answered me with a laugh, "Serious, you will have to keep to your bed for three weeks, and make new blood."

I turned my face to the wall, not wishing to show my tears. And with my heart's eyes I perceived Babet and my uncle Lazare stretching out their arms towards me. I had finished with the sanguinary struggles of my su mer day.

III
AUTUMN

It was nearly fifteen years since I had married Babet In my uncle Lazare's little church. We had sought happiness in our dear valley. I had made myself a farmer; the Durance, my first sweetheart, was now a good mother to me, who seemed to take pleasure in making my fields rich and fertile. Little by little, by following the new methods of agriculture, I became one of the wealthiest landowners in the neighborhood.

We had purchased the oak-tree walk and the meadows bordering on the river at the death of my wife's parents. I had had a modest house built on this land, but we were soon obliged to enlarge it; each year I found a means of rounding off our property by the addition of some neighboring field, and our granaries were too small for our harvests.

Those first fifteen years were uneventful and happy. They passed away in serene joy, and all they have left within me is the remembrance of calm and continued happiness. My uncle Lazare, on retiring to our home, had realized his dream; his advanced age did not permit of his reading his breviary of a morning; he sometimes regretted his dear church, but consoled himself by visiting the young vicar who had succeeded him. He came down from the little room he occupied at sunrise, and often accompanied me to the fields, enjoying himself in the open air, and finding a second youth amidst the healthy atmosphere of the country.

One sadness alone made us sometimes sigh. Amidst the fruitfulness by which we were surrounded, Babet remained childless. Although we were three to love one another we sometimes found ourselves too much alone; we would have liked to have had a little fair head running about amongst us, who would have tormented and caressed us.

Uncle Lazare had a frightful dread of dying before he was a great-uncle. He had become a child again, and felt sorrowful that Babet did not give him a comrade who would have played with him. On the day when my wife confided to us with hesitation, that we would no doubt soon be four, I saw my uncle turn quite pale, and make efforts not to cry. He kissed us, thinking already of the christening, and speaking of the child as if it were already three or four years old.

And the months passed in concentrated tenderness. We talked together in subdued voices, awaiting some one. I no longer loved Babet: I worshipped her with joined hands; I worshipped her for two, for herself and the little one.

The great day was drawing nigh. I had brought a midwife from Grenoble who never moved from the farm. My uncle was in a dreadful fright; he understood nothing about such things; he went so far as to tell me that he had done wrong in taking holy orders, and that he was very sorry he was not a doctor.

One morning in September, at about six o'clock, I went into the room of my dear Babet, who was still asleep. Her smiling face was peacefully reposing on the white linen pillow-case. I bent over her, holding my breath. Heaven had blessed me with the good things of this world. I all at once thought of that summer day when I was moaning in the dust, and at the same time I felt around me the comfort due to labor and the quietude that comes from happiness. My good wife was asleep, all rosy, in the middle of her great bed; whilst the whole room recalled to me our fifteen years of tender affection.

I kissed Babet softly on the lips. She opened her eyes and smiled at me without speaking. I felt an almost uncontrollable desire to take her in my arms, and clasp her to my heart; but, latterly, I had hardly dared press her hand, she seemed so fragile and sacred to me.

I seated myself at the edge of the bed, and asked her in a low voice:

"Is it for to-day?"

"No, I don't think so," she replied. "I dreamt I had a boy: he was already very tall and wore adorable a little black moustache. Uncle Lazare told me yesterday that he also had seen him in a dream."

I acted very stupidly.

"I know the child better than you do," I said. "I see it every night. It's a girl."

And as Babet turned her face to the wall, ready to cry, I realized how foolish I had been, and hastened to add:

"When I say a girl, I am not quite sure. I see a very small child with a long white gown. It's certainly a boy."

Babet kissed me for that pleasing remark.

"Go and look after the vintage," she continued, "I feel calm this morning."

"You will send for me if anything happens?"

"Yes, yes, I am very tired: I shall go to sleep again. You'll not be angry with me for my laziness?"

And Babet closed her eyes, looking languid and affected. I remained leaning over her, receiving the warm breath from her lips in my face. She gradually went off to sleep, without ceasing to smile. Then I disengaged my hand from hers with a multitude of precautions. I had to maneuver for five minutes to bring this delicate task to a happy issue. After that I gave her a kiss on her forehead, which she did not feel, and withdrew with a palpitating heart, overflowing with love.

In the courtyard below, I found my uncle Lazare, who was gazing anxiously at the window of Babet's room. As soon as he perceived me he inquired, "Well, is it for to-day?"

He had been putting this question to me regularly every morning for the past month.

"It appears not," I answered him. "Will you come with me and see them picking the grapes?"

He fetched his stick, and we went down the oak-tree walk. When we were at the end of it, on that terrace which overlooks the Durance, both of us stopped, gazing at the valley.

Small white clouds floated in the pale sky. The sun was shedding soft rays, which cast a sort of gold dust over the country, the yellow expanse of which spread out all ripe. One saw neither the brilliant light nor the dark shadows of summer. The foliage gilded the black earth in large patches. The river ran more slowly; weary at the task of having rendered the fields fruitful for a season. And the valley remained calm and strong. It already wore the first furrows of winter, but it preserved within it the warmth of its last labor, displaying its robust charms, free from the weeds of spring, more majestically beautiful, like that second youth, of woman who has given birth to life.

My uncle Lazare remained silent; then, turning towards me, said:

"Do you remember, Jean? It is more than twenty years ago since I brought you here early one May morning. On that particular day I showed you the valley full of feverish activity, laboring for the fruits of autumn. Look; the valley has just performed its task again."

"I remember, dear uncle," I replied. "I was quaking with fear on that day; but you were good, and your lesson was convincing. I owe you all my happiness."

"Yes, you have reached the autumn. You have labored and are gathering in the harvest. Man, my boy, was created after the way of the earth. And we, like the common mother, are eternal: the green leaves are born again each year from dry leaves; I am born again in you, and you will be born again in your children. I am telling you this so that old age may not alarm you, so that you may know how to die in peace, as dies this verdure, which will shoot out again from its own germs next spring."

I listened to my uncle and thought of Babet, who was sleeping in her great bed spread with white linen. The dear creature was about to give birth to a child after the manner of this fertile soil which had given us fortune. She also had reached the autumn: she had the beaming smile and serene robustness of the valley. I seemed to see her beneath the yellow sun, tired and happy, experiencing noble delight at being a mother. And I no longer knew whether my uncle Lazare was talking to me of my dear valley, or of my dear Babet.

We slowly ascended the hills. Below, along the Durance, were the meadows, broad, raw green swards; next came the yellow fields, intersected here and there by grayish olive and slender almond trees, planted wide apart in rows; then, right up above, were the vines, great stumps with shoots trailing along the ground.

The vine is treated in the south of France like a hardy housewife, and not like a delicate young lady, as in the north. It grows somewhat as it likes, according to the good will of rain and sun. The stumps, which are planted in double rows, and form long lines, throw sprays of dark verdure around them. Wheat or oats are sown between. A vineyard resembles an immense piece of striped material, made of the green bands formed by the vine leaves, and of yellow ribbon represented by the stubble.

Men and women stooping down among the vines, were cutting the bunches of grapes, which they then threw to the bottom of large baskets. My uncle and I walked slowly through the stubble. As we passed along, the grape-pickers turned their heads and greeted us. My uncle sometimes stopped to speak to some of the oldest of the laborers.

"Heh, Father André," he said, "are the grapes thoroughly ripe? Will the wine be good this year?"

And the country folk, raising their bare arms, displayed the long bunches, which were as black as ink, in the sun; and when the grapes were pressed they seemed to burst with abundance and strength.

"Look, Mr. Curée," they exclaimed, "these are small ones. There are some weighing several pounds. We have not had such a task these ten years."

Then they returned among the leaves. Their brown jackets formed patches in the verdure. And the women, bareheaded, with small blue hand-kerchiefs round their necks, were stooping down singing. There were children rolling in the sun, in the stubble, giving utterance to shrill laughter and enlivening this open-air workshop with their turbulence. Large carts remained motionless at the edge of the field waiting for the grapes; they stood out prominently against the clear sky, whilst men went and came unceasingly, carrying away full baskets, and bringing back empty ones.

I confess that in the centre of this field, I had feelings of pride. I heard the ground producing beneath my feet; ripe age ran all powerful in the veins of the vine, and loaded the air with great puffs of it. Hot blood coursed in my flesh, I was as if elevated by the fecundity overflowing from the soil and ascending within me. The labor of this swarm of work-people was my doing, these vines were my children; this entire farm became my large and obedient family. I experienced pleasure in feeling my feet sink into the heavy land.

Then, at a glance, I took in the fields that sloped down to the Durance, and I was the possessor of those vines, those meadows, that stubble, those olive-trees. The house stood all white beside the oak-tree walk; the river seemed like a fringe of silver placed at the edge of the great green mantle of my pasture-land. I fancied, for a moment, that my frame was increasing in size, that by stretching out my arms, I would be able to embrace the entire property, and press it to my breast, trees, meadows, house, and ploughed land.

And as I looked, I saw one of our servant-girls racing, out of breath, up the narrow pathway that ascended the hill. Confused by the speed at which she was traveling, she stumbled over the stones, agitating both her arms, and hailing us with gestures of bewilderment. I felt choking with inexpressible emotion.

"Uncle, uncle," I shouted, "look how Marguerite's running. I think it must be for to-day."

My uncle Lazare turned quite pale. The servant had at length reached the plateau; she came towards us jumping over the vines. When she reached me, she was out of breath; she was stifling and pressing her hands to her bosom.

"Speak," I said to her. "What has happened?"

She heaved a heavy sigh, agitated her hands, and finally was able to pronounce this single word, "Madame."

I waited for no more.

"Come, come quick, uncle Lazare, Ah, my poor dear Babet,"

And I bounded down the pathway at a pace fit to break my bones. The grape-pickers, who had stood up, smiled as they saw me running. Uncle Lazare, who could not overtake me, shook his walking stick in despair.

"Heh, Jean, the deuce," he shouted, "wait for me. I don't want to be the last."

But I no longer heard Uncle Lazare, and continued running.

I reached the farm panting for breath, full of hope and terror. I rushed upstairs and knocked with my fist at Babet's door, laughing, crying, and half crazy. The midwife set the door ajar, to tell me in an angry voice not to make so much noise. I stood there abashed and in despair.

"You can't come in," she added. "Go and wait in the courtyard."

And as I did not move, she continued: "All is going on very well. I will call you."

The door was closed. I remained standing before it, unable to make up my mind to go away. I heard Babet complaining in a broken voice. And, while I was there, she gave utterance to a heartrending scream that struck me right in the breast like a bullet. I felt an almost irresistible desire to break the door open with my shoulder. So as not to give way to it, I placed my hands to my ears, and dashed downstairs.

In the courtyard I found my uncle Lazare, who had just arrived out of breath. The worthy man was obliged to seat himself on the brink of the well.

"Hallo, where is the child?" he inquired of me.

"I don't know," I answered; "they shut the door in my face. Babet is in pain and in tears." We gazed at one another, not daring to utter a word.

We listened in agony, without taking our eyes off Babet's window, endeavoring to see through the little white curtains. My uncle, who was trembling, stood still, with both his hands resting heavily on his walking-stick; I, feeling very feverish, walked up and down before him, taking long strides. At times we exchanged anxious smiles.

The carts of the grape-pickers arrived one by one. The baskets of grapes were placed against a wall of the courtyard, and bare-legged men trampled the bunches under foot in wooden troughs. The mules neighed, the carters swore, whilst the wine fell with a dull sound to the bottom of the vat. Acrid smells pervaded the warm air.

And I continued pacing up and down, as if made tipsy by those perfumes. My poor head was breaking, and as I watched the red juice run from the grapes I thought of Babet. I said to myself with manly joy, that my child was born at the prolific time of vintage, amidst the perfume of new wine.

I was tormented by impatience, I went upstairs again. But I did not dare knock, I pressed my ear against the door, and heard Babet's low moans and sobs. Then my heart failed me, and I cursed suffering. Uncle Lazare, who had crept up behind me, had to lead me back into the courtyard. He wished to divert me, and told me the wine would be excellent; but he spoke without attending to what he said. And at times we were both silent, listening anxiously to one of Babet's more prolonged moans.

Little by little the cries subsided, and became nothing more than a painful murmur, like the voice of a child falling off to sleep in tears. Then there was absolute silence. This soon caused me unutterable terror. The house seemed empty, now that Babet had ceased sobbing. I was just going upstairs, when the midwife opened the window noiselessly. She leant out and beckoned me with her hand, "Come," she said to me.

I went slowly upstairs, feeling additional delight at each step I took. My uncle Lazare was already knocking at the door, whilst I was only half way up to the landing, experiencing a sort of strange delight in delaying the moment when I would kiss my wife.

I stopped on the threshold, my heart was beating double. My uncle had leant over the cradle. Babet, quite pale, with closed eyelids, seemed asleep. I forgot all about the child, and going straight to Babet, took her dear hand between mine. The tears had not dried on her checks, and her quivering lips were dripping with them. She raised her eyelids wearily. She did not speak to me, but I understood her to say: "I have suffered a great deal, my dear Jean, but I was so happy to suffer, I felt you within me."

Then I bent down, I kissed Babet's eyes and drank her tears. She laughed with much sweetness; she resigned herself with caressing languidness. The fatigue had made her all aches and pains. She slowly moved her hands from the sheet, and taking me by the neck placed her lips to my ear, "It's a boy," she murmured in a weak voice, but with an air of triumph.

Those were the first words she uttered after the terrible shock she had undergone.

"I knew it would be a boy," she continued, "I saw the child every night. Give him me, put him beside me."

I turned round and saw the midwife and my uncle quarrelling.

The midwife had all the trouble in the world to prevent uncle Lazare taking the little one in his arms. He wanted to nurse it.

I looked at the child whom the mother had made me forget. He was all rosy. Babet said with conviction that he was like me; the midwife discovered that he had his mother's eyes; I, for my part, could not say, I was almost crying, I smothered the dear little thing with kisses, imagining I was still kissing Babet.

I placed the child on the bed. He kept on crying, but this sounded to us like celestial music. I sat on the edge of the bed, my uncle took a large arm-chair, and Babet, weary and serene, covered up to her chin, remained with open eyelids and smiling eyes.

The window was wide open. The smell of grapes came in along with the warmth of the mild autumn afternoon. One heard the trampling of the grape-pickers, the shocks of the carts, the cracking of whips; at times the shrill song of a servant working in the courtyard reached us. All this noise was softened in the serenity of that room, which still resounded with Babet's sobs. And the window-frame enclosed a large strip of landscape, carved out of the heavens and open country. We could see the oak-tree walk in its entire length; then the Durance, looking like a white satin ribbon, passed amidst the gold and purple leaves; whilst above this square of ground were the limpid depths of a pale sky with blue and rosy tints.

It was amidst the calm of this horizon, amidst the exhalations of the vat and the joys attendant upon labor and reproduction, that we three talked together, Babet, uncle Lazare, and myself, whilst gazing at the dear little new-born babe.

"Uncle Lazare," said Babet, "what name will you give the child?"

"Jean's mother was named Jacqueline," answered my uncle. "I shall call the child Jacques."

"Jacques, Jacques," repeated Babet. "Yes, it's a pretty name. And, tell me, what shall we make the little man: parson or soldier, gentleman or peasant?"

I began to laugh.

"We shall have time to think of that," I said.

"But no," continued Babet almost angry, "he will grow rapidly. See how strong he is. He already speaks with his eyes."

My uncle Lazare was exactly of my wife's opinion. He answered in a very grave tone, "Make him neither priest nor soldier, unless he have an irresistible inclination for one of those callings to make him a gentleman would be a serious."

Babet looked at me anxiously. The dear creature had not a bit of pride for herself; but, like all mothers, she would have liked to be humble and proud before her son. I could have sworn that she already saw him a notary or a doctor. I kissed her and gently said to her, "I wish our son to live in our dear valley. One day, he will find a Babet of sixteen, on the banks of the Durance, to whom he will give some water. Do you remember, my dear? The country has brought us peace: our son shall be a peasant as we are, and happy as we are."

Babet, who was quite touched, kissed me in her turn. She gazed at the foliage and the river, the meadows and the sky, through the window; then she said to me, smiling:

"You are right, Jean. This place has been good to us, it will be the same to our little Jacques. Uncle Lazare, you will be the godfather of a farmer."

Uncle Lazare made a languid, affectionate sign of approval with the head. I had been examining him for a moment, and saw his eyes becoming filmy, and his lips turning pale. Leaning back in the arm-chair, opposite the window, he had placed his white hands on his knees, and was watching the heavens fixedly with an expression of thoughtful ecstasy.

I felt very anxious.

"Are you in pain, uncle Lazare?" I inquired of him, "What is the matter with you? Answer, for mercy's sake."

He gently raised one of his hands, as if to beg me to speak lower; then he let it fall again, and said in a weak voice, "I am broken down," he said. "Happiness, at my age, is mortal. Don't make a noise. It seems as if my flesh were becoming quite light: I can no longer feel my legs or arms."

Babet raised herself in alarm, with her eyes on uncle Lazare. I knelt down before him, watching him anxiously. He smiled.

"Don't be frightened," he resumed. "I am in no pain; a feeling of calmness is gaining possession of me; I believe I am going off into a good and just sleep. It came over me all at once, and I thank the Almighty. Ah, my poor Jean, I ran too fast down, the pathway on the hillside; the child caused me too great joy."

And as we understood, we burst out into tears. Uncle Lazare continued, without ceasing to watch the sky, "Do not spoil my joy, I beg of you. If you only knew how happy it makes me, to fall asleep for ever in this armchair, I have never dared expect such a consoling death. All I love is here, beside me and see what a blue sky, The Almighty has sent a lovely evening."

The sun was sinking behind the oak-tree walk. Its slanting rays cast sheets of gold beneath the trees, which took the tones of old copper. The verdant fields melted into vague serenity in the distance. Uncle Lazare became weaker and weaker amidst the touching silence of this peaceful sunset, entering by the open window. He slowly passed away, like those slight gleams that were dying out on the lofty branches.

"Ah, my good valley," he murmured, "you are sending me a tender farewell. I was afraid of coming to my end in the winter, when you would be all black."

We restrained our tears, not wishing to trouble this saintly death. Babet prayed in an undertone. The child continued uttering smothered cries.

My uncle Lazare heard its wail in the dreaminess of his agony. He endeavored to turn towards Babet, and, still smiling, said, "I have seen the child and die very happy."

Then he gazed at the pale sky and yellow fields, and, throwing back his head, heaved a gentle sigh.

No tremor agitated uncle Lazare's body; he died as one falls asleep.

We had become so calm that we remained silent and with dry eyes. In the presence of such great simplicity in death, all we experienced was a feeling of serene sadness. Twilight had set in; uncle Lazare's farewell had left us confident, like the farewell of the sun which dies at night to be born again in the morning.

Such was my autumn day, which gave me a son, and carried off my uncle Lazare in the peacefulness of the twilight.

IV
WINTER

There are dreadful mornings in January that chill one's heart. I awoke on this particular day with a vague feeling of anxiety. It had thawed during the night, and when I cast my eyes over the country from the threshold, it looked to me like an immense dirty grey rag, soiled with mud and rent to tatters.

The horizon was shrouded in a curtain of fog, in which the oak-trees along the walk lugubriously extended their dark arms, like a row of specters guarding the vast mass of winter imparts health and strength to one's frame when the sun is clear and the ground dry. The air makes the tips of your ears tingle, you walk merrily along the frozen pathways, which ring with a silvery sound beneath your tread. But I know of nothing more saddening than dull, thawing weather. I hate the damp fogs which weigh one's shoulders down.

I shivered in the presence of that copper-like sky, and hastened to retire indoors, making up my mind that I would not go out into the fields that day. There was plenty of work in and around the farm-buildings.

Jacques had been up a long time. I heard him whistling in a shed, where he was helping some men remove sacks of corn. The boy was already eighteen years old; he was a tall fellow, with strong arms. He had not had an uncle Lazare to spoil him and teach him Latin, and he did not go and dream beneath the willows at the riverside. Jacques had become a real peasant, an untiring worker, who got angry when I touched anything, telling me I was getting old and ought to rest.

And as I was watching him from a distance, a sweet lithe creature, leaping on my shoulders, clapped her little hands to my eyes, inquiring, "Who is it?"

I laughed and answered, "It's little Marie, who has just been dressed by her mamma."

The dear little girl was completing her tenth year, and for ten years she had been the delight of the farm. Having come the last, at a time when we could no longer hope to have any more children, she was doubly loved. Her precarious health made her particularly dear to us. She was treated as a young lady; her mother absolutely wanted to make a lady of her, and I had not the heart to oppose her wish, so little Marie was a pet, in lovely silk skirts trimmed with ribbons.

Marie was still seated on my shoulders.

"Mamma, mamma," she cried, "come and look; I'm playing at horses."

Babet, who was entering, smiled. Ah, my poor Babet, how old we were, I remember we were shivering with weariness, on that day, gazing sadly at one another when alone.

Our children brought back our youth.

Lunch was eaten in silence. We had been compelled to light the lamp. The reddish glimmer that hung round the room was sad enough to drive one crazy.

"Bah," said Jacques, "this tepid rainy weather is better than intense cold that would freeze our vines and olives."

And he tried to joke. But he was as anxious as we were, without knowing why. Babet had had bad dreams. We listened to the account of her nightmare, laughing with our lips but sad at heart.

"This weather quite upsets one," I said to cheer us all up.

"Yes, yes, it's the weather," Jacques hastened to add. "I'll put some vine branches on the fire."

There was a bright flame which cast large sheets of light upon the walls. The branches burnt with a cracking sound, leaving rosy ashes. We had seated ourselves in front of the chimney; the air, outside, was tepid; but great drops of icy cold damp fell from the ceilings inside the farmhouse. Babet had taken little Marie on her knees; she was talking to her in an undertone, amused at her childish chatter.

"Are you coming, father?" Jacques inquired of me. "We are going to look at the cellars and lofts."

I went out with him. The harvests had been getting bad for some years past. We were suffering great losses: our vines and trees were caught by frost, whilst hail had chopped up our wheat and oats. And I sometimes said that I was growing old, and that fortune, who is a woman, does not care for old men. Jacques laughed, answering that he was young, and was going to court fortune.

I had reached the winter, the cold season. I felt distinctly that all was withering around me. At each pleasure that departed, I thought of uncle Lazare, who had died so calmly; and with fond remembrances of him, asked for strength.

Daylight had completely disappeared at three o'clock. We went down into the common room. Babet was sewing in the chimney corner, with her head bent over her work; and little Marie was seated on the ground, in front of the fire, gravely dressing a doll. Jacques and I had placed ourselves at a mahogany writing-table, which had come to us from uncle Lazare, and were engaged in checking our accounts.

The window was as if blocked up; the fog, sticking to the panes of glass, formed a perfect wall of gloom. Behind this wall stretched emptiness, the unknown. A great noise, a loud roar, alone arose in the silence and spread through the obscurity.

We had dismissed the workpeople, keeping only our old woman-servant, Marguerite, with us. When I raised my head and listened, it seemed to me that the farmhouse hung suspended in the middle of a chasm. No human sound came from the outside. I heard naught but the riot of the abyss. Then I gazed at my wife and children, and experienced the cowardice of those old people who feel themselves too weak to protect those surrounding them against unknown peril.

The noise became harsher, and it seemed to us that there was a knocking at the door. At the same instant, the horses in the stable began to neigh furiously, whilst the cattle lowed as if choking. We had all risen, pale with anxiety, Jacques dashed to the door and threw it wide open.

A wave of muddy water burst into the room.

The Durance was overflowing. It had been making the noise that had been increasing in the distance since morning. The snow melting on the mountains had transformed each hillside into a torrent which had swelled the river. The curtain of fog had hidden from us this sudden rise of water.

It had often advanced thus to the gates of the farm, when the thaw came after severe winters. But the flood had never increased so rapidly. We could see through the open door that the courtyard was transformed into a lake. The water already reached our ankles.

Babet had caught up little Marie, who was crying and clasping her doll to her. Jacques wanted to run and open the doors of the stables and barns, but his mother held him back by his clothes, begging him not to go out. The water continued rising. I pushed Babet towards the staircase.

"Quick, quick, let us go up into the bedrooms," I cried.

And I obliged Jacques to pass before me. I left the ground-floor the last.

Marguerite came down in terror from the loft where she happened to find herself. I made her sit down at the end of the room beside Babet, who remained silent, pale, and with beseeching eyes. We put little Marie into bed; she had insisted on keeping her doll, and went quietly to sleep pressing it in her arms. This child's sleep relieved me; when I turned round and saw Babet, listening to the little girl's regular breathing, I forgot the danger, all I heard was the water beating against the walls.

But Jacques and I could not help looking the peril in the face. Anxiety made us endeavor to discover the progress of the inundation. We had thrown the window wide open, we leant out at the risk of falling, searching into the darkness. The fog, which was thicker, hung above the flood, throwing out fine rain which gave us the shivers. Vague steel-like flashes were all that showed the moving sheet of water, amidst the profound obscurity. Below, it was splashing in the courtyard, rising along the walls in gentle undulations. And we still heard naught but the anger of the Durance, and the affrighted cattle and horses.

The neighing and lowing of these poor beasts pierced me to the heart. Jacques questioned me with his eyes; he would have liked to try and deliver them. Their agonizing moans soon became lamentable, and a great cracking sound was heard. The oxen had just broken down the stable doors. We saw them pass before us, borne away by the flood, rolled over and over in the current. And they disappeared amid the roar of the river.

Then I felt choking with anger. I became as one possessed, I shook my fist at the Durance. Erect, facing the window, I insulted it.

"Wicked thing," I shouted amidst the tumult of the waters, "I loved you fondly, you were my first sweetheart, and now you are plundering me. You come and disturb my farm, and carry off my cattle. Ah, cursed, cursed thing. Then you gave me Babet, you ran gently at the edge of my meadows. I took you for a good mother. I remembered uncle Lazare felt affection for your limpid stream, and I thought I owed you gratitude. You are a barbarous mother, I only owe you my hatred."

But the Durance stifled my cries with its thundering voice; and, broad and indifferent, expanded and drove its flood onward with tranquil obstinacy.

I turned back to the room and went and kissed Babet, who was weeping.Little Marie was smiling in her sleep.

"Don't be afraid," I said to my wife. "The water cannot always rise. It will certainly go down. There is no danger."

"No, there is no danger," Jacques repeated feverishly. "The house is solid."

At that moment Marguerite, who had approached the window, tormented by that feeling of curiosity which is the outcome of fear, leant forward like a mad thing and fell, uttering a cry. I threw myself before the window, but could not prevent Jacques plunging into the water. Marguerite had nursed him, and he felt the tenderness of a son for the poor old woman. Babet had risen in terror, with joined hands, at the sound of the two splashes. She remained there, erect, with open mouth and distended eyes, watching the window.

I had seated myself on the wooden handrail, and my ears were ringing with the roar of the flood. I do not know how long it was that Babet and I were in this painful state of stupor, when a voice called to me. It was Jacques who was holding on to the wall beneath the window. I stretched out my hand to him, and he clambered up.

Babet clasped him in her arms. She could sob now; and she relieved herself.

No reference was made to Marguerite. Jacques did not dare say he had been unable to find her, and we did not dare question him anent his search.

He took me apart and brought me back to the window.

"Father," he said to me in an undertone, "there are more than seven feet of water in the courtyard, and the river is still rising. We cannot remain here any longer."

Jacques was right. The house was falling to pieces, the planks of the outbuildings were going away one by one. Then this death of Marguerite weighed upon us. Babet, bewildered, was beseeching us. Marie alone remained peaceful in the big bed with her doll between her arms, and slumbering with the happy smile of an angel.

The peril increased at every minute. The water was on the point of reaching the handrail of the window and pouring into the room. Any one would have said that it was an engine of war making the farmhouse totter with regular, dull, hard blows. The current must be running right against the facade, and we could not hope for any human assistance.

"Every minute is precious," said Jacques in agony. "We shall be crushed beneath the ruins. Let us look for boards, let us make a raft."

He said that in his excitement. I would naturally have preferred a thousand times to be in the middle of the river, on a few beams lashed together, than beneath the roof of this house which was about to fall in. But where could we lay hands on the beams we required? In a rage I tore the planks from the cupboards, Jacques broke the furniture, we took away the shutters, every piece of wood we could reach. And feeling it was impossible to utilize these fragments, we cast them into the middle of the room in a fury, and continued searching.

Our last hope was departing; we understood our misery and want of power. The water was rising; the harsh voice of the Durance was calling to us in anger. Then, I burst out sobbing, I took Babet in my trembling arms, I begged Jacques to come near us. I wished us all to die in the same embrace.

Jacques had returned to the window. And, suddenly, he exclaimed, "Father, we are saved. Come and see."

The sky was clear. The roof of a shed, torn away by the current, had come to a standstill beneath our window. This roof, which was several yards broad, was formed of light beams and thatch; it floated, and would make a capital raft, I joined my hands together and would have worshipped this wood and straw.

Jacques jumped on the roof, after having firmly secured it. He walked on the thatch, making sure it was everywhere strong. The thatch resisted; therefore we could adventure on it without fear.

"Oh, it will carry us all very well," said Jacques joyfully. "See how little it sinks into the water; the difficulty will be to steer it."

He looked around him and seized two poles drifting along in the current, as they passed by.

"Ah, here are oars," he continued. "You will go to the stern, father, and I forward, and we will maneuver the raft easily. There are not twelve feet of water. Quick, quick, get on board, we must not lose a minute."

My poor Babet tried to smile. She wrapped little Marie carefully up in her shawl; the child had just woke up, and, quite alarmed, maintained a silence which was broken by deep sobs. I placed a chair before the window and made Babet get on the raft. As I held her in my arms I kissed her with poignant emotion, feeling this kiss was the last.

The water was beginning to pour into the room. Our feet were soaking. I was the last to embark; then I undid the cord. The current hurled us against the wall; it required precautions and many efforts to quit the farmhouse.

The fog had little by little dispersed. It was about midnight when we left. The stars were still buried in mist; the moon which was almost at the edge of the horizon, lit up the night with a sort of wan daylight.

The inundation then appeared to us in all its grandiose horror. The valley had become a river. The Durance, swollen to enormous proportions and washing the two hillsides, passed between dark masses of cultivated land, and was the sole thing displaying life in the inanimate space bounded by the horizon. It thundered with a sovereign voice, maintaining in its anger the majesty of its colossal wave. Clumps of trees emerged in places, staining the sheet of pale water with black streaks. Opposite us I recognized the tops of the oaks along the walk; the current carried us towards these branches, which for us were so many reefs. Around the raft floated various kinds of remains, pieces of wood, empty barrels, bundles of grass; the river was bearing along the ruins it had made in its anger.

To the left we perceived the lights of Dourgues, flashes of lanterns moving about in the darkness. The water could not have risen as high as the village; only the low land had been submerged. No doubt assistance would come. We searched the patches of light hanging over the water; it seemed to us at every instant that we heard the sound of oars.

We had started at random. As soon as the raft was in the middle of the current, lost amidst the whirlpools of the river, anguish of mind overtook us again; we almost regretted having left the farm. I sometimes turned round and gazed at the house, which still remained standing, presenting a grey aspect on the white water. Babet, crouching down in the centre of the raft, in the thatch of the roof, was holding little Marie on her knees, the child's head against her breast, to hide the horror of the river from her. Both were bent double, leaning forward in an embrace, as if reduced in stature by fear. Jacques, standing upright in the front, was leaning on his pole with all his weight; from time to time he cast a rapid glance towards us, and then silently resumed his task. I seconded him as well as I could, but our efforts to reach the bank remained fruitless. Little by little, notwithstanding our poles, which we buried into the mud until we nearly broke them, we drifted into the open; a force that seemed to come from the depths of the water drove us away. The Durance was slowly taking possession of us.

Struggling, bathed in perspiration, we had worked ourselves into a passion; we were fighting with the river as with a living being, seeking to vanquish, wound, kill it. It strained us in its giant-like arms, and our poles in our hands became weapons which we thrust into its breast. It roared, flung its slaver into our faces, wriggled beneath our strokes. We resisted its victory with clenched teeth. We would not be conquered. And we had mad impulses to fell the monster, to calm it with blows from our fists.

We went slowly towards the offing. We were already at the entrance to the oak-tree walk. The dark branches pierced through the water, which they tore with a lamentable sound. Death, perhaps, awaited us there in a collision. I cried out to Jacques to follow the walk by clinging close to the branches. And it was thus that I passed for the last time in the middle of this oak-tree alley, where I had walked in my youth and ripe age. In the terrible darkness, above the howling depth, I thought of uncle Lazare, and saw the happy days of my youth smiling at me sadly.

The Durance triumphed at the end of the alley. Our poles no longer touched the bottom. The water bore us along in its impetuous bound of victory. And now it could do what it pleased with us. We gave ourselves up. We went downstream with frightful rapidity. Great clouds, dirty tattered rags hung about the sky; when the moon was hidden there came lugubrious obscurity. Then we rolled in chaos. Enormous billows as black as ink, resembling the backs of fish, bore us along, spinning us round. I could no longer see either Babet or the children. I already felt myself dying.

I know not how long this last run lasted. The moon was suddenly unveiled and the horizon became clear. And in that light I perceived an immense black mass in front of us which blocked the way, and towards which we were being carried with all the violence of the current. We were lost, we would be broken there.

Babet had stood upright. She held out little Marie to me, "Take the child," she exclaimed. "Leave me alone, leave me alone,"

Jacques had already caught Babet in his arms. In a loud voice he said, "Father, save the little one. I will save mother."

We had come close to the black mass. I thought I recognized a tree. The shock was terrible, and the raft, split in two, scattered its straw and beams in the whirlpool of water.

I fell, clasping little Marie tightly to me. The icy cold water brought back all my courage. On rising to the surface of the river, I supported the child, I half laid her on my neck and began to swim laboriously. If the little creature had not lost consciousness but had struggled, we should both have remained at the bottom of the deep.

And, whilst I swam, I felt choking with anxiety. I called Jacques, I tried to see in the distance; but I heard nothing save the roar of the waters, I saw naught but the pale sheet of the Durance. Jacques and Babet were at the bottom. She must have clung to him, dragged him down in a deadly strain of her arms. What frightful agony, I wanted to die; I sunk slowly, I was going to find them beneath the black water. And as soon as the flood touched little Marie's face, I struggled again with impetuous anguish to get near the waterside.

It was thus that I abandoned Babet and Jacques, in despair at having been unable to die with them, still calling out to them in a husky voice. The river cast me on the stones, like one of those bundles of grass it leaves on its way. When I came to myself again, I took my daughter, who was opening her eyes, in my arms. Day was breaking. My winter night was at an end, that terrible night which had been an accomplice in the murder of my wife and son.

At this moment, after years of regret, one last consolation remains to me. I am the icy winter, but I feel the approaching spring stirring within me. As my uncle Lazare said, we never die. I have had four seasons, and here I am returning to the spring, there is my dear Marie commencing the everlasting joys and sorrows over again.

A Note on the Text

The task of assembling the short fiction of Émile Zola has been formidable for a number of reasons. It would be facile to say that any work rendering Zola (or any non-English writer) into English is problematic at the very least, impossible at the worst. We are simultaneously blessed and cursed with existing translations. Blessed because they introduced Zola to a much admiring public; cursed because such translations are so of their time. The Vizetelly family which has always been applauded for their efforts in this regard worked under a threat that few people in the western world face; they were not only fearful of being imprisoned, but were in fact put in jail merely for the act of translating Zola into English. As a result their translations suffer on two counts: they are expurgated almost to the point of nonsense and they are Victorian in the extreme, which is to say that they are insufferably stuffy, overblown and laden with a vocabulary that only the most forsaken scholar living in a cave somewhere and avoiding all contact with contemporary culture could understand.

Translators generally build upon each other's work and it is our misfortune that the foundation of Zola translations are the firm of Vizetelly and Co. I know this will stir the ire of mainly the British scholars of Zola because they are covetous of the prestige which surrounds the "bravery" of the Vizetellys in taking on the task in the first place. But being first does not mean doing a great job; a passable job, yes. A better than no job at all, also yes. But I can be quite certain that their translations destroyed any chance Zola had of being widely accepted in the United States and I can assure you that his influence is so potent as for any student to safely be able to assert that without Émile Zola, American literature from 1880 to 1940 would be completely and utterly different. This influence, however, is based on our American authors' ability to read the master in his original French, a talent widely accepted in the years mentioned but woefully absent today where our literati are considered learned if they have mastered MSWord. Fortunately, the same cannot be said of America's great contemporary film directors who religiously observe French films all to the general good of American cinema.

The problems with translations notwithstanding, there are even greater problems assembling Zola's short works because they were often published in newspapers and other periodicals with a heavy editorial hand. A story such as "Nantas" has at least three variations within the French language itself. So it was with some temerity that I chose the version closest in my opinion to what Zola, hopefully, intended. Most, if not all, of his short fiction was written quickly, under deadline, and with considerably less care than his novels. Many are simply sketches reminiscent of an author's working notebooks where ideas for novels are set down looking to the day when they might be fleshed out. If that day never comes, the sketches or notes will suffice to satisfy the hungry reading public whose appetite has been stimulated by the passion that intelligent readers everywhere have for the novels. Interestingly, many of his stories are so short that in their day they would have been considered ridiculous (and were by many critics.) But today, such short fiction has been "invented" in the form of what is colloquially and now in some more refined circles referred to as "flash fiction."

As a scholar of Zola, but more importantly as an adoring fan (a term I have no qualms with), I would never recommend to any reader unfamiliar with the man to start with his short stories. I think many of Thomas Hardy's short stories, most of William Faulkner's and Herman Melville's and all of Guy DuMaupassant's would make an excellent introduction to those great writers. But unequivocally, Zola is a novelist and even his best stories, while excellent by anyone's standards, pale in comparison to his full-length fiction. Nonetheless, his short works often provide an insight into his genius and, I might say, into his thought processes as a craftsman of fiction. His early stories collected in Stories for Ninon are maudlin, immature, hopelessly romantic and often vicariously embarrassing. But this could be said of any writer, great and small, who for the first time takes up his pen and presents his soul to the world. A careful reading of these stories might remind many readers of their first forays into fiction where wearing one's heart on one's sleeve was not the opprobrium it is today.

The other difficulty in a presentation of so much material is the order in which it is presented. Like any very popular author, publishers scrambled to get work of any kind into print no matter how many times it was rejected when the fellow was unknown. Profit is always the motivating force behind the publishing trade and it is little wonder that works by Jane Austen, Charles Dickens and a slew of others are foisted upon the reading public when, in fact, they were not only unedited by their authors, but not even finished! I have had the good fortune to have had access to a lengthy letter from the London firm of Chatto & Windus which had proposed to the Zola estate a publication of his complete short works. For reasons unknown, the project never proceeded. However, a proposed "table of contents" was included with a precise statement that the order was to be precisely that used in the eventual publication. While I am no fan of the Chatto & Windus English translations, I much admire their dedication to the master's works and, I might add, they even "updated" some of the expurgations and made some of them a little more accurate and a little less befuddling in the early years of the 20th century. There is a reference in said letter that Zola himself had been consulted on the matter and while there is no evidence that he dictated the order of the stories, it is my opinion that it represents a better version than one I could evolve. It would be very simple to have the order dictated by the chronology of their appearance in print. This would be very difficult indeed and would belie the fact that many were written years before they found their way into print and actually pre-date others which were written later but published earlier. My own opinion is that by 1900, Zola wouldn't have cared. The fact that he consented to the publication of his early novel, The Mysteries of Marseilles, proves to me at least that whatever brought in a royalty check was good enough for him. And why not? He might have seen that novel and his first, Claude's Confession, with the same affection that many writers view their early work: "Well, this isn't bad at all." His reputation was already made and he could have written a poem sang to the tune of "Yankee Doodle Dandy" and his renown would have suffered not a whit.

What little obeisance I have made to the early translations and to some of the later ones is to retain some of their now obsolete punctuation and archaic syntax. The fact remains that Zola was a writer very much of his time and his MSS indicate that, for example, he often used a colon before a piece of dialogue and not a comma as we universally do today. Sometimes he used single quotation marks, sometimes double. And perhaps his most annoying habit, at least to the eye of a 21st century reader is his absurd overuse of the exclamation point. Today, I'm afraid, we are less apt to license our writers to shout their lines at our sophisticated faces. But in Zola's time when the novel was novel, such excesses were not only permitted but encouraged. Black marks on a white page may be many things but the 19th century reader felt privileged to feel the passion the writer felt and no punctuation accomplishes that so well as the exclamation point!

These volumes of his Complete Stories were years in the making and it is my genuine hope that they entertain, amuse and enlighten the American reader to one aspect of Émile Zola they might not otherwise have encountered.

Stephen R. Pastore, 2011.

www.ingramcontent.com/pod-product-compliance
Lightning Source LLC
Chambersburg PA
CBHW030331030726
47499CB00003B/733